D1391619

A TERMINAL CASE

The parishioners of Bryntaf, a leafy Cardiff suburb, are far from being shocked when the vicar of St Samson's announces he is divorcing his wife. Some are surprised, though, when he adds that he expects to remarry – an attractive, young widow – *and* still keep his job. But his intentions go for nothing when the widow, a hospital consultant, is brutally murdered, her body mutilated with one of her own scalpels. When the circumstances and timing of the crime come out, it follows that any number of interested parties could have committed it – including the vicar's distracted wife, her saturnine student son, the consultant's jealous accountant, her single-parent cleaner, and at least one spinster of the parish who everyone agrees would die for the vicar, and may well have killed for him. Only the wily Chief Inspector Parry is sharp enough ultimately to work out the subtle motive which exposes the true culprit.

In this fourth mystery featuring DCI Merlin Parry and his assistant Sergeant Gomer Lloyd, David Williams further refines the balance of his Welsh series, which is rapidly earning equal status with his much acclaimed Mark Treasure stories – strong on plot, a lively appreciation of local mores, engaging characterization, the whole spiced with humour and written with elegance.

A TERMINAL CASE

David Williams

*For Mike and Mary
with many thanks for
medically immaculate advice!

Love

David Williams

Wentworth, 1997*

HarperCollins*Publishers*

Collins Crime
An imprint of HarperCollins*Publishers*
77–85 Fulham Palace Road, London W6 8JB

First published in Great Britain
in 1997 by Collins Crime

1 3 5 7 9 10 8 6 4 2

Copyright © David Williams 1997

David Williams asserts the moral right to
be identified as the author of this work

A catalogue record for this book
is available from the British Library

ISBN 0 00 232635 3

Set in Meridien and Bodoni

Typeset by Rowland Phototypesetting Ltd
Bury St Edmunds, Suffolk
Printed and bound in Great Britain by
Caledonian International Book Manufacturing Ltd, Glasgow

This one for
David and Eileen Pearce

1

'You haven't forgotten you're seeing Bronwyn Hughes at twelve, have you, Peter?' asked Sybil Treace. She was squinting at the kitchen wall diary through the wrong spectacles and half-closed eyes, while contriving simultaneously to refill the teapot. It was Tuesday, March 25th, the week before Palm Sunday, and her husband had a lot of engagements.

'No. You told me yesterday.' The Vicar of St Samson's, Bryntaf, buttered a second piece of toast. His words were precise, but the intonation was somehow preoccupied. Then he looked up. 'Bronwyn Hughes. Did she sound agitated?'

'Worried, more like.' The short, plump Sybil pushed a lock of greying hair from her face. As a forty-eight-year-old vicar's wife, she fancied she was used to fine-gauging motivations in the voices of parishioners, even if her husband didn't share this opinion about her. 'It's about Dilys, the daughter, I should think.'

'Not necessarily, and I'd have expected her to tell you if it was. I thought you and she were close?' He drank what was left of his tea. 'Dilys always was a difficult child, wasn't she? Flighty. I heard she's living with a boyfriend in central Cardiff somewhere. Wasn't she in the same class as Janet for a bit?' Janet was the younger of their two children.

'That's right. From when they were both twelve. She'll be nineteen now, same as Janet. Handful for Bronwyn to bring up on her own. It's ten years since that husband deserted her. Time flies.' Though the implication was it probably hadn't for Bronwyn Hughes. Sybil came back to the table in the kitchen of the postmodernist, red-brick vicarage that had been been built, eleven years before this, in Tesco mode, to replace its rambling predecessor. Still standing, she filled her husband's cup as she continued. 'Anyway, Bronwyn's arranging special help in the shop so she can get away before lunchtime. I think it's important.' Mrs Hughes owned Bryntaf's only fashion boutique.

'She could have seen me some evening. Unless it's urgent as well. She'll be involved in the special parish meeting tonight, of course.' He had stopped eating, and was watching his wife like a hunter stalking prey. Instead of resuming her seat at the table, she had gone back to the blue worktop next to the cooker.

'I can do an extra sandwich,' she offered. 'If you want to ask Bronwyn to lunch here. Nuisance for you, the extra parish meeting, what with Easter coming up.'

He wished she'd refer to the great religious festivals less as though they rated equal with the Cup Tie or Guy Fawkes day. It wasn't that she was actually disrespectful; it was just the way the words came out. 'Can't be helped,' he said. 'And don't do a sandwich for Bronwyn. I shan't have that much time.' He pushed his cup and saucer away from him in what might have been a nervous gesture, except that the dark, spare, striking-looking priest wasn't normally given to nervous gestures. Like a good many handsome, healthy men approaching fifty who have kept their hair and figures, and who excel at their jobs, he was physically and mentally pretty sure of himself. 'Could you stop what you're doing, Sybil, and come and sit down,' he ordered, too sharply. 'There's . . . there's something we need to talk about.' He had sworn he would get through it today, now, after breakfast, no fail.

She turned about, the look on her face undisguisedly apprehensive, not in the remotest sense hopeful or joyfully expectant. 'Of course, love.' She wiped her hands on a tea towel. She had been peeling apples to go in a pie for their supper. 'Look, if it's about last Wednesday night, I've said I'm sorry.' She took her seat at the table, as she continued confusedly, the fingers of her raised right hand grasping at the heavy frame of the spectacles without purpose. 'It wasn't a relapse. Not a proper relapse. I promise faithfully –'

'It's not about Wednesday night. I'm sure what you say is right,' he interrupted with more tolerance in his voice than she'd looked for in the circumstances.

'Well, that's good.' She shifted awkwardly in her seat. 'I didn't mean it to happen. I was so lonely all day, that's all. I just had to –'

'Look, I've told you, it's nothing to do with that, Sybil. Honestly.' He paused, then leaned across the narrow table, and reached out to take one of her hands in both of his. The intimate gesture pleased as much as surprised her. 'I'm afraid it's . . . it's sad news. Inevitable, but very sad. You've got to be strong about it, though. We both of us have to be strong.' He breathed in and out quite slowly. 'You see, we've come to the end of the line. You and I. To the end of our marriage. It's over. Has been for some time, hasn't it? You know that.' He swallowed at the sudden but utter look of despond in her eyes. He was only glad that it was that and not disbelief she was showing. 'The fact is, I want a divorce.'

'A divorce? Oh, no. Please, not that.' Now there was disbelief. The little cupid's bow mouth in the over-fed face stayed open for a full second. 'You're not serious? You're not . . .' She stopped suddenly as she paled, visibly paled, as the blood drained from her face and neck. She pulled her hand away from his and drew back in the chair. 'There's someone else, isn't there, Peter? You've found someone else? Oh, how could you? Leave me for another woman. I . . . I just shan't be able to face that.'

He frowned, momentarily fazed by her response. 'There is someone else involved, yes. I –'

'I knew it. So who is it? It's not Bronwyn Hughes is it? Oh, no. Is that why she's coming –'

'No, Sybil, it's not Bronwyn Hughes.' But Sybil's taste was sounder than her guesswork, he thought. Bronwyn was quite a looker, and one of the unattached females who could never do enough for him. But he'd never pictured her as a lover – nor, in fairness, had he pictured any of his parishioners as that until very recently. 'Who it is doesn't matter, not for the moment.'

'Well it matters to me, Peter. Who is it? You've got to tell me now. Someone I know? Someone in the congregation, is it? Bound to be.'

He sighed. 'You hardly know her. It's Delia Bewen. The doctor I've been counselling,' he said quietly.

'Oh, God, not her? I can't believe it. She's half your age.'

'No, Sybil, she's a lot older than that. She's thirty-four.'

'She looks younger. And sexy with it, and educated, and intelligent.' She got up from the chair, moved to the sink, then held on to the front of it with both hands, her back to him. 'God in heaven. I wondered why she needed counselling. Now I know.'

'No you don't.' He seriously thought she might be about to throw up in the sink.

So did she. 'Yes I do,' she uttered breathily. 'She was . . . she was after you. She never even came to church before –'

'You're wrong, Sybil,' he interrupted, 'quite wrong. She was broken-hearted about her husband's death. It's true, she only turned to the church for help in her grief. Then, I have to admit, it was one of those things that happen. As time went on, as we came to know each other better . . . well, we couldn't help ourselves. We fell in love.'

'Oh yes, I'm sure.' She turned to face him, her back now against the sink. 'Oh Peter, what's happened to you, love? Can't you see, she's making a fool of you? She was lonely, you're very attractive, she decided to go for it. But she'll ruin you. Your future, our future, our family. And where's the point? She'll chuck you the same way she picked you up. As soon as she meets someone she fancies more. And what about your . . . your vocation? You know the church won't stand for –'

'I should tell you, I've been to see the archdeacon.'

His words seriously took her aback. 'About us? Already? Before you told me?' With an unbalanced movement she went back to her chair, sitting on it where she'd left it, a foot or so clear of the table, and angled half away from it.

'The archdeacon's since spoken with the bishop,' Treace went on, ignoring her comment. 'Obviously they don't feel comfortable about the divorce. Well, they can't really. But they understand. That there's no chance of reconciliation. Yes, they definitely understand.' The last words sounded like reassurance from the speaker to himself as he completed. 'The archdeacon and I prayed together about it all. We prayed deeply and long. Not everything can be resolved immediately, but some provisions are possible now. Counselling has been arranged for you. Beginning today. This evening.'

'Counselling? For me?' She shook her head slowly. 'Peter, I can't believe this is happening.' She let out a little whimper, then, searchingly and desperately she looked around the kitchen, her kitchen, as if she had never been in it before.

He would have leaned forward again across the table, but she was too far off for his hands to reach her. 'We thought the counselling should start as quickly as possible. There's a woman in Cardiff, at St John's. She's expert in cases like this, and she's been briefed.'

'Who by?' So she was a case now.

'The . . . the archdeacon.' Ignoring the fresh incredulity in her expression, he pressed on. 'You have an appointment with her at six, if you want to take it, and I hope you will. Obviously you won't want to attend the parish meeting tonight. In fact I'd rather you gave that a miss in any case.' He had looked away from her at the last sentence. 'Things are bound to be a bit traumatic at the start. Better to face up to that now before you er . . . before

11

there's the chance you'll go under with it. That's what I meant about being strong. We – '

'Before there's a risk I'll hit the bottle, you mean?' she broke in. He had thought she was about to burst into tears. Her eyes were still watery, but she was willing herself not to break down, not yet. There might still be a chance, but not if she gave in now – not if she didn't put up a fight. Oh, please God, don't let it be over: 'So you, and the archdeacon, and the bishop, you've all arranged it . . . so I go quietly like? No scandal. No falling over at evensong. No being carried home like before.' Both her hands, fingers spread, went to hold her temple for a moment. 'That's why they're being so understanding, is it? The archdeacon and the bishop? You've had so much to put up with in the past. You deserve a nice civilized divorce now. A fresh start.'

'No, no, you've got it wrong, Sybil. It's not like that at all. We've all got your best interests at heart.'

'Have you? Haven't they been thinking, he's got her on her feet again, so he deserves rewarding? Compensation with a nice new, sexy wife. That way, there's a chance yet he'll fulfil his early promise. A deanery perhaps? Even a bishopric, with a suitable . . . what's the word? . . . consort standing beside him. Not like the old one, old Sybil. They going to let you keep the living here, are they? That came into the prayers, did it?'

'Whether I stay on here is, er . . . is yet to be decided,' he answered evasively, his eyes shifting to study his teacup. In fact, he was quite confident he would be keeping the living. Of course, nothing firm had been said: no commitment had been made – but in all the circumstances, and in the present ecclesiastical climate, yes, he was confident.

'Yet to be decided, is it, when you're sleeping with another woman? Living in adultery? Fine parish priest you make, I must say.' Except it really wasn't what she'd wanted to say. She had blurted it out before she could stop herself.

'I'm not sleeping with anybody, Sybil. Not with Delia,

and not with you either,' he responded stonily. 'I'll move into the spare room tonight.' He put his hands together in a prayerful way. 'Whether I stay here as vicar depends a lot on how the parish take what's happening.' He touched his lips with the end of his long fingers. 'I've put a lot of work in at Bryntaf over the ten years.'

'And you don't believe they'll want to chuck you out? No, I think you're right, Peter. Many of them won't. Maud Davies and . . . and Agnes Craig-Owen for starters, and plenty of others, my friend Bronwyn Hughes included, I shouldn't wonder. And if you survive here for a bit, it'll make it a lot easier when you want to move on.'

'That's not my motive, at all. I was sent here to do a job, and I feel, deeply, it's not finished yet. If others feel as I do, clearly they'll want me to stay.' His fine chin lifted as if to meet the formidable challenge ahead.

'I see. So, you'll be telling the whole parish as well, will you? And when's that going to be then?' Her mouth opened again, but it was a moment before she uttered. 'Oh, God, it's tonight, isn't it?' Her head was nodding as she went on. 'The special parish meeting. About the supermarket. Except you're going to tell them all you're leaving your useless, pathetic wife.'

Peter Treace clenched his fists and brought them together in front of him. 'You're not pathetic, Sybil,' he said with unctuous insistence, 'and you're not useless either. There's plenty of time for you to make a new life, as I'm going to. But we can't go on as we are.'

'Because of Delia Bewen. What's she a doctor of, by the way?' She was fighting to seem normal now, not to show the utter misery she was enduring.

He ran a finger over the front of his clerical collar. 'She's a specialist. A gynaecologist.'

'Is that right? Well that's useful. Knows about male sexual problems as well, does she? Like your little mid-life hang-up?'

He ignored the slight. 'Anyway, the archdeacon feels there's no point in letting news like this just trickle out.

13

I'm sure he's right. We don't want the local newspapers picking up ugly rumours. It's better we control things ourselves.'

'You mean *you're* controlling things. I'm not being consulted. Calling a press conference, are you?'

'Of course not. I'll simply announce at the end of the meeting tonight that we've decided to part, amicably. To have our marriage dissolved. All in our own good time.'

'But not too much time, because Delia's waiting. So do the children know anything about this?'

'Not yet, no.'

'Well, that's something, I suppose.'

'But frankly, I don't believe either of them will be exactly surprised.'

'I see. You know they'll be home tomorrow morning?'

'Of course. Janet's meeting Simon in London tonight. They're going to a party together. He's bringing her down in his car.' He had already calculated that their arrival together would balance things out well enough, meaning in his favour, Janet being the forceful one – Janet, the high-flyer, the scholarship girl. She was reading modern languages at Cambridge, at his own college, and was set on a diplomatic career. She was her father's favourite. He felt she took after him: he knew she adored him. Simon was two years older than his sister, and not bright academically. He was struggling to keep his place in the engineering school at a northern university. He was very close to his mother, and in some ways shared her weaknesses of will. 'We can see them together. Explain things,' he completed.

'If there's anything to explain, Peter.'

'How d'you mean?'

'What I say. I'm not buying it, love. Not any of it. Archdeacon or no archdeacon.' She took a very deep breath. 'I'm not having counselling. I'm not leaving this vicarage, and I'm certainly not giving you a divorce. I love you. You're my husband. We made vows. I've kept them. If

14

you haven't kept yours then ... then I'll forgive you. That's the Christian thing, isn't it?'

His dark eyebrows lifted. He had never seen her so defiant. It was not at all her style, or within her capacities to sustain. He sensed it was an act that could collapse at any moment. 'If only it was as simple as that. It isn't, I'm afraid.' He smiled tolerantly, shaking his head. 'I thought I'd made it clear; you don't need to leave the vicarage straight away. We can both live here for a bit, if that's what you want. Certainly while the children are here, and perhaps until we get some sense of what's to happen.'

'I know what's to –'

'I mean whether I'll be staying on in the living,' he interrupted, ignoring what she had clearly intended to say. 'Meantime, you'll need to decide where you want to live. Why don't you talk it over with Janet and Simon tomorrow? Janet especially. She'll be here the whole of the Easter vacation, won't she? I'm sure she'll have ideas about your future.' Having invoked his daughter in that way, he wished now he'd explained everything to her in advance, but it had been an awkward thing to do on the telephone. He'd felt it was better left till she was here. It was then that he also felt the first niggling suspicion of doubt that perhaps, just perhaps, his daughter wouldn't be as wholly on his side as he'd been assuming. 'I thought perhaps you'd want to move nearer your mother,' he added. Sybil's widowed mother lived fifty miles away, near Swansea, at the seaside, where she shared a flat with another widow.

'Where I'd live if I left here would be up to me, wouldn't it?' Sybil countered. 'It wouldn't have anything to do with Janet or Simon, or with you, come to that. But since I'm not leaving here, it doesn't matter, does it?'

He gave an irritated sigh. 'I'm really afraid that's not a long-term option, Sybil. Whatever happens.' Why was his mind suddenly being assailed by all kinds of subjective doubts about his carefully prepared plan? He steeled himself not to go back on it now, not any of it. He couldn't afford to vacillate. What he had decided had appeared to him to be well timed, sensible, equitable, and, above all, practical – as it could easily do to someone as naturally if unknowingly ruthless as he was. Underlying his resolve was also the fact that he'd given his word to Delia Bewen that he would see the matter through as planned. 'You'll thank me in the end, Sybil,' he continued. 'Thank me for mapping the way through a difficult impasse. Difficult for all of us, but capable of . . . of a resolution.' He had been on the point of saying 'and a Christian solution', but had thought better of it.

Silently, Sybil got up from the chair, moved toward him, then dropped on her knees in front of him, grasping one of his hands and forcing it against her cheek. 'Peter, I'm sorry if I've failed you,' she half whispered. 'But please don't leave me. For your sake as well as mine. In my heart I know it's wrong. That you'll regret it later, but I don't know how to explain why. I know you too well. In the end you're going to hate yourself if you go through with this, any of it. And you'll hate this Delia, as well. But I feel so helpless at the moment. I'm not strong like you. And . . . resolute. I need time to explain. To find the words. Now I'm just shocked . . . and helpless . . . and useless.' Her voice had broken on the last word. 'If you give me another chance, I promise I'll be a better wife to you. Better in every way. Better in bed, if that's what you want. Better in the house. Better in the parish. I'll work, I'll slave to keep you. I love you. Oh, please don't desert me.' She was sobbing now, but she was still forcing out the words. 'Give us time, love. Give us both time. And please, please don't tell them tonight . . . not at the meeting. Don't do that. Don't shame me.' Weeping piteously now, she buried her face in his lap.

Inwardly he was sensing relief. He could cope with her as a supplicant.

2

Bryntaf is a village of ancient origin. It lies several miles due north of Cardiff, in the Taff River valley. It was after the Second World War that developers expanded Bryntaf to the west, away from the river, and up the hillside, converting it – in estate agent's terms – into one of the Welsh capital's most desirable outer suburbs. It still retains a rural ambience, something its newer inhabitants, in their substantial executive villas, have naturally been anxious to protect. The still surviving original villagers might have been expected to enjoin this view, except they feel that the cause was lost years ago, and that there is nothing truly rural left to protect. Their view is of no great account since they don't have the financial clout of the new-comers. Sometimes, though, the two sections of the community find issues that bind them.

Certainly no one could gainsay that the pretty, twelfth-century village church of St Samson was, and still is, the gem feature of old Bryntaf. It stands a hundred yards to the west of the old Valley Road that runs due north through the village. The church has a stout, squat central tower made of flint, and firmly defensive in aspect. Tower and chancel are said to date from even earlier than the rest of the building which, in any case, was largely restored when the nave was extended in 1846. The church's sylvan setting is well protected by a modest-sized graveyard (full up since 1961), and four acres of old glebe land on which a church hall and the present vicarage were built, still leaving enough green space for the staging of church fêtes.

This whole section might have been surrendered for development a dozen years ago had the church authorities not been offered a munificent price for the old, unmanageable and inconveniently sited vicarage. This Gothic monster was thereafter demolished and an unprepossessing block of twenty-four flats erected in its place – but distant enough not to spoil the immediate church environment.

It was in the church hall that the special parish meeting had been convened, and which was now drawing to what should have been its formal close.

'So, from that show of hands, it's clearly the wish of all those present that a strong objection in the name of the Parochial Church Council should be sent from this meeting to the Local Authority,' pronounced Alwyn Gorse, the stocky, sixty-seven-year-old chairman of the St Samson's PCC, and a retired Cardiff solicitor. 'This will register our total opposition, for environmental and other reasons, to the erection of a supermarket on the Carmen Lane field,' he completed, smoothing the top of his bent and nearly bald head. He stared out questioningly over the top of his gold-framed half-glasses at the sixty or so strong audience below the platform on which he was seated, between the vicar and the honorary secretary.

Before the noise of general assent had died, a buxom, auburn-haired, middle-aged woman in the second row came majestically to her feet. In her own time, she adjusted the set of her open green cardigan over its matching jumper and her substantial bosoms, then offered in a penetrating contralto voice: 'Could we add to that, Mr Chairman, that if the Authority is so blind to the desires of the people of this area, and to the need to protect its natural beauty and present infrastructure, as to approve this ridiculous application, that we'll take our case to the Department of the Environment in London, and demand an official inquiry?' After over-effusively acknowledging the only just audible murmurs of support from people sitting close to her, she then resumed her seat, her torso ramrod straight, her face a study in self-satisfaction at a job well done.

'Thank you very much, Mrs Craig-Owen.' Gorse cleared his throat. 'I'm sure you're right about the action you predicate, but we did deal with that aspect of the matter earlier. I took the feeling of the meeting then that it'd be better to wait till the Planning Committee votes on the application next week, before we outline any action we might take if it's approved. Ours is not the only important objection that'll be registered, and in my view it's highly likely the application will be dismissed. So, to . . . to embellish our attitude now may well be like pushing on an open door, antagonizing members of the Committee unnecessarily, at a . . . a crucial point in their deliberations,' he ended solemnly.

This time, there were many more calls of 'Hear! Hear!' from the body of the hall than had followed Mrs Craig-Owen's statement. The lady herself sniffed, but said nothing more. Her displeasure over the chairman's judgement seemed to be manifested in the angry glare she fixed upon the small man to her left. This was her husband, enveloped in an oversized, herringbone jacket, and who parried the glare with a tranquil smile of sympathetic understanding. It was well known to most of those present that in addition to being the proprietor and operator of the only grocery store in the village, Agnes Craig-Owen also owned the freehold of four more of the twelve retail premises that comprised Bryntaf's total shopping parade. Since there was little doubt that a substantial supermarket would put many of these emporia out of business altogether, including probably three of those controlled by Mrs Craig-Owen, it seemed likely that her opposition to it was bedded in self-interest rather than an altruistic desire to protect the remaining natural attractions of the area. In any case, the Carmen Lane site ran along the railway line: it was hardly a beauty spot.

A skinny, unprepossessing younger woman of aesthetic mien, wearing round, metal-framed spectacles and a

19

hand-knitted jumper with poppies on it, now half rose to her feet in the centre of the hall. Then, immediately, she sat down again confused, and in deference to another would-be questioner. A second later, though, she was obliged to come to her feet again when the other contender, an older man, indicated gallantly that he was yielding her the floor.

'Yes, Miss Davies?' said Gorse encouragingly, but with just a touch of impatience. The time to air additional views had really passed with the vote just taken.

'I feel it's a pity,' she began nervously, her thin arms folded in front of her.

'Can't hear. Speak up,' someone called loudly from the back.

The speaker reddened, gulped hard, and began again. 'I feel it's a pity,' she uttered, this time in a strangled and piercingly high-pitched voice, 'not to make the point about er . . . about how much we're against Sunday opening. Of supermarkets, I mean. On the Lord's Day. I'm sure the vicar would agree.'

Peter Treace, on Gorse's right, leaned forward. 'Good point, Chairman. And I think some reference to the adverse affect Sunday opening of supermarkets has on Sunday observance in general should be included in our letter. We could make special reference to church attendance, and to supermarket staff being obliged to work on Sundays, often against their will. I think this is a consideration that could weigh heavily in the minds of some members of the Planning Committee.' He beamed broadly at Miss Davies, whose gaze dropped demurely.

'Can I have a show of hands from all those in favour of what Miss Davies said?' asked the chairman.

Something over three-quarters of the audience raised their hands – this was still traditional Sabbath-keeping Wales.

'Well, that's clear enough. We'll include the point in the letter,' Gorse concluded, confirming this with a nod to the honorary secretary, a pimply, earnest youth of about

20

twenty, with political aspirations and the conviction that they were being furthered by his volunteering for the PCC. The chairman then made a show of looking at the time. 'Although that concludes the formal business of the meeting,' he said, 'the vicar wants to take the opportunity of making a . . . a personal statement.'

Treace stood up in one energetic movement. 'Thank you, Mr Chairman.' He touched the front of his collar, then rested his hand on the black stock below it. 'Ladies and gentlemen, friends – and I count you all as friends – I have some unhappy news to share with you.' He dipped his head, then raised it again. 'After long and often agonizing deliberation, my wife and I have decided to divorce and go our separate ways.' There was an immediate, excited buzz from the audience as he continued. 'This will not be unexpected news to many of you, I know, but I'm sure it will sadden all of you. Our marriage has been a difficult one for some time, for . . . for a variety of reasons.' He paused briefly, giving several of his listeners the opportunity to nod their heads in a sage, understanding way. 'For the sake of my work, Sybil and I have tried to keep an appearance of marital unity going. Tried, and, latterly I fear, failed, especially since a new element has entered the equation. I'll come to that later.

'The circumstances I now find myself in are difficult for someone in holy orders, most particularly for a vicar who loves his parish, and all those in it, with all his heart. A parish where he has some reason to feel his work has been blessed with a measurable amount of success, and where he hoped – still hopes – to continue ministering for some time to come.' The pause at this point was greeted by a substantial, growing murmur of warm assent.

'Some may say that a divorced vicar has no business to continue in his job, particularly a divorced vicar who intends, as I do, to remarry.' The speaker raised his chin to a more combative angle. 'Yes. That's the new element I referred to. I fear I couldn't contemplate going on without the support of a chosen, strong, and God-fearing helpmate, who, as it happens, is a talented and responsible widow of the parish, known to many of you. I have thought and prayed about the matter deeply.' He took a deep inward breath. 'So have the archdeacon and the bishop, who have known about the situation for some time.' The pause here was made to even greater effect than any of the others, as it was timed to do. That the two most senior clergy in the diocese were privy to what was going on put a quite different focus on the vicar's predicament – and a somehow sympathetic one, almost absolving, in advance, everyone else from having to make an awkward judgement in the matter.

'In all the circumstances, the feeling is,' Treace went on, implying that this might well include the feeling of the bishop and the archdeacon, 'in all the circumstances,' he repeated, with emphasis now on the word 'all', 'that the way ahead needs to be determined in large part by you, the faithful, responsible members of my congregation. Personally, I feel very strongly that this is how it should be – indeed, how it has to be. In all conscience, I couldn't even contemplate continuing here without the wholesome support of the parishioners.' He took another deep breath. 'Well, that's all I have to say. Thank you for bearing with me. Mr Chairman, I don't believe there's any purpose in discussing the matter further now. Simply I wanted you all to know what Sybil and I have decided.' He sat down, wearing a sober and valiant expression.

It was Mrs Craig-Owen who straight away rose to comment, despite the vicar's contrary admonition. 'Mr Chairman, I'm sure I speak for all the regular members of St Samson's when I say how very sorry we are about Peter's situation, and how much we understand and sympathize over what he's been through, poor man, and Sybil too, of course. It's typical of Peter that he's come clean, bared his breast like, in front of all of us, although many of us have known about the situation for years, and the way he's coped with it manfully, and without grumbling. That's why I think it's up to us straight away to say we support him, and want him to stay. There's plenty of other clergymen these days who've been allowed to do the same in similar circumstances, but none I know of as deserving as our Peter Treace, a vicar in a thousand.' She gave a forceful nod, and sat down amidst loud, though not universal clapping.

'Thank you, Mrs Craig-Owen,' a somewhat uncomfortable-looking Alwyn Gorse responded. 'I'm not sure –'

'Mr Chairman,' called a middle-aged man who had stood up at the back. 'Since the vicar has been so forthcoming over everything else, could I ask if he can give us the name of the lady he intends to marry after the divorce? There are such a lot of widows in the parish, he won't want speculation running riot, will he?' The speaker had ended with a grin, which was quickly followed by tension-breaking laughter from various parts of the hall.

'Perish the thought, Cyril,' exclaimed the vicar lightly, and getting to his feet again. 'I'm so sorry, I fully intended to tell you, of course. The lady is Delia Bewen, Dr Delia Bewen, whose husband died so tragically in a car accident eighteen months ago.'

'Good luck, vicar,' called one man.

'Congratulations, Peter,' shouted another.

'Shame,' cried a woman at the back whose admonition quickly revived the earlier pall of embarrassment.

'Well, ladies and gentlemen,' said a now thoroughly uneasy Alwyn Gorse, his well-developed legal instincts rebelling against his continuing to preside over an assembly as unstructured as this one, where views were being expressed which he found distasteful. 'I think that must conclude the meeting. Thank you for your attendance. We shall –'

'But we're not divorced yet. Oh, no. Not by a long shot.' The interruption had come from Sybil Treace who had appeared through the swing doors at the rear of the hall. Her words had been loud and clear, but her progress down the centre aisle between the seats was less steady than it was purposeful.

23

Gorse's stomach suddenly felt distinctly hollow.

'I've heard everything Peter's said,' the vicar's wife continued, as she came to a halt between the first and second row of seats. She turned about, swayed slightly, leaned out to grasp the back of the nearest chair, missed it, and indecorously fell into the lap of the elderly man sitting at the end of the third row, and who tried, as best he could, to prop her up once more, and away from him. 'Whoops,' she observed, on her feet again, beaming at the audience, though still leaning on the man's shoulder. Many had now had the opportunity to see that the button-through dress she was wearing was inexpertly arranged, its second button engaged in the top buttonhole, giving dress and wearer a lopsided look. This impression was deepened by the crooked way in which Sybil had applied both lipstick to her mouth and rouge to her cheeks.

'And I want you all to know the divorce is not a fate accom . . . a fate acco . . . it's not . . . not decided. Not by me, it . . . it t'isn't. Maybe it is by Peter and his new friend, the doctor, but not by me. And it takes two to . . . to tango, doesn't it?' She giggled over her last words, while at the same time appearing to be sinking towards the floor.

By this time Peter Treace had descended from the platform and was beside her. He put a supporting arm about her firmly but very tenderly. 'Quite right, Sybil,' he said to her quietly, but even a whisper would have been heard by almost everyone in the dead silence that had fallen. 'Let's see if you and I can tango back to the vicarage, shall we?'

'Isn't he lovely?' Sybil exclaimed as he led her away. 'We're not going to split up, you know? Not on your life. It's all a mira . . . mira . . . it's all a mistake . . . She's not going to get him . . . He's still mine . . . Always has been . . . Always will be . . . What God hath joined together let no man . . . no . . . no woman, put asun . . . ass . . . oh dear, I don't feel very well.'

Most people looked down as the couple moved past. It was as the two neared the door that a fashionably dressed,

24

pretty woman pushed through to the aisle from her seat. 'Let me help, Sybil,' she said, and the three disappeared into the vestibule. The thud of the outside door beyond followed shortly afterwards. It was not till then that the swell of comment broke, but not so swiftly that anyone could have missed Mrs Craig-Owen's fortissimo summary. 'She's a disgrace. No wonder he can't go on. We've got to back him.'

Which couldn't have served Peter Treace's case better if he'd written the whole scene and its poignant end line himself – which some were later to wonder if, in some way, he'd actually contrived to do.

3

'Cooked her goose proper, she did, coming in like that,' said Agnes Craig-Owen. Clad now in a slip, she was carefully folding her cashmere twinset on the bed.

'But was the vicar telling the truth, d'you think?' replied her husband tentatively, while draping his trousers over a hanger. Roland Craig-Owen had learned to be tentative in his approach to most things during twenty-one years of marriage. This was from fear of being called to account for an avoidable lapse. He accepted having to endure the other kind of lapse. Life with Agnes was largely a balancing exercise in damage limitation.

The main bedroom of the Craig-Owen's five-bedroomed, two-bathroomed villa was south-facing, with a Venetian window opening on to a diminutive imitation stone balcony of the kind that house buyers invariably admire, but later never find occasion to use. The furnishings here, like those in the rest of the house, were ponderous – with too many satin cushions, and too much gold fringing, notably on the presently closed curtains which looked as though they ought to be gracing a small opera house, or a travelling circus. Roland didn't care for the appearance of this or any other room in the place, but it was Agnes who personally supervised all interior decoration. There was the compensation, of course, that she supervised it afresh quite often, so that one rarely had to live with any single set of her mistakes for very long.

The Craig-Owens had bought the house – one of Bryntaf's middle range of superior abodes – fifteen years before this. The grocery store, inherited from Agnes's parents, had been showing obscene profits for a number of years. These she had shrewdly invested in other shop premises, for renting, in the increasingly affluent suburb. The price of the house had been a benefit generated by the success of her enterprises.

'I don't know what you mean saying Peter was lying, I'm sure,' Agnes responded, turning about. At the same moment, she removed the slip over her head in a deft single movement worthy of a striptease artiste with only a fraction of the frame to unveil.

'I only asked if you thought he had, love.'

'Well, I don't. Peter's truthful to a fault. It's partly his undoing. That, and the hours he puts in.' Now she was folding the slip with the same care she had earlier applied to the woollens and her skirt, while remaining erect, and a living testimony to the efficacy of the Gossard engineering now revealed to be encasing her person. Her prow, as it were, seemed ready to cleave through forward resistance like a well-founded catamaran. Her stern, in turn, was well rounded and palpably inviolate to any interference from that quarter.

'I mean she couldn't have agreed to their getting a divorce,' said Roland. 'Wasn't that the whole point of her coming in like that? To say there'd be no divorce.'

'Huh. The point of her coming in like that was because she was too drunk to know what she was doing. There's no doubt about that, none at all.'

Roland had mislaid his pyjama bottoms and felt vulnerable and inadequate standing about in his shirt-tails, exhibiting skinny white knees, but he still responded, and daringly for him. 'But if she'd really agreed to a divorce, like he'd said, she wouldn't have had a leg to stand on, would she?'

Agnes's mouth stiffened. 'Of course she'd agreed. Then went back on her word. Typical. Most probably she forgot what she'd said before. Drink does that to people.'

'She was supposed to be cured of drinking, wasn't she?'

'That was months ago. There've been many relapses, apart from the ones we all know about. Peter's hinted that to me, often.' Agnes gave a knowing nod.

Roland had found his pyjama bottoms and was putting them on. 'But now he's said he's involved with Dr Bewen, there's no going back, is there? Not with the bishop knowing, and everything?'

'And the archdeacon. No, you're right.' Agnes dropped her nightdress over her head and began decorously to remove the rest of her underclothes from beneath it. 'I wonder what Peter can do to force a divorce through, if Sybil's against it?' she added.

'Nothing much, I don't think,' he answered. 'Not straight away. He'll have to wait five years. Or so I've read somewhere,' Roland added carefully, not wishing to give the impression that he had ever made too specific enquiries on his own account. His life was far from fascinating, but he was reasonably content. With no money problems, he'd found genuine satisfaction through the Open University course he was doing in dramatic art, and most particularly in the residential study weeks his wife allowed him to attend on his own, twice a year.

The couple had met when Roland, aged forty, had been hired as senior counter hand at Agnes's father's shop, with little prospect of his getting further advancement, there or anywhere else. He owed his present affluent circumstances to Agnes and the fact that he had still been a bachelor at the time. She had married him at a period in her life when she had realistically come to the view that it was going to be Roland or nothing. There had never been any children.

'Well, I don't see Peter waiting any five years. You ready, then?' Agnes demanded. They each advanced along opposite sides of the massive double bed and grasped a top corner of the satin cover that encased it. They then folded the cover back, neatly, in two-foot widths, before lifting it from the bed and bringing the two sides, and themselves, together at the bottom. It was something between a military drill and steps in the maypole dance. Removing that bedcover was the only truly joint activity they engaged in here, in their bedroom, but it was a ritual they both unspokenly recognized as a consoling sublimation. 'And I don't see Dr Bewen wanting to hang about either,' Agnes continued, as they climbed in under the bedclothes. 'They're neither of them getting any younger.'

'D'you suppose they're sleeping together already?' he asked, though if sleeping together described what he and Agnes were currently engaged in, it was a blameless enough process.

'Of course not. Peter wouldn't be so daft. There'd be no chance of him keeping his job if there'd been any hanky-panky between them.' To Agnes, hanky-panky covered all aspects of intimate heterosexual activity – or all the aspects she knew about.

'You really think so?'

'Certainly,' said Agnes, who wasn't as certain as all that.

For his part, Roland was genuinely surprised at the alleged self-denial being practised by the vicar and his lady friend. He knew Dr Bewen by sight, though she didn't shop in the village. Allowing he had no direct experience of extramarital affairs, he was given to fantasizing, and his Open University 'away weeks' were not entirely without what he considered to be romantic temptations – all, to date, unrealized. Even so, if he had begun a serious relationship with another woman, he reckoned he'd have made certain they suited each other in 'that way' before he got a divorce on her account.

'But that's where the muck will be spread,' Agnes added, meaningfully. 'There's a lot of people who'll try to prove the opposite, I expect. Plenty there tonight, too. You could feel the anti faction at work, straight off. People who'll side with Sybil, come what may.'

'Of course, to some it might look as if she had right on her side. I only said some, mind,' Roland amended quickly.

'Like Bronwyn Hughes, you mean?' She hadn't challenged his contention, which surprised him.

'Yes, Bronwyn, and . . . and Maud Davies.'

'Huh.' Agnes redistributed the feather filling of her top pillow with some energetic punching of its middle. 'Bronwyn never really forgave Peter for being in favour of women's ordination.'

'But didn't he change his mind before that first vote?'

'Yes, and changed it back again before the second. I don't believe he ever really altered his view.' The ordination of women had been rejected by the Church in Wales shortly after it had been accepted by the Church of England. But the Welsh decision had been reversed on a second vote a few years later. 'Anyway, he'll need Bronwyn's support over this, as one of the more zealous Christians in the parish. May not get it, of course. As for Maud Davies, the vestment virgin,' Agnes continued, 'she's against divorce because of Bible teaching. Of course, she's potty about Peter, so she'll have to make a choice as well, won't she?'

'She was good tonight on the supermarkets and Sunday opening,' Roland offered.

'Yes, I'll give her that,' Agnes admitted. Their grocery store had never opened on Sundays, less for religious reasons than because Agnes was against paying staff overtime, especially as she didn't believe the extra turnover would justify the change. It would be different if she had competition from a supermarket.

'So what's the next move on the vicar, do you think?' asked Roland, despite his being about ready for sleep.

'Well, you heard at the meeting. The archdeacon wants to know what the parish feels about the divorce, and Peter staying on in the job.'

'That's if Peter's right about the archdeacon's view, and the bishop's,' Roland commented, sucking breath in, noisily, through his teeth. '*Duw, Duw*, couldn't have been any doubt in the old days, could there? A divorced clergy-

30

man wouldn't have been allowed in the church, let alone to stay on as a vicar.'

'Yes, well, things have changed,' Agnes replied, sounding a touch dispirited.

Roland sniffed to indicate he too thought the change hadn't been for the better, though, in fact, it didn't bother him one way or the other. 'But how're they going to find out what the parish thinks?' he asked.

Agnes pondered for a moment. 'Officially, through the Parochial Church Council, I suppose. And . . . and then by hearing direct from opinion formers like us. Yes.' She was warming to the second idea. 'You'll have to write to the archdeacon tomorrow, saying we're both behind Peter.'

'Me? Write to the archdeacon?' Roland reacted with surprise, but without directly refusing instructions.

'That's right. You should do it, not me, since I'm a member of the PCC anyway. I'll tell you what to put tomorrow.' She reached out and extinguished the central bedhead light. The switch was on her side of the bed, like the telephone.

'It's only me, Dad,' Maud Davies called from the front door as she let herself in. She and her father lived in a three-bedroomed, ground-floor flat in what had been named Old Vicarage Mansions, the still new-looking, red-brick block that stood a few hundred yards from the church.

'Well, I never thought you were a burglar. So how did your meeting go, then?' Smiling at his daughter, Gareth Davies looked up from his book, over his glasses, and took hold of his empty pipe as she entered the room.

Davies was a big man with a heavy square head, bushy eyebrows, sad eyes, and fleshy, horizontal folds on either side of a down-turned mouth – giving him the appearance of a wise and ageing Saint Bernard dog. Sixty-nine years of age, he had sold his timberyard business after the death of his wife three years before this. He had since also

31

disposed of the house they had lived in, twenty miles away, up the Rhondda Valley. He had bought the Bryntaf flat in Maud's name, and moved in with her. He had two other children, both younger than Maud, and both married. His only son lived in London, his other daughter in Norwich. He stayed with them for a month or so at different periods in the year. This arrangement suited everybody, until such time, Gareth Davies was careful always to point out, as Maud decided to get married.

Nobody actually expected Maud to get married, including Maud – saving only, in her case, if Peter Treace's wife met with a nasty accident or succumbed to serious illness, and was 'taken from us' as a result. Such an event never even occurred in Maud's conscious thinking, though it did often enough in her subconscious. Thus it was never necessary rationally to define whether a suddenly widowed Peter Treace would actually turn to Maud for permanent, or even temporary consolation in his grief. It was just a hazy, poignant mirage – or had been, up to tonight.

Maud was fulfilled in her occupation as Bryntaf's senior librarian, and her unpaid work as St Samson's vestment verger, the editor of the church's parish magazine, and the supervisor of its electoral roll, along with other, one-off tasks, most of which other parishioners were not prepared to take on from Peter Treace at short notice. Maud was always ready in that particular circumstance, her availability being less a measure of a willing nature than her need to be in close, if always decorous, contact with her vicar.

She kissed her father lightly on the forehead, then dropped into the armchair opposite the one he was occupying. 'My side won about opposing the supermarket,' she said, modestly drawing her skirt down over her knees, then slipping off her shoes. 'The PCC is going to send a formal protest to the Council.'

'Hm. Suppose that's a good thing,' he responded, but

doubtfully. 'In a way, the shops in the village could do with a bit more competition.'

'But not the kind that'll close them outright, Dad.'

'No, perhaps not. Trouble is, if the supermarket plan is turned down, Agnes Craig-Owen will go on making her millions till kingdom come.' He smiled ruefully. 'Can't stand that woman. Bet she had plenty to say tonight.'

'She did, I'm afraid.'

'Yes, well, that's the reason I didn't come. Seems to me she's had it all her own way for too long in these parts. I don't know how that husband of hers survives. Weedy little runt, but he's a good darts player.' He blew through the pipe, and then began filling it. 'Anything else come up at the meeting?'

His daughter bit her lip. 'Nothing really, except . . . well, one other thing.' She swallowed. 'The vicar . . . he announced he and his wife are getting a divorce.'

'Good God.' Davies looked up from the pipe. 'That's pretty drastic isn't it? I'm no churchman, well you know that, but is it allowed for vicars to get divorced? I mean, can he stay on in his job?'

Maud dipped her head as one hand went awkwardly to push the fringe of mouse-coloured hair away from her face. 'That's what he was asking the meeting. Whether the congregation thought he should stay.'

'Oh yes? And what did the congregation decide in its manifold wisdom?'

'Nothing. Well, not straight away, that is. He's left it for the Parochial Church Council to . . . to sort of gather opinions.'

'But isn't it up to his bosses to make the decision? The church elders, his bishop, or whatever?'

'Yes. Except he seemed to think the parishioners could influence things a lot.'

'I see. So is it the wife who's going off with someone else?'

'No, Dad. It's . . . it's the other way round.' She seemed to have had some difficulty in getting out the last words.

33

'Is that right?' He busied himself lighting the pipe, but he was still watching her through the billowing smoke. 'You must know them both pretty well, of course. Isn't she a bit of a drinker? Is that the excuse?'

'I'm . . . I'm not sure.'

'And did he say who the other woman is?'

'Yes. Her name's Delia Bewen. She's a doctor.'

'Never heard of her, have you? Local is she?'

'Yes, but she's a hospital specialist, not a GP.'

'Good looker is she? Glamorous, like? Well she would be, if she's got him off the straight and narrow.'

'I'm sure I wouldn't know, Dad.' Maud had got up from the chair and was already halfway out of the room. 'I'll make some tea.'

'No hurry, love,' he began, but she had gone already, and he wondered why she had gone quite so suddenly. Perhaps she was upset, and didn't want to show it. He'd always thought she was a bit too awestruck by that vicar, and always at his beck and call. Now she knew he had feet of clay, like everyone else, perhaps she regretted her past loyalty. But he'd been careful not to imply he'd been thinking on the same lines. He considered himself a perceptive man, especially where Maud was concerned, because she was more sensitive than his other children. He was much more conscious of her feelings than she imagined, and very much more protective.

Maud closed the door behind her and leant against it, tears streaming down her face as she muffled her sobs with her handkerchief. Up to now she had managed to stem any show of emotion. It was her father's last question that had broken her. But the tears were from anger, not sorrow – the manifest indignation of a woman deeply wronged.

4

'But Daddy, how could she have done that?' demanded Janet Treace.

'To make an exhibition of herself, in front of all those people? I expect she'll say I drove her to it,' her father answered in a philosophical voice.

'That's what she is saying. But it was still stupid. OK, you'd given her a shock. But it'd been coming for ages. Deep down, she knew that. In fact she almost admitted it to Simon and me just now.'

'I'm surprised. That wasn't her attitude last night.'

'Well, it'll make things a bit easier for you, I suppose. In the parish, I mean. But not with Simon. He's terribly hurt for her. I'll try to make him see your side, but . . .' Janet shrugged to demonstrate that the effort was going to be in vain.

Janet was a dark, slim beauty, with long straight hair, strikingly large blue eyes, and a languorous manner which camouflaged a capacity for boundless mental energy. People said she was the image of her father. Certainly she bore little resemblance to her lacklustre mother.

'What are they doing now?' Treace asked. He was leaning against a worktop in the kitchen, his arms folded in front of him.

'Simon's helping her to pack. She obviously didn't want me there any more.'

'I'm sorry, Janet. I've put you on the spot. Divided loyalties and so on.'

'You can say that again. Honestly, it would have been

a lot better if you'd waited till Simon and I were here.' Father and daughter were habitually very frank with each other.

Treace opened his hands. 'There were reasons. They seemed sound to me. Still do.'

'Not to Mummy they don't, nor to Simon.'

It was nearly lunchtime. Janet was preparing a snack meal with the food available in the house. She and her brother had arrived home mid morning. Their mother had not emerged from her bedroom before then. Their father had straight away told them what had happened the day before, and why. The 'why' had taken rather longer than the description of the exhibition the inebriated Sybil had made of herself.

Janet had gone through the motions of affecting objectivity over the reasons for her parents' estrangement. It should have been difficult for her not to sympathize with her mother over her father's admitted involvement with another woman – but she had managed it all the same. Her mother was an alcoholic, ostensibly a cured alcoholic, except the performance last night, and other recent lapses, one only a few days earlier, had given the lie to that. Janet was well aware of what having a wife with a 'problem' had done to her father, and his career, over the years. She chose not to question whether the problem had been in any part of her father's own making. Janet had met Delia Bewen a few times, and she liked – even admired – her. Her father's ambivalent claim that he wasn't sleeping with Delia she tacitly took to mean that they had never done so – which is what he had wanted her to believe.

Nothing his father had said had impressed Simon Treace. From the start he had taken his mother's side. He lacked his sister's cogency – as surely as he lacked his father's striking looks. He took much more after his mother in acumen, temperament and appearance. Although taller than his sister, he had a bulky frame, was slow to react physically, and was mentally ponderous and irresolute. At one point during the confrontation earlier it had seemed he'd been close to telling his father what he thought of him for deserting his mother. Instead, though, he had got up and abruptly left the room, slamming the door behind him, and noisily climbing the stairs to see his mother. This had been before his father had finished delivering a well-prepared justification for his actions.

After hearing her father out, Janet had gone up to join Simon in her mother's bedroom, but she had returned to her father's study quite soon afterwards.

'So she's really going to stay with Bronwyn Hughes?' Treace asked her now.

'Yes. She seems determined on that,' Janet answered, breaking eggs into a bowl. 'Simon's going to drive her.'

'Last night she was making it pretty plain she was going to stay here and . . . and put up some kind of fight.'

'Did she? By the way, she says she begged you not to make any announcement at the parish meeting. That you promised –'

'She asked me not to make the announcement, yes. I didn't promise her I wouldn't.'

Janet frowned, but didn't look up from what she was doing. 'Wasn't that pretty unfeeling, Daddy?'

He shook his head. 'Her reaction would have been the same however I'd handled things. I planned what I thought would be the least upsetting way. In the long run. If I'd waited for you and Simon to be here, for instance, we'd have been arguing the toss for days. And it wouldn't have made any difference. I'd made up my mind at last to do what I should have done years ago – would have done if you and Simon had been older. I didn't want either of you feeling you were sharing in the responsibility. Not either way. Your mother and I have grown deeply wrong for each other. I'm convinced staying together is a hundred times worse for her, and for her . . . her problems, than it is for me. It sounds hard, un-Christian, probably, but . . . but she's had her chances.

37

I've given her every opportunity, time after time, and she's blown them all.'

'You said that before, Daddy. I believe you. It's just that Delia –'

'If I'd left your mother for Delia without telling the parishioners in advance, or the archdeacon, there'd have been no hope of my being allowed to stay on,' he had interrupted sharply. 'I still have work to do here, you know.'

'You believe you'll be allowed to stay if you get a divorce and marry Delia?' There was doubt in Janet's voice, and even more in her mind.

'I think there's a chance, yes. And if we survive at all here, it'll be that much easier when we move on.' He was acutely conscious that he was reiterating something Sybil had said.

'Simon thinks you're being arrogant as well as callous,' Janet replied flatly, without emotion or recrimination, as she grated some cheese for the omelet she intended making. 'In some ways he's right. But I see the other side.'

'Thanks, but, as I said, the responsibility is entirely mine. You shouldn't feel part of it.'

'Sure, Daddy. I was going to say, I don't know what other people will think.'

'I'll take my chances on that. Do you know why Mummy's decided to go to Bronwyn's?'

'Because of something Bronwyn said to her last night. Mummy's going to take a few days to think things through.'

'We'd arranged professional counselling for her, you know?'

'Oh Daddy, you don't really believe she was going to take that up? If it was a sop for your conscience, you could have saved yourself the trouble.' She sometimes thought her father had blank spots in his mental make-up, and he had just exposed one of them. 'It'll be better for Mummy to talk to Bronwyn,' she went on. 'They've a lot in

38

common. Remember, Bronwyn's husband left her years ago? He had a drink problem, as well.'

Treace's eyebrows lifted. 'I must say, Bronwyn was pretty good with your mother last night.'

'Helping you get her out of the church hall, you mean? Mummy told us that. She's pretty ashamed at what happened. Anyway, she'd remembered Bronwyn's invitation.'

'I'm surprised. She really was pretty plastered. And the idea was for her to go with Bronwyn right then. I must admit, I wouldn't have been against that, either. And I'm not going to try stopping her today.' He shook his head. 'It looks as though the last alcohol cure went for nothing. Absolutely nothing.'

'I thought there was no liquor in the house, Daddy?'

'There wasn't. Your mother's been buying it on the quiet. Anyway, I suppose I have to blame myself for the relapse. Well, partly, at least.'

'No you don't, Daddy. You said she hit the bottle last week, too.'

'Yes. Because I'd left her alone all day, or that's what she said. She went out and bought a bottle of gin in the village.' He sighed. 'Honestly, I can't be with her all the time. I've got my job to do.'

'Of course you have.' Janet left what she was doing and moved across to where he was standing with his back to the window. She put her arms around his neck, hugged him, and kissed him lightly on the cheek. 'Did you talk to Delia this morning?'

'On the phone, yes. She's in Cardiff all day, at the hospital.'

'But she knows all about last night?'

'Sure. I rang her after Bronwyn left. Incidentally, I was supposed to see Bronwyn at noon yesterday, but I made a late excuse. I had to see Delia. It was the only chance I had.'

'Was Bronwyn sore about the cancellation?'

He shrugged. 'I don't think so. It didn't come up. I'd apologized earlier. Before the meeting started.'

'Do you know what she wanted to see you about? I mean, was it important?'

'I don't know that either. Neither did your mother. The appointment was made through her. Bronwyn didn't know the real reason I'd cancelled, of course.'

'She doesn't seem the type to want counselling from her vicar.'

'She isn't, no. Very self-sufficient. And quite hard with it. Probably it was a parish matter.' But he sounded doubtful as he went on: 'Anyway, she's not likely to want to pursue it now. Not if she's taking on your mother.'

'But you, a parson's wife, Delia? Doesn't fit somehow.' Olaf Lewis, a dark, swarthy Celt in his late forties, nodded at the waitress as she put the two drinks down on the table – a double whisky for him, a tonic water for Dr Delia Bewen, his companion. It was early in the evening, but the popular Henry's Café Bar in Cardiff's central Park Place was filling up. The two were at a corner table.

The thumb and forefinger of Dr Bewen's right hand went involuntarily to caress the plain gold ring on the third finger of her other hand. The ring was tight, bulging the flesh around it. 'Lots of things haven't been fitting since Ralph died,' she responded thoughtfully, 'but being in love again fits me fine, thank you very much. Cheers.' The look she offered him over the top of her glass was indulgent, not reproachful. It was the kind of look she might have given a usually well-behaved child whose conduct had fallen a little below standard. She was a pretty woman, a blonde with soft contours, hazel eyes, generous lips and fresh pink cheeks. She wore no make-up, and the only jewellery she had on, other than the wedding ring, was a pair of gold oyster earclips.

'Cheers. I just meant that you having a clergyman for a lover seems a bit . . . well, incongruous, like.'

'If you mean lover in the physical sense, I never said

40

he was. We intend to marry as soon as possible.' Her words were matter of fact, not prim.

'But I gather he's married already.' He adjusted the double cuffs of his white shirt to make them protrude more from under the grey pinstripe sleeves of his suit. He was a sharp dresser.

'I expect most people have gathered that, in double quick time,' she replied, crossing well-shaped legs under the short, green linen skirt. 'Yes, Peter's married, and for years very unhappily.'

'So you haven't exactly broken up his marriage?'

She grinned. 'No, Olaf darling. Not in the way we might have broken up your marriage. That's if we'd both put our minds to it, like one of us tried to.' She took another sip of her drink. 'Peter's marriage was effectively over before I met him. Yours is one of the best marriages I know. That's when you're not forgetting how incredibly lucky you are. You know, one of these days Sheila's going to find you out. In fact, I'd be surprised if she doesn't suspect you of being unfaithful already. Even if she hasn't, it's a terrible risk for you to take. To spoil everything for no lasting gain. And potentially she could be a very jealous lady. I know her type. Professionally, I mean. You really ought to give up your ... your philandering. It's not as though you're serious about it. Any of it.'

He frowned in protest, leaned closer to her, and pressed a leg against hers under the table. 'I'm damned serious about you, Delia. We could be very happy together.'

'No we couldn't. You know, my dear, you're at your least convincing when you try to be earnest. It's just not your style,' She chuckled. 'You're much better when you're being your natural, charming, fun-loving self. Anyway, I don't love you for a start – not in the right way, at least. And you'd tire of me in no time, like you have all your other girlfriends.'

'Come off it, there haven't been that many others.' His righteous indignation would have done justice to a wrongly accused Welsh lay preacher – which is what his

41

father had been. 'And none of them was serious, except for you.'

'Except I wouldn't have been content to be your current bit on the side,' she interrupted. 'Not like the others.'

'That wasn't the idea. You know it wasn't. I wanted you to marry me. Still do, for that matter.'

'And that's why you had to see me so urgently this evening?'

'Well . . . yes. After I heard about your . . . your engagement to this clergyman. In case there was still a chance for me.'

'I'm touched. How did you get the news, by the way? From the afternoon paper, was it?'

'No. It was before that came out. One of the secretaries in the office. She lives in Bryntaf, with her parents.'

Delia stretched out a hand to squeeze one of his. 'I really am touched, Olaf. But, honestly it wouldn't have worked, the two of us. It would just have been the ruination of everyone – you, Sheila, those sweet kids, and not forgetting me. I mean, how selfish can you get? With all that happiness at stake. OK, we clicked when we first met, the two of us. But Ralph was alive then. It was just a . . . a chemical attraction, and should have been a transitory thing. Would have been if Ralph had survived, even for you.'

He shook his head. 'I don't know how you can be so lacking in perception. No, it was never a transitory thing with me. And how can you know it had to be that with you in . . . in different circumstances?'

Her eyebrows rose a fraction. 'If I have no perception, as you say, then through instinct, probably. Anyway, I care for Sheila too much – much too much. Oh, and for you, come to that. I haven't forgotten how marvellous you both were after Ralph's death, and I hope in your case that wasn't just because you were on the make. I don't believe it was.' It was her turn to sound earnest. 'What might have developed later between us, if we'd let

42

it, would have been so unfair to Sheila. Unfair, unnecessary, and . . . and very selfish.'

'Yes, teacher.' He leaned back, and smoothed his crinkled dark hair. 'And the Reverend Peter Treace isn't being selfish?' he asked, pouting like a schoolboy done out of a treat.

'He's been very unselfish for a long, long time, doing the decent thing by an incurably alcoholic wife. They have two kids as well. He's waited for them to grow up before doing anything about his marriage.'

'He'd have left his wife anyway, you mean? Whether you'd come on the scene or not?'

She blinked, studying the contents of her glass. 'To be honest, I don't know. Perhaps not – not till he did meet me, or someone like me.'

'But what if you hadn't met him? Would there have been a chance for me then?'

'Perhaps. Who knows?' she answered, but without meaning it – to let him down lightly. She figured that the hurt would be short-lived and was only affecting his irrepressible self-esteem.

'So what's going to happen to the vicar's wife?'

Delia looked up. 'You're really getting your pound of flesh, aren't you? Hopefully she'll be shaken into doing something about her problems, instead of being propped up by an indulgent husband. As I said, he's sacrificed a hell of a lot for her up to now. So, no, I don't feel particularly guilty on her account.'

'I didn't mean that.'

'Yes, you did, but I don't mind.'

'Alcoholics don't usually change because of a shock.'

'Oh, so you've become an expert on alcoholism have you?'

He gave a confident grin. 'Oh, I've known quite a few drunks.'

'Well, it's true, there's no guarantee about Peter's wife. Except he's convinced that this way she'll be forced to change her attitude to everything. Into making a fresh start.'

'With two grown-up children, it doesn't sound as if she's got much time left to do that.'

'He says she has. If she puts her mind to it.'

'And you think that's right?'

She hesitated. 'I said I don't believe her rosy future's spoken for. It's up to her. But I don't believe she should be allowed to go on spoiling other people's chances either.'

'Peter's and yours, you mean? And that's not selfish?'

'Olaf, stop pretending to be a bad loser. There was really no contest. You know that.'

His face showed hurt surprise. 'But you said just a minute ago, if it hadn't been for this Peter, I might have stood a chance.'

'So I shouldn't have said it,' she responded with evident irritation. 'I didn't mean it. And now can we change the subject, please?'

He leaned back in his chair holding his hands up in surrender. 'All right, and I hope you'll be very happy with your vicar.' He paused, taking a long swallow of Scotch before asking: 'Tell me, though, what about his job? It's a long time since I was in a church. Do they accept divorced clergymen these days?'

'Sometimes, yes. If they don't accept Peter, he'll find something else to do. He has other qualifications. He taught for a while, before he was ordained.'

'He wouldn't mind giving up being a vicar?'

'I think he'd mind a good deal, but it hasn't come to that yet. I hope it won't.' She switched her gaze, half closing her eyes to see something better on the other side of the room. 'That woman over there in blue, the one who's just come in, was she waving at you or at me?'

He looked in the same direction. 'You, I expect. I don't think I know her. Can't see her face. Perhaps we shouldn't have come here.' He sounded uneasy.

'Doesn't bother me in the least. It's come to a pretty pass if a medical consultant can't have an innocent drink

44

with her accountant.' She leaned forward to touch one of his hands again. 'Even if he does still want to go to bed with her,' she added with a mischievous smile. 'And don't think I'm not flattered, dearest Olaf.' She made a kissing motion with her lips. 'Anyway, our consciences are clear, aren't they?'

'I suppose so. Up to now,' he replied levelly, suppressing his very real frustration and anger – and weighing up his chances of qualifying tonight for a consolation prize if he tried hard enough.

5

'And I thought I was through for the night,' said Detective Chief Inspector Merlin Parry of the South Wales Constabulary, as he urged his middle-aged, soft-top Porsche northwards, away from the centre of Cardiff.

It was shortly after eleven on the same evening. The theatres, cinemas and most of the drinking places had just closed, with the homebound traffic heavy for that reason.

'Ah, no peace for the wicked. Not after closing time,' commented the stout, and – like the car – middle-aged Detective Sergeant Gomer Lloyd from the passenger seat in a deep sepulchral tone. He smoothed the back of one hand over his bushy moustache. 'For the wicked or the innocent, of course. No offence intended, boss,' he added with a grin, but also a precautionary sideways glance. He didn't take liberties with superiors when on duty, even the younger ones.

'None taken, Gomer.' The good-humoured tiny wrinkles at the sides of the speaker's eyes multiplied. 'Anyway, better class of victim for us this time,' Parry completed, but less lightly.

'Would have to be in Bryntaf, boss. And couldn't be much worse than we've just had, could it?' Two hours before, there had been a brawl in a Custom House Street pub on the southern side of the city. This had culminated in two serious assaults before the uniformed police had arrived. Parry and Lloyd, summoned to the scene later, had arrested a pimp on holding charges of causing grievous bodily harm to another man, as well as to one of the pimp's own girls. Depending on the state – or survival – of the victims, one or both the charges were likely to be moved up to something a lot more serious before the night was out. 'Even the guilty don't have previous records where we're going now. Very law-abiding lot. Does credit to the community,' completed the sergeant, like an ingenuous pastor magnanimously commending his congregation for group admission at the Pearly Gates.

'The victim, Dr Delia Bewen. She was a consultant?' asked Parry, in his habitually clipped delivery. It was the sergeant who had been briefed, by phone, at the Central Police Station on the so far inexplicable slaying of Dr Bewen at her home. This had been while Parry had been completing formalities as arresting officer of the miscreant they had brought in there.

'That's right, boss. She was a gynaecologist. Mainly worked at the RCI.' The initials stood for the Royal Cardiff Infirmary. Lloyd was pushing a peppermint into his mouth as he added, 'Terrible thing. She was quite young, too. Oh, and recently widowed.'

'How long's recently?'

'Eighteen months, I think. Yes, a twelve-month last October.' The sergeant was referring to his notebook under the dashboard light.

'Do we know how the husband died?' Parry's questions sounded casual enough, unlike the motive spawning them.

'Road accident, boss. She was with him at the time. A lorry hit their car. He was some kind of architect.' Lloyd looked up. 'Your Perdita would have known her, would she?'

'Possibly. Not necessarily.' Perdita Jones was Parry's girlfriend. Although they were unofficially engaged, he would still have hesitated to call her his Perdita. She had resumed studying medicine in London, something abandoned at her marriage and taken up again some time after her divorce. In between, she had qualified as a physiotherapist and had practised in Cardiff. 'It's nearly a year

47

since Perdita worked around here,' the chief inspector, a thirty-nine-year-old widower, went on. 'Senior medical staff change a lot.'

'A year? *Duw, Duw*. Time flies, doesn't it? So she'll be qualified in how long?'

'In fourteen months.' Parry answered accurately, as if he'd counted recently – which he had – then he blinked, something he seemed to do less than most people. 'Except she's gone back to nearly convincing herself she's going to fail.'

'She won't fail. It'd be letting you down, for one thing. After you'll have waited all that time for her, like.' The sergeant, happily married for twenty-eight years, and the father of five largely dutiful and definitely grateful grown-up children, was a solid believer in the power of obligation. Indeed, Gomer Lloyd had a determined, quite unsentimental trust in a number of old-fashioned values that many policemen, with much less service than he had, would cynically have questioned existed at all nowadays.

Parry's pale blue eyes had been reflecting his under-standing of Lloyd's meaning, but without signifying agreement. He moved their speed up a bit over the limit as they joined the broad, six-lane Northern Avenue, where traffic was thinning, then he accelerated harder as they crossed under the M4 motorway. 'Who's on the scene at Bryntaf?' he asked, changing the subject as well as the gears.

'Detective Sergeant Norris is there, boss. Arrived at 10.48, with two detective constables from the Cardiff sec-tion. A SOCO team's on its way from headquarters. Detec-tive Sergeant Glen Wilcox in charge. Should be there by now.'

'Good.' The recently promoted Mary Norris was a ser-geant with the small permanent section of the Serious Crime Support Unit attached to Cardiff Central – estab-lished there to provide a quick response. Parry and Lloyd were stationed at the Unit's headquarters in Cowbridge, nine miles west of the capital. DS Wilcox was one of the most experienced Scene of Crime Officers in the Unit. 'So when was the body found?' Parry went on.

'At 10.32, boss. Nothing on time of death yet.'

The chief inspector nodded as they overtook a speeding articulated lorry with the message emblazoned on its side 'Europe's largest suppliers of decorative laminates', which prompted him to wonder idly, but still professionally, why supplying the Rhondda Valley with decorative laminates was such an urgent matter at eleven fifteen at night. 'What about cause of death?' he asked. 'There's a nasty head wound you said?'

'Yes. Can't be sure it was the cause, though, because there's stabbing to the abdomen as well.'

'Any weapons identified?'

'None reported before we left, boss. Not the knife, nor what caused the head wound. Body's a bloody mess according to the senior of the two uniformed constables who answered the call. Her partner, young fellow, he threw up at the sight, apparently.' The sergeant gave a deprecating grunt, implying that male constables, no matter how junior, ought to be made of sterner stuff, especially when partnered by members of what he affectionately regarded as the weaker sex.

'I think women usually cope better with gore,' Parry observed, with a sniff. 'So who found her?'

'The local vicar. The Reverend Peter Treace. When he called at the house.'

'At 10.32? Had he been sent for?'

'Don't know yet, boss. They say he's very upset, poor chap. Well, you'd expect that, wouldn't you?' The vicar was evidently not to be equated with young policemen who inexcusably balked at the sight of bleeding entrails.

'So how did he get in? Was the door left open?'

'No. Seems he had a key.'

'Go on.' Parry slowed as he approached a roundabout, accelerated the car off it to the left, crossed a river bridge almost immediately, then swung left again, into the outskirts of Bryntaf. 'Does he have keys to all the widows' houses in the parish, I wonder?' he asked, a touch cynically.

'Ah, there's a reason he'd have had one to Dr Bewen's. He announced last night they were getting married. It was in the *Echo* this evening, as a matter of fact.' Lloyd paused briefly. 'They couldn't go ahead though, not till after the vicar had got a divorce.' The last words were delivered with pious and judgemental disapprobation, which was understandable in a Methodist – though less so, perhaps, in a largely lapsed Methodist.

Dr Bewen's house, Kingfishers in Picton Grove, was a mock Georgian, U-shaped detached villa, with its substantial, single-storey projections on the northern, driveway side. The building was set back from the road, and well shielded from it, by several close-set mature birch trees, leafless still, and a larger number of tall evergreen bushes. There was no fence or entrance gate.

Kingfishers closed the end of Picton Grove. This was a short cul-de-sac lined by similar houses, all built in the mid eighties, on a wooded site, for sale to the upwardly mobile. Kingfishers boasted a pillared, elevated front door, painted royal blue, under a pierced white wooden pediment. An integral double garage occupied the projection to the left. The balancing projection on the other side evidently provided living space, with no window to the north, but with two presently illuminated ones to the west.

Because of the house's position, its garden – of nearly an acre – was bigger than that of the others in the road. It even contained a tennis court, the perimeter netting just discernible on one side. So much was clear immediately because the exterior of the house was brightly lit all around by tungsten security lights. Kingfishers was not one of Bryntaf's most expensive residences, most of which had been individually designed for placing on larger plots and even higher ground, but it still looked pricier than the majority of houses in the developed village.

'Tidy-sized place just for one person,' remarked Lloyd,

as he and his chief walked up the drive to the front door, after acknowledging the salute of the uniformed constable standing guard at the entrance.

'I was thinking the same,' Parry responded. He had left the Porsche in the circle of road that terminated Picton Grove. Already there were a number of vehicles parked at the top of the drive, and more still seemingly abandoned outside in the haphazard pattern that typifies the vicinity of an accident, a crime scene – or, less excusably, a building site. A twelve-seater police van was the largest conveyance on view in the street, left with one side humped on to the mown grass verge – pavements didn't exist in the better parts of Bryntaf – and indicating that the SOCO team had arrived from Cowbridge. As the two men mounted the step to the open front door, the chief inspector nodded at the policeman on duty there, whom he knew well. 'Evening, Constable Brunnow, where's DS Wilcox?' he asked.

'Through the hall, sir. Door facing you. Er ... shoe covers in the box, sir.'

'Thanks, I thought they'd be somewhere.' Parry grinned approvingly. He and Lloyd each tore open the packing to a pair of laundered, white, ankle-length canvas shoe covers with elasticized tops, then pulled the covers on over their shoes and trouser bottoms. Glen Wilcox was a stickler for having scene-of-crime regulations observed.

The double-doored, L-shaped living room they entered was quite large, its dimensions seeming to be reduced by both the number of policemen present already, and, more, by the numerous and disparate items of furniture it normally accommodated, though these last impressed most for the unpredictable harmony they achieved. The well-maintained exterior of the building, the front garden, and the pink tarmac drive, had suggested not just affluence but also a degree of stolid uniformity: in contrast, this room reflected an individual and original taste, a touch of impudence – and, possibly, a slim-pursed owner.

Apart from the fitted rust-coloured velvet curtains, and

51

green self-coloured carpeting, most of the contents had the look of times past – of second-hand pieces, not ripe to be elevated to quite the status of antiques, but the kind of items an imaginative buyer might have acquired cheaply, at unfashionable country auctions, or city street markets.

There were four severely unmatching armchairs, two of them Victorian, and an over-large, heavily cushioned sofa of twenties vintage. An assortment of *objets d'art* and old industrial artefacts were displayed on three side tables, two lacquered, the other in natural oak, and in two hand-painted, glass-topped cabinets. There seemed to be too many mirrors, in assorted shapes and sizes, except in a way they helped to re-extend the dimensions of the room, especially when, as now, the curtains were closed. The windows provided aspects to the west (as noted from the drive) and the south. Three identically shaped art deco-lamps, but with shades in contrastingly multicoloured painted glass, were providing most of the illumination, including subdued lighting for the solid north wall of very closely hung pictures – nineteenth-century landscapes by probably forgotten artists, contemporary watercolours, contemplative pastels, rousing, art school forays in poster paint, and a *bonne bouche* of etchings. None of these was immediately arresting on merit, but the tight display was engaging as a total artistic experience.

Parry, who had a taste for the unusual, took in the unexpected interior without remarking on it. Both the newcomers were too involved with the aftermath of the drama that had just taken place here to be distracted by decor, except to note, which both did automatically, that there was no evidence of violent upheaval in the room, or anything else exceptional – save for the very dead body of a woman.

The earthly remains of Delia Bewen were lying before the empty fireplace. This was to the right of the doors, the area where policemen and others, most of them dressed in white SOCO overalls and hoods, were engaged with, or near, the body.

While Lloyd moved across to join Sergeant Wilcox, Parry went to crouch beside a busy older man in the same posture, incongruously dressed in a dinner jacket – albeit a dinner jacket as worn as its weather-beaten owner – which, sartorially, was proving more distinguishing than distinguished in the present company. The white shoe covers and the surgical gloves the man had on added a bizarre element to his appearance.

'Evening, Doctor,' said the chief inspector.

George Maltravers, the unkempt, mildly eccentric, and most experienced of the area's police surgeons, glanced briefly over his shoulder and grunted an acknowledgement. He then returned to extracting a thermometer, with some delicacy, from the human orifice favoured by medical practitioners required to take the temperature of the recently deceased.

It was not altogether surprising, Parry thought, breathing deeply and slowly, that one of the uniformed officers first on the scene had been physically upset by the appearance of the murder victim: he had viewed the remains of many such cadavers, but this one was, for a conspicuous reason, especially stomach churning.

The body was nearly naked, with the lolling head appearing to be propped up, because the neck was pressed against the lower front of the sofa. There was an ice blue silk dressing gown draped carelessly over the back of the sofa, and a pair of expensive, white leather high-heeled shoes on the seat beside it. The only whole piece of clothing in place on the body was a low-cut, delicate white lace bra, still supporting the well-developed breasts. For the rest, there was only stark flesh, some of it hideously mutilated.

The victim's shoulders and arms were collapsed inwards and downwards, like the limp upper limbs of an abandoned rag doll. The hands were half open and turned upwards, with fingers closed together, as though they had been preparing to grasp some object from underneath. Both little fingers were resting against the outside of the thighs on either side. The legs were roughly spreadeagled, the right one a little straighter than the other, as if the subject might have been dragged a short distance on that side. In contrast, the left leg was acutely bent at the knee, the upper part pointing outwards at an angle if not unnatural then at best, in the circumstances, unseemly. The lower half of the leg was curled inwards, with the ankle and foot crookedly tucked behind the right knee.

The head, like the whole body, was inclined a little to the right, chin sunk downwards, with the hair and scalp on the more exposed left side matted in blood. A rivulet of blood had also run down behind the ear, which was still incongruously decorated with a gold oyster clip. There was no blood on the face, but the extent of the bleeding was evident from the very heavy staining of the sofa cover, indicating that the blow responsible for the damage had been to the unexposed back of the skull.

But it was on the abdomen that the killer had perpetrated a callous, bestial havoc on the flesh and what lay under the flesh.

Two savagely deep knife cuts had been made – one down from the navel to terminate in the mount of flaxen pubic hair below, the other, running at right angles to it, from hip to hip. The two incisions made a roughly cruciform design. Many more smaller cuts, without a matching geometric, or methodical pattern, had crisscrossed the first two. None of these lesser incisions were deep, or long, but they had served to extend the sickening exposure of subcutaneous tissue and organs – mixed with the blood-soaked, tattered remains of what had been a pair of lace panties, their colour impossible to divine.

Since there was surprisingly little blood spilled to witness what had been wreaked on the lower part of the body, the effects were chillingly graphic. This was why it had been relatively simple for Parry to guess at the likely sequence in the assault, without explanation from the

54

doctor who was presently too preoccupied to give one.

'Seems like the work of a demented butcher,' muttered the policeman.

'Demented, or amateur. Or both,' Maltravers responded a few moments later, again over his shoulder. 'Semantically acute comment of yours though, Merlin.' He paused as he gently touched a lump of dissected flesh with two glove-encased fingers. 'That's if you were meaning to mark the difference between a family butcher and a . . . a slaughterman,' he continued. 'I think we can assume whoever did all this felled her first with the blow to the head from behind. Then he got his perverted kicks making these . . . these choice cuts afterwards.'

'Any idea what sort of weapons were used?'

'The head wound was caused by something solid. Solid and heavy, most likely with an uneven surface. The lacerations –' the heavy shoulders heaved – 'They could have been made by any kind of narrow-bladed sharp knife, a small one probably.' He looked about him, then back down at the body. 'Depending on the size, the knife could be inside her still. And that wouldn't be for the first time in my experience. But I'm thankful to say it's not my job to go searching for it now.'

6

———

'The Reverend Treace says he rang Dr Bewen at ten, sir. That was as promised. But he got no answer, not even from her machine. When the same thing happened at ten-twenty, he decided to come up, and check she was all right.'

Detective Sergeant Mary Norris, petite, with dark hair cut in a page-boy style, looked as efficient as she sounded – if shorter than usual – in a brown, cotton trouser suit, green polo-neck sweater, black stockings and no shoes. She had arrived at the house ahead of the SOCO team – and the shoe covers. She had removed her own shoes on first entering, and hadn't made time since to do anything else about her feet.

'Have you asked if he touched the body?' Parry asked, standing with the young woman in the middle of the room where Dr Maltravers was still completing his examinations.

'Yes, sir. He checked the neck for a pulse.'

'Pretty pointless seeing the state she was in.'

'But a natural, caring reaction, sir.' The response had been very prompt.

'Quite right.' He was amused by the gentle implied reproof. He had been one of those responsible for Mary Norris's transfer out of the uniformed branch, and, later, for her promotion. Diplomacy had come high on her list of merits, he remembered.

'Then he tried to cover her, he said, with the scraps of her carved-up panties,' she went on. 'He meant, to cover her genitals. As you saw, that didn't work. The material was too damaged and bloodstained, and anyway, that part of her was too violated.' Mary Norris was twenty-five, but looked a lot less. She was very aware of her over-youthful, waiflike appearance. Had she been a man, she would probably have grown a moustache, or a beard. As it was, she tended to wear an unendearing frown, often when it was uncalled for, because she felt it aged her. She also steeled herself always to look senior male officers unwaveringly in the eye when making verbal reports, especially verbal reports on subjects like lacerated female genitalia.

'I suppose we should be grateful he didn't use important evidence to cover her, like the dressing gown,' said Parry.

The sergeant lowered her voice. 'It's hard to explain, sir, but I don't believe he was that keen on . . . on covering her. Not all over.' She swallowed. 'When he and I were looking at her, he seemed, well, sort of mesmerized, not grief-stricken like he was before that. For instance, he didn't hear two of the questions I put to him, not first time.'

'That's interesting, Sergeant,' Parry smiled in commendation. 'He'll have left expensive genetic prints on the body, of course. All probably useless to us,' he added, in a grudging voice.

Anyone involved in a murder who, though professing innocence, admits to close contact with the victim, before or after the crime, can be costly to the police. Unidentified DNA samples taken at the scene may need to be checked against matching samples voluntarily supplied by that person. And processing DNA samples is pricey. Further, as Parry's last comment implied, even if the Reverend Treace later became a genuine suspect, there was little chance now that he would be proved guilty merely because a stray hair from his head was found on the victim. If samples of, say, his blood or sperm were discovered on or in the body, of course, that would not be incidental.

'At least the vicar knew about not moving the body, sir,' Sergeant Norris volunteered.

'Well, bully for him.' Parry was still entertaining negative thoughts about Mr Treace.

'Yes, sir. And after he'd rung for the police, he says he stayed clear of the body and . . . and prayed for Dr Bewen.'

'I see.' Parry cleared his throat. 'Did you ask him where he did his praying? Where and how?'

'On his knees, sir, over there in front of the red chair. I've told SOCO.'

'Good. It was a bit late for him to be staying clear of the body, of course. Still, as you said, he could hardly have avoided touching it earlier. How long was it before he rang for the police?'

The sergeant checked her notes. 'Two minutes, sir. If he got here at 10.32. And that's his estimate.'

'Any corroboration?'

'We think so, sir. But we have to check it out. He says he was talking to his daughter Janet at home, at the vicarage, from about ten past nine up to the time he left. He estimates that's a five-minute walk from here.'

'He walked here?'

'That's right, sir.'

'And was he at the vicarage all evening otherwise?'

'Not between 7.25 and just after 9 p.m. He gave his regular Wednesday Lent lecture in the church hall at 7.30.'

'Lasting all that time?'

'I assumed so. From what he said. Shall I check with him again, sir?'

'No, I will, when I see him.' He was waiting on the doctor for a rough estimate on the time of death, aware already, though, that it was more likely to be offered in hours than minutes. 'Get someone to see the daughter before the vicar leaves here, will you?' he asked. 'No, better still, do it yourself, in the next fifteen minutes. And find out anything else you can from her about his movements. Like how long this Lent lecture lasted.'

'I don't think she was there, sir. Nor her brother. His name's Simon. They're both away at university. Came home together this morning.'

'Was Simon at home tonight as well?'

'No, sir. So far as Mr Treace knows, he's spent the evening with his mother. She's staying with someone locally called . . . Mrs Bronwyn Hughes.'

'Is that because the Treaces are splitting up?'

'I don't know, sir. I didn't know they were splitting up.'

'Well they are. The vicar didn't tell you he and Dr Bewen were planning to get married?'

'No, sir.' The sergeant looked surprised. 'I assumed they were just close friends, his having a key to the house.'

Parry nodded. 'Too shocked to mention it, perhaps. He said his wife was staying the night with this Mrs Hughes, did he?'

'Yes, sir. Simon may be home at the vicarage by now, of course,' the speaker was looking at her notes again.

'OK. Go to Mrs Hughes's address before the vicarage, and check if Simon Treace is still there. If he isn't, find out from Mrs Hughes and Mrs Treace what time he left. Where's Mr Treace now?'

'In Dr Bewen's consulting room, sir, across the hall. He says she used it for seeing her local patients. Private patients, mostly. I got SOCO to sweep it before Mr Treace went in there. I told him we'd be grateful if he'd stay for further questioning.'

'That was tactful.'

The sergeant smirked at the approbation, showing even, snow white teeth. 'He was quite co-operative about that, sir. He's very upset. I think he was glad to have some time alone.'

'Had Dr Bewen been seeing private patients this evening?'

'There's an appointment at 9 p.m. entered in the organizer in her handbag, sir. It says KF, then the name Audrey S. But the entry's been crossed through with a pencil.'

'Meaning it was cancelled?'

'Or kept, sir. She's crossed through a lot of items in the organizer. It could mean she always crossed things off after she'd done them.'

Parry looked doubtful for some reason. 'Her secretary at the RCI will know if she did. She should also know who Audrey S. is. So where's this organizer now?'

'It's being checked for fingerprints, sir, in the kitchen. Shall I get it?'

'No, tell them to let me see it when they've done. Incidentally, I want you to stay on the case for the next twenty-four hours at least. We'll draft in a substitute for you at Cardiff Central. Only I want you on the day relief tomorrow, with overtime, if required. Can you manage that?'

'Yes, sir.' She seemed dutifully resigned, not fazed, at the prospect of going without some of her sleep tonight. 'About the organizer, sir, we're only guessing KF stands for Kingfishers. There aren't many appointments entered with that against them. Some have the initials BCH after the times and before the patient's name. They're usually late in the afternoon, except Tuesdays are different because –'

'BCH stands for what?' he interrupted.

'We're pretty certain it's Bryntaf Cottage Hospital, sir. Mr Treace says Dr Bewen had a regular clinic there every Tuesday. I was going to say, most Tuesday afternoons are crossed through in the organizer, with BCH written above.'

Parry pinched the end of his nose. 'Do we know anything yet about her movements today?'

'So far, only that she was at the RCI all day, and left at 6.20, sir. We're asking neighbours now if anyone saw her come home. The only message on the answering machine was recorded at 7.28 p.m.'

'So she, or somebody, switched it off at some time between then and ten o'clock, when the vicar called the first time. Who was the message from?'

'Her hairdresser's, sir, in Cardiff. About an appointment. They closed at eight. Do you want us to get the manager at home?'

'Yes. Find out if she rang them back.'

60

'That's not likely, sir. Their message was to confirm an appointment.'

'I see. Well, still check, in case she did ring them. If she did, the time of the call could be critical. If you can't find the manager, BT can give us the same information, and tell us about any other calls she made this evening. If she has a mobile –'

'She has, sir.'

'Right. Get the log of calls she made on that as well. Anything else?'

'Not yet, sir.'

'So, any ideas about why she was in her living room half-dressed?' As he spoke, he looked over the woman detective's shoulder to check that the doctor was still busy with the body.

'Possibly she wasn't, sir. Not when she came down. There's the silk dressing gown she probably had on earlier.'

'Earlier than what?'

'Whatever she came down to do, sir.'

'Like . . . like entertain a caller?'

'Could be, sir. It looks like she had a shower when she got home, put on a clean bra and panties, the old ones are near the laundry basket in her bedroom – thrown at it, I'd say because –'

'Then she came down here in the dressing gown,' he broke in, thinking aloud, 'to watch TV, make some supper, read, listen to the radio or a CD.' He looked around the room. There was no television set in here, but there was a radio and CD player in one corner. 'Any signs she'd been making supper in the kitchen?'

'No, sir. I'd say it hadn't been used at all tonight. The dishwasher's empty, so's the waste bin, and there are no dirty plates in the kitchen, nor in here, or any of the other rooms. Of course, she could have been interrupted before getting round to doing what she'd planned.'

Parry nodded. 'But she wasn't getting ready for bed, was she? Not if she put on clean undies.'

'Doesn't seem likely, sir, no. And the bed wasn't turned down. It's only a guess, but it looks as if she might have showered and changed in a terrific hurry. Either that, or she was a very untidy person.'

'No signs of violence in the bedroom, though?' Parry put in quickly.

'No, sir. It's just that she left everything where she dropped it – the other clothes she must have been wearing are scattered all over the place, on the floor, some of them, like the undies, and the bathroom towels. Her dressing table is the same – the top left off a moisturizer bottle. A drawer left open.'

'Is the whole bedroom a mess?'

'No, sir. Nor the bathroom, either. Everything neat and tidy except the stuff she'd been using.'

'So if she was in such a tearing hurry, she must have had a deadline to meet. Someone coming any second. But not to take her out. Not if she hadn't put a dress on.'

'Or not to take her out straight away, sir.'

'Might have been a lover, I suppose.'

Mary Norris frowned. 'That wouldn't follow, would it, sir? I mean, for a lover, a sexy nightie under the dressing gown would have been just as likely. And . . . and nothing on underneath, more likely still. Depends what switches people on, doesn't it?'

Parry noted that the woman sergeant was looking him straight in the eye again with more than usual determination. 'Yes, I'm sure that's right,' he replied. An awkward pause followed, during which he couldn't stop himself speculating that Sergeant Norris had just inadvertently described what she, Sergeant Norris, would or would not have worn under a dressing gown when getting ready to let in a lover. He was also half certain that the sergeant knew exactly what he was thinking, because despite her fiercely dispassionate gaze and sternly set mouth, her cheeks had gone an attractive shade of pink. 'But can we assume this lover, if there was one, has to have been Mr Treace?' he went on in an overly matter-of-fact voice.

'Not according to him, sir. I mean, I asked him if she could have been expecting him. He said no.'

'But he'd arranged to ring her at ten?'

The sergeant nodded. 'He says that was because he couldn't see her during the evening, but wanted a word before she went to bed. He wasn't going to say he was coming round, and she wasn't expecting him to. And he's sure she wasn't going to ask him round either.'

'How could he possibly be sure of that?'

The sergeant made a face. 'He seems to know her habits pretty well,' she offered, but without a lot of conviction.

'But what he's said is what we'd assume he'd say. Whether he was telling the truth or not,' said the chief inspector, rubbing the space between his eyebrows. Then he smiled as he dropped his hand. 'It's all speculation at this point, of course. Right. You carry on. I'll see Treace in a minute.' He moved across to the white-suited Detective Sergeant Glen Wilcox who was with Gomer Lloyd a few feet away, comparing notes. 'So, what have we got?' he asked.

'House was well secured, sir. No locks or windows forced,' said Wilcox, an ambitious and dedicated young graduate who was as economical with words as Parry – excepting only when he came to lauding the virtues of his pretty wife, something he did at every opportunity. The lady was a Tupperware distributor, and the sergeant's colleagues had been led to believe, amongst other things, that she earned a good deal more than he or they did.

'So she most probably let in whoever killed her, boss,' put in Gomer Lloyd. 'Unless he had a key, of course.'

'And perhaps the vicar's not the only one with one of those,' said Parry. There was a momentary silence as all three men debated that possibility, or lack of it.

'She was out all day, most days, including Saturdays. That's what a neighbour told one of the uniform constables who answered the call, boss. There's a regular cleaning lady who comes in every morning except Sundays. She'd have a key most likely.'

Parry nodded. 'And what about your sweep in here, Glen? Any trace of the weapons yet?'

'Not yet, sir. Plenty of sharp knives in the kitchen. Surgical ones, too, in the consulting room. None bloodstained. Any of them could have been used in the stabbing and washed after. We're sending them for forensic checks. Plenty of blunt instruments about, as well, of course. The doctor may be telling us what kind was used on her head.' Wilcox had removed his white hood and was displaying a close-cut crop of carrot-coloured hair. Long hair is discouraged in Scene of Crime Officers for obvious reasons, at least amongst the male ones, who are not expected to run the risk of wasting police time and money vacuuming up strands of their own hair for laboratory examination later. 'We're finished, really, sir, on both floors, including photographs. That was done first thing. So we have to see what we get from the vacuum bags tomorrow. Place seems to have been cleaned this morning. No dust anywhere. Same in the kitchen, and most of the other rooms.' The fact seemed to have displeased Wilcox, even though it had simplified the immediate job.

'Including the consulting room?' asked Parry.

'Cleanest place of the lot, sir.'

'No fingerprints in there?'

'None found, sir.'

'And what about upstairs? I haven't been up there yet.'

'Bathroom carpet outside the shower cubicle's a bit wet. Bathmat's the same. Few stray hairs there, blonde ones. That suggests they're all hers. She's a natural blonde. My wife's the same,' Wilcox completed, a hint of pride entering his voice compared to his previous mundane delivery.

Parry and Lloyd glanced solemnly in the direction of the body, both affecting not to be thinking about Glen Wilcox's wife's now formally attested blonde pubic hair.

'Fingerprinting's pretty well done everywhere, boss,' said Lloyd, scratching his stomach.

'Yes, but we shan't get much from that,' supplied Wilcox.

64

'Thanks to Dr Bewen's conscientious cleaning lady,' the chief inspector smiled. 'We'll need a set of her prints for elimination.'

'Yes, sir. Hoped to get them off the Hoover handle, but no luck. Wears household gloves all the time, I expect.'

'Were the surfaces in this room cleaner than anywhere else?' Parry asked.

'Not really, sir. Less so in one sense. There's quite a few of Dr Bewen's prints in here. At least, we're guessing they're all hers at the moment.'

'Same in the bedroom?'

'Yes, sir. But I think all the action happened down here.'

'And the murderer wore gloves too, like the cleaner?'

'Not necessarily, sir. Or maybe not all the time.' Wilcox's freckled brow knitted. 'If he came to the house meaning to kill her, he could have avoided touching anything. Or wiped anything he did touch after, like. But he'd have stuck to one room if he could, for that reason. That's why I don't believe he went upstairs.'

'Could be. Excuse me,' Parry moved away from the two detective sergeants. He had watched Dr Maltravers get to his feet after apparently ending his ministrations on the body. 'Going back to your posh dinner, Doctor?' the chief inspector enquired lightly.

'Oh, very droll, Merlin. Boring medical do at the Park Hotel, it was. One of the pharmaceutical outfits suavely flogging a new nostrum. It was over before I was called here. I was on my way home to a good night's rest. Teach me to keep my mobile switched on.' He rolled off a surgical glove, then poked a bare finger into the hairy orifice of one ear, screwing up his face as he did so.

'Are you finished with the body?'

Maltravers turned about slowly to gaze again at the dead Dr Bewen. 'Just about,' he said. 'They'll be taking her to the morgue tonight.'

'The pathologist doesn't want to look at her here?' Parry was surprised.

'Would do normally, Merlin, only it's a bad night for

65

pathologists. There's not one available till mid-morning tomorrow, and we can't have her hanging about here in this state. Anyway, I don't suppose there's anything to be learned here that won't be just as clear at a post mortem. I can't help you any more on the weapons, I'm afraid. Skull was badly fractured with something heavy. That's what killed her. Oh, and the stabbings definitely came after she was dead.'

'Can you give us an estimate on the time of death?'

'Not a very precise one, no.' Maltravers folded his arms across his barrel chest. 'Did I hear she left the RCI a bit after six?'

'At 6.20, yes. So if she drove straight to Bryntaf, she could have made it by, say, 6.45. There's an appointment in her diary for nine o'clock, here.'

'Private patient, was that, Merlin?'

'Probably, but we don't know yet. Also the appointment may have been cancelled. At some point after about 7.30, she, or someone, switched off her answering machine. It's most likely to have been her, of course, which means she was alive then, also that she probably didn't come straight home. If she had, she'd most likely have switched the machine off earlier, and before a message that was recorded at 7.28.'

'Well, that'd strengthen my guess she died between eight and nine,' said Maltravers. 'The body temperature I got suggests that, although this house would have kept her pretty warm, meaning she could have died earlier.' The speaker moved away a pace to examine an etching of a large and, to Parry, unprepossessing pig. 'If you can find out when she last ate, the post mortem might give you a closer time of death than mine, though I doubt it. My word, that's a handsome porker, isn't it? Wessex Saddleback. Magnificent.' The doctor reared champion pigs as a hobby. He had put on a pair of half-spectacles to study the picture more closely. 'Date on it reads 1872. Well I never.' He moved back, his gaze now taking in the whole wall of closely hung paintings and drawings. 'Fine collection of pictures she had. Her late husband's doing, I expect, not hers.'

'You knew them both, doctor?'

Maltravers took off the spectacles and blinked as he slipped them back into their case. 'Not really. Met him once, with her, at a hospital party. Emaciated-looking chap. Architect. No money in that, of course. That's why he ran an interior design business, I think. Enterprising of him, but I don't believe that paid very much either.' He cleared his throat with a deep grumble, then attempted to flick a crumb off the silk lapel of his faded dinner jacket, except the crumb proved to be a well-established food stain. 'As for her,' he continued, with a malicious last look at the stain, 'she hadn't been at the Infirmary all that long. Three years, I think, or possibly a bit longer. One forgets these things. Didn't come across her much. Different ends of the business, in a way. Me too often taken up with the dead and wounded, she with the just born and the yet unborn.' The doctor sat himself in a nearby upright chair. 'Of course, as a gynae, she had a bit to do with thinning them out as well.' The outdoor, wizened countenance tightened in what might have been perplexity – or at the effort involved in removing the first of the shoe covers.

7

'Sorry to keep you waiting, sir,' said the chief inspector as he entered Dr Bewen's home consulting room. 'My name's Merlin Parry. I'm Senior Investigating Officer on the case. Terrible business, of course. You have my . . . my deepest sympathy.'

'Thank you, Mr Parry.' Peter Treace got up from behind the single pedestal metal desk set at the far end of the quite narrow room, under the only window. He shook hands with the policeman, then went on. 'I hung on because the lady officer, er . . . Miss Norris, I think, she said you'd want to see me tonight.' The cleric's manner was dignified. He seemed more tired than distraught, and his eyes were red.

'That's right, sir. Thanks very much. Won't keep you longer than necessary.'

Treace shook his head. 'I still can't bring myself to believe what's happened.' He paused. 'I'm usually the one who has to persuade the bereaved to . . . to face the facts. To accept God's will, mysterious and unaccountable as it might seem. But this was no work of God's. Only the Devil's.' He gave a bitter smile, then straightened his back. 'Do you want to sit here?' He made to move out from behind the desk.

'No, sir. I'll be all right this side. Please sit down again.' Parry pulled out the chair intended for patients. The room was austere compared to what he had seen of the rest of the house. To the left of the door was an examination couch, covered in brown plastic, with a wide, adjustable

68

examination light at the end. On the right was a wash-basin, after which the lower part of the wall was lined with closed cupboards, with glazed-in shelves at a higher level exhibiting a variety of medical impedimenta, including some neatly stacked white cartons, and a battery of shining chrome implements. There was a computer set on a metal extension to one side of the desk, and a two-tier filing cabinet on the other – this last topped by a telephone and a book rack holding a set of medical directories and some heavy textbooks.

'You know Delia Bewen and I were getting married, Mr Parry? As soon as I've got my divorce. We were very much in love. Deeply, deeply in love. There were problems, of course, because of my . . . my situation. I mean my being married already, and my job as parish priest here. But all that would have been overcome. One way or another. We intended to marry, whatever else had to be given up – sacrificed.' There was another brief pause before he completed: 'I thought you should know that.'

Treace's delivery had been deliberate, and his tone strangely devoid of emotion. He had offered an unprompted recital of what he evidently believed was necessary information – though Parry was not wholly sure why he had done it.

'Yes, I gathered you were going to marry, sir. That you announced it last night.' Parry squeezed his lips together before he added. 'Does anyone come to mind who might have murdered Dr Bewen because of that announcement? From anger, jealousy, or –'

'No, Mr Parry,' the other man interrupted. 'I can see what you mean, of course. Some people might have been upset. I'm afraid my wife for one. No, no,' he added quickly, with a dismissive gesture because Parry had made as if to break in after the mention of Mrs Treace. 'My wife wouldn't hurt a fly. And neither would any of the people who may have thought I was doing the wrong thing. That's all I meant about them, you see? No, I understand what you're getting at. But I can tell you, honestly, I don't know anyone who'd have wanted physically to harm Delia.'

'Not even another close male friend, sir, angry about her decision to marry you? The most unlikely, normal sort of people are sometimes capable of sudden, horrendous reactions to information like that.'

Treace considered for a moment. 'No,' he said slowly. 'You see, surprising as it may seem, there weren't any other close male friends. When she came to me a year ago, for pastoral help, she was a heartbroken widow, emotionally and spiritually very much alone. There really was no one else in her life then, and hasn't been since. I'd know if there had been. People may find her loneliness then hard to believe. I did. After all, she was a young – well, comparatively young – intelligent, and very attractive woman.'

Parry nodded. 'I know a bit about how she must have felt, sir. I've been a widower for some time myself. People can't credit the loneliness, or the reasons for it.'

'That's very perceptive of you, Mr Parry.' He wet his lips. 'You possibly find it difficult to understand, to condone even, a parish priest who lets himself become emotionally caught up in the way I did. I can only say that human loneliness, isolation, can take many forms, and that clergymen are not immune to any of them, despite a comforting trust in the fellowship and companionship of our Lord.'

'Of course, sir.' Once again Parry was surprised, and in this instance, a touch embarrassed that Treace had felt obliged to unburden himself unnecessarily for a second time. 'Anyway, if a name does come to mind later, sir, please tell us. We'll need all the help we can catching whoever did this.' He paused, shifting a little in his seat. 'Now, I'm afraid I have to ask you to go over your own movements this evening again, in more detail, for the record. Routine, you understand, but important.' He opened a notebook in front of him on the desk.

'The rest can't wait till tomorrow, Mr Parry? I'm feeling pretty done in.'

'Better not, sir, if you can possibly stand it for a bit longer. One forgets things otherwise. Things that can be important to our finding the doctor's killer. I promise we'll be through quickly. Now, I gather you gave a lecture at 7.30 this evening?' he completed at a brisker pace.

'Lenten talk, yes.' Treace responded flatly, but clearly resigned to having the interview continue. 'It was part of a weekly series. In the church hall.'

'And it was over at what time, sir?'

'Oh, questions finished about 8.20, but people tend to hang about. Probably I locked up the hall ten minutes after that. Say at 8.30 or 8.35. Does it matter?'

'It might do, sir. You never know at this stage,' Parry responded, off-handedly. 'Was anyone with you when you left the hall, by any chance?'

There was a moment's hesitation. 'For once, no. A Miss Davies, Maud Davies, one of the very faithful, she usually leaves at the end with me. Does the locking up, too. But she wasn't there tonight. I don't know why. I meant to ring her to find out. In case she's ill. But I'm afraid I forgot.'

'And did you go straight back to the vicarage, then, sir?'

'Yes . . . sorry, no. I had a few things to do across at the church on the way. Must have got back a little after nine. Ten past, perhaps.' He shook his head. 'My daughter will know, probably.'

'That's your daughter Janet, sir?'

'Yes. We only have the one daughter. And one son, Simon. Janet was in my study, using my computer.'

'Was Simon in too, sir?'

'No. I believe he was with his mother. She's er . . . she's staying a night or two with a friend. It's taking everybody a bit of time to settle in to the er . . . the new situation.'

'You mean your intended divorce and remarriage, sir? But presumably your wife and children knew about both, before you announced it to everyone else?'

71

Treace's expression became pained. 'My wife, yes. But not long before. Yesterday morning, to be exact. Though she was aware for some time we'd have to part sooner or later.' He made the last comment as though he was thinking aloud, before adding in a stronger voice. 'The children I told this morning, when they got home. From university. The whole thing has been difficult. Not least in judging the timing.'

'I'm sure, sir. And you and Janet were together tonight, until you came here?'

The cleric sighed heavily. 'That's right.'

'Sergeant Norris told me you first rang Dr Bewen by arrangement? At ten o'clock, was that?'

'Yes. But there was no answer.'

'Had you been planning to see her later this evening, sir?'

Treace looked surprised. 'No, I hadn't. For several reasons, all of which I now regret bitterly. I mean, if I'd been with her earlier, she'd be alive now, wouldn't she?' He gave another deep sigh, then leaned forward, forearms resting on the desktop, head bowed, his eyes on the hands clasped in front of him. 'I told you, Janet and Simon got back this morning. I felt I owed it to them to be at home today. Well, as much as possible. To talk things through. With them, and my wife. I'm afraid, it didn't quite work out that way.'

'Because your wife left to stay with the friend, sir? Mrs Hughes? And Simon went with her?'

'Yes. Well, not quite with her. He drove her over, and went back there again later. It's not far away, and it was just for the evening for him, I think. Probably he's home by now.'

'How did Simon and Janet take the news, sir?'

'Janet was . . . resigned about it. Realistic, too. She'd seen it coming for years. She's . . . sympathetic, to both of us.'

'To yourself and your wife, sir?'

The cleric looked up in a questioning way. 'I'm sorry?

Oh, yes. Well, to all three of us involved. She completely accepts my intention to remarry.' He breathed in heavily, his eyes once again dropping to study his hands. 'Simon didn't take the news at all well, I'm afraid. He's very loyal to his mother, despite her . . . problems.'

'Her problems, sir?'

'She's an alcoholic, Mr Parry. It's no secret. Indeed, I sometimes think it's the best-advertised known fact in the parish.' The response had been bitter.

'I'm sorry, sir.' Parry swallowed, then continued. 'Is Simon a headstrong young man?'

Treace looked up sharply. 'The opposite. And he's certainly not the type to commit murder, if that's what you're suggesting, Mr Parry.'

'I was enquiring about his nature, sir, that's all. But people sometimes behave out of character when they're shocked or angry, or when someone dear to them has been badly hurt. I'm sure he's as level-headed as you say. I'm afraid we'll need to see him anyway, but, again, that's routine.' The policeman waited for a response, but when there was none, he asked: 'If we could just go back to what you did when there was no reply to your ten o'clock call?'

'As I told Miss Norris, I tried again twenty minutes later. When there was still no answer, I decided to come up here, to make sure everything was all right.'

'You walked here, I believe? Not the quickest way in an emergency, sir.'

'It was hardly an emergency at that point. I take physical exercise whenever I can. Also . . . also we've, that's Delia and I, we've always been discreet. For instance, where possible I've avoided leaving my car in the drive here. That's so people can't work out how long I've stayed.' He shrugged. 'I suppose it was a reflex thing to do the same tonight, although our relationship is out in the open now. In any event, that's why I walked here.'

'Thank you, sir. Did you have any solid reason to think things might not be all right for Dr Bewen?'

Once more the other man was slow to answer. 'No reason. Well, not exactly,' he said eventually, but his tone was uncertain.

'A premonition, perhaps?'

'That's too strong a word. A number of possibilities went through my mind, though. One has heard about hate mail, for instance, following the kind of . . . episode we were going through.'

'Following the announcement of your plans, sir?'

'Yes. It occurred to me that it might just have spawned hate mail or . . . or cruel phone calls. I thought Delia might have forgotten I was going to telephone, that she wasn't answering the phone because someone had rung up already and been unkind to her. It was a reason why she might have switched off the answering machine as well.' He shrugged. 'Of course, all kinds of bizarre ideas go through one's mind in situations of that kind.'

'Quite so, sir. But there was no reason for you to think she might have had doubts, misgivings?'

'About what?'

'Perhaps the sense of making the announcement last night, sir.'

'Why should she possibly have had doubts about that? It was something we'd been planning together for weeks. She had no doubts then.'

'Sure. But you mentioned your personal circumstances just now. I suppose it's always possible some busybody might have upset her in some way since the announcement.'

'Upset her, maybe, but not altered her mind. I'm sure of that.'

'I understand, sir. And presumably you'd seen Dr Bewen since the parish meeting?'

Treace looked uneasy. 'No, as a matter of fact, I hadn't. And that's something else I'll regret for the rest of my life.' There was a long pause before he went on, after evidently fighting back the emotion that had shown in his voice. 'I'd meant to come up after the meeting was over. To tell her how it had gone. But with my wife in the state she was in . . . very drunk, I'm afraid, I couldn't get away. I phoned Delia instead, quite late on, and again this morning. That was when I promised to call her tonight at ten. We'd agreed not to meet today. That was partly because of possible newspaper interest in us.'

'There was a report about you in this evening's *Echo*, sir.'

'Yes, I saw it. I know one of the senior editorial people there quite well. I phoned him early this morning, gave him the same facts I'd given the meeting last night, and answered some questions. I thought in that way I could keep media interest at a low level, and I think I might have succeeded. It really wasn't that much of a story. So, all in all, Delia and I thought it best to go about our usual jobs in our usual ways.'

'And you really had no intention of coming up to see her tonight, sir?'

There was another of the long sighs. 'I suppose, if I'm absolutely honest about it, I might have changed my mind on that, especially if Delia had asked me to come. My daughter thought I should have come here in any case. I told you, she's been very understanding.'

'And when you did arrive here, sir, on foot, you let yourself in with your own key?'

'I rang the bell first. That's another of the . . . discreet habits I'd developed up to now. In case Delia had someone with her, a patient, or, well, anybody. But, yes, when she didn't come to the door, I used my own key.'

'That's a key to the front door, sir?'

'Yes. I don't have one to the back door.'

'Did you know Dr Bewen was supposed to be seeing a patient at nine, sir?'

'No. But she often did see private patients here in the evening.'

'The appointment in her diary was with an Audrey S. Does Audrey S. mean anything to you, sir?'

'Nothing at all, no. Should it?'

'Probably not, sir. I wondered if the lady might have been local.'

'The chances could well be she wasn't, Mr Parry. Delia had patients coming to her here, and at the hospital, from all over South Wales. She was a brilliant gynaecologist.'

'I'm sure, sir. Well, we'll probably find out who Audrey S. is tomorrow. And whether she kept the appointment.'

'Is there some doubt about that?'

'Only that this room didn't appear to have been used recently. Not since it was cleaned this morning, sir.'

Treace shook his head. 'Delia didn't always see patients in here. If no examination was necessary, no physical examination, I think she sometimes just talked to them in the sitting room. A lot of her work was ... well, I suppose you could say, psychological. Explaining the pros and cons of treatment. Whether an operation was advisable. That kind of thing. I think she must have been a very sympathetic physician. People say so. Women, I mean.'

'I understand, sir.' Parry leaned back in the chair. 'And when you came into the house, what did you do?'

'I . . . I called out for Delia. Several times.'

'And which room did you go to first?'

'This one. The door was half-open, and there was a light on. When I found she wasn't here, I went to the sitting room. You know the rest.'

'And, sorry to ask this, sir, did you notice the body immediately?'

'Yes, because I looked automatically to the right. To the chair she always uses, on the far side of the sofa. I thought she might have fallen asleep there.'

'Thank you. It must have been the most terrible shock,' said Parry quietly. When the other man made no reply, he went on: 'Can you remember, was there anything else strange about the room, sir? A piece of furniture missing, or . . . or in a different place from normal. Or anything new, even.'

Treace began to shake his head in denial, but then he looked up and said, 'There was one thing. I didn't notice

76

it then, it was later. After I'd telephoned for the police. It was something quite trivial though. The ornaments on one table had been moved about.'

'What kind of ornaments, sir?'

'Principally an old-fashioned miner's lamp. It's nothing very special, but it's noticeable. And Delia was fond of it. I think her husband picked it up cheaply, like most of the other things in the room. It's on the table between the two windows overlooking the garden. Well, you wouldn't know that with the curtains drawn tonight. There's a mirror on the wall behind it.'

'And the lamp had been moved, sir?'

'To one side, yes. About a foot or so. You asked if I noticed anything different. I noticed that. Delia didn't move things about in that room. Not furniture or ornaments. Everything seemed to have its regular, permanent spot.'

'Thank you, sir. Did you put the lamp back in its normal place, by any chance?'

'No.'

'Excuse me just a second.' Parry got up quickly and left the room, reappearing again shortly afterwards. 'I've just arranged for the lamp to be checked, sir. May be nothing to learn from it, but it's worth a try. It's an interesting piece. Bit of history, I suppose. I can see why Dr Bewen liked it.' He took his seat again. 'So, one last question. Have you any idea why Dr Bewen was dressed the way she was? In er . . . in just bra and panties.'

'There was a dressing gown as well, Mr Parry. It was on the back of the sofa. And the white shoes, of course.' It was almost as though he was defending the victim's sense of propriety.

'I know that, sir, but it's unlikely she had those on when she died. There was no blood on the dressing gown anywhere. Not on the collar even, where there'd almost have to have been blood if she was wearing it when she was hit on the head.'

The cleric frowned. 'I see what you mean. But if you

want to know why she was in her own living room just in her underwear, I can't tell you. She wasn't in the habit of going about half-dressed at home. That's why I still think the dressing gown and the shoes are important.'

'You think she was made to take those things off before she died, sir?'

'If the murderer was a man, that has to be so. She'd never have taken them off otherwise.'

'What if the man was a doctor, sir?'

There was a momentary silence. 'Delia had nothing wrong with her,' Treace said eventually. 'Why should she be examined by a doctor when she was well? And in her own home? She spent most of her days in a hospital. If she'd wanted a . . . a check-up, say, she'd have had one there.'

'I think that's probably right enough, sir. So why was she dressed that way in the first place? If she was going to bed, we think she'd have had a nightdress on, not underwear.'

'Perhaps she was getting undressed for bed when whoever killed her arrived. You're thinking she let him in, aren't you? So am I.'

'We don't think she was preparing for bed, sir, because she'd just showered, and the underclothes were clean ones.'

Treace gave a weary look, as though he was tired of being pressed for information he couldn't supply, but then he said, 'What if she'd been in the middle of dressing properly again, but had to throw on a dressing gown to do something quickly. Answer the door or the telephone, perhaps? Well, not the telephone, I suppose. There's one in the bedroom.'

Parry waited to see if Treace intended to speculate further; when he didn't, the policeman offered, 'Well, thanks for trying to help us on that one, sir. I can tell you, it's got us baffled for the moment.' He closed his notebook. 'And now I'll have you driven home.'

'That won't be necessary, Mr Parry. I can walk.'

'I think it's better you're driven, sir. I've just been told there are a lot of reporters outside, and a TV camera crew's just arrived.'

8

'And those Welsh cakes, they're for eating, not looking at. Only don't let Gomer scoff the lot. Sorry there's only those left, but they're fresh made this afternoon. I shan't expect to see any back in the tin, either, not when I come down in the morning. Well, it's morning already, isn't it?' the comely, well-padded, garrulous Gracie Lloyd had looked at the time as she brought the teapot to the table.

Gracie, her husband, Gomer, and Merlin Parry were in the kitchen of the Lloyds' large semi-detached, thirties-built house in Fairwater, an inner suburb on the north-west side of Cardiff. It was just gone midnight, and the two men had left Fairwater police station a few minutes earlier, after going over her report with Mary Norris.

'Now, you súre that's all you want?' Gracie asked, standing back a little from the table, and eyeing especially the six home-made, well-sugared bakestone cakes on the plate. Welsh-speaking, like her husband, and, again like him, a one-time trophy-winning amateur ballroom dancer, she was also a tireless knitter of sweaters and an accomplished cook – 'nothing fancy, or Gomer will turn his nose up', being her yardstick for culinary excellence. She had still been up, ironing in front of the television, when they had come in.

'That's just perfect, Gracie,' said Parry, a favourite of his hostess, and a frequent visitor to the Lloyd house and table, more particularly during the period following the death of his wife. 'And you shouldn't have troubled.'

'No trouble, I'm only bothered you haven't had a proper

supper, and in your case you won't have a proper breakfast either,' she completed, genuine concern showing in the caring blue eyes and the set of the heavily dimpled cheeks. 'I can do you bacon and eggs in no time, and there's some laver bread, you love laver bread, I know.'

'Not as much as I love you, Gracie. But no thanks. Tea and cakes will do me very well, and I promise to make breakfast for myself.'

'Well, mind you do. It's high time Perdita was back here to look after you.'

'That won't be till she's qualified, next year at the earliest.'

Gracie gave a heave of her well-rounded bosoms. 'There's more to life than qualifications. Still, none of my business. So, *nos dda*, both of you.'

'Good night, Gracie. I won't keep him long.' Parry had got up and kissed her on the cheek. They watched her as she left the room, still with a dancer's poise and easy movement, despite being more than a touch overweight.

'And that brings us to this Mrs Hughes, Bronwyn Hughes,' Lloyd was commenting some minutes later, brushing sugar off his shirt front. 'She sounds a very responsible, sensible sort of woman. Well, from what Mary Norris says about her.'

'And seems to have coped well enough with the pitiful Sybil Treace,' Parry replied, sipping his tea from the large, willow-pattern cup.

'Not so pitiful though, is it? Not if she gets her husband back?' the sergeant said slowly, in his deepest and significant-sounding bass register.

'Hm. You may be right about that, of course. Anyway, she has to be a suspect, in spite of her parlous state before the murder happened.'

'That's right, isn't it, boss? Deserted, angry wife, with time to have got to Picton Grove and back before Mrs Hughes got home again from the shop.' Lloyd paused. 'Or perhaps not. Timing's too tight. Pity the son hadn't stayed with her all evening. Pity for mother and son, really. More tea?'

'No thanks, Gomer.' Parry looked at the time. 'I should be going.' He had driven Lloyd the mile home from Fairwater police station, which was the closest one to Bryntaf village. An incident room was being set up there on the Delia Bewen case.

'Have the last Welsh cake then?' Lloyd urged. 'Go on. It'll please Gracie.'

'No, I couldn't. You have it, Gomer.'

The sergeant hesitated, but only briefly. 'So what time do you want to start tomorrow?' he asked, munching his fourth cake.

'I'll pick you up here at 7.45, and we'll go straight to Bryntaf vicarage,' said Parry.

'To see Janet and Simon Treace?'

'Yes. Assuming the boy gets home at all. I told their father we'd be round early. After that I want to see Mrs Treace and Mrs Hughes.'

Sergeant Norris had got both women out of bed when she had called at Mrs Hughes's bungalow. This was on the western side of Bryntaf, on the outskirts of the community, but quite close to Dr Bewen's house. As the woman sergeant later reported, Simon Treace had eaten supper with his mother and her hostess at 7.30. Afterwards, at about 8.20, Mrs Hughes had gone alone to her shop – a three-minute drive away – quickly to finish unwrapping and price-ticketing a delivery of garments which had arrived late that afternoon. It had been easier to complete that then, she had explained, than in the morning, before the shop opened, especially when she had someone staying in the house, which always delayed things a bit. She had left mother and son to have a private talk together, or so she had thought, except that on her return twenty minutes later, Simon was no longer there. According to his mother's very sleepy statement, he had left soon after Mrs Hughes, though she hadn't been sure of the exact time.

It had been 11.40 when Mary Norris had moved on to the vicarage, leaving the two ladies to go back to bed – but only after she had checked with Lloyd, through her radio, that he and Parry were not intending to see them tonight.

Janet Treace had still been up, anxiously waiting for her father to return. He had telephoned her while waiting to be interviewed by Parry, telling her of Delia Bewen's death. Her statement to Mary Norris had as good as corroborated her father's – that the two of them had been together from the time he'd returned from giving his talk that evening, until he had left for Kingfishers. The only difference in what Janet had said had related to the time he had joined her in his study. She thought it had been at around 9.20, later than he had estimated himself. She had certainly been a witness later to his twice attempting to telephone Dr Bewen.

'You didn't say to do anything more about Simon Treace tonight,' said Lloyd, more questioning than commenting.

Parry shrugged. 'Nothing much else we can do, is there? He could be anywhere. It's his first night back from university. He's probably doing something as innocent as seeing old friends.'

'Not the ones we've tried, boss. And it's funny he didn't tell his mother where he was going.'

'Perhaps he's with a girl. One she doesn't approve of, for instance.'

'Ah, that's a thought, boss.'

Parry made a pained face. 'The other thought being that he's done in his father's lover, and scarpered. But I don't think he has, all the same. From what we know about him, he might have hit her over the head, but the other doesn't fit, does it?'

'The knifings, you mean? No. But you never know these days. What they see on video nasties. Gives them ideas.' The voice was in deep register again.

The chief inspector looked dubious. 'Well, we've got an area call out for him and his car, and his family know we want to hear from him. If he's not shown up by dawn, the port and airport alert will have gone out on him. There aren't any more flights or ferries till six in the morning.'

Lloyd scratched his forearm. 'Well, by then, as you said, he'll most probably be home. His sister didn't know whether he had his passport with him or not.'

'And wasn't surprised when Mary Norris asked about that, with the obvious implication that we thought he might be making a flit after doing the murder.'

'She surprised Mary, though, boss, who said it didn't sound like there was much love lost between brother and sister. Nor between daughter and mother, come to that. Different when it came to Janet's relations with her dad.'

'Which doesn't necessarily mean the daughter would have resented Dr Bewen any less than the son did. Though in her case it would have been jealousy more than straight resentment,' Parry offered ruminatively. 'But Simon's certainly his mother's favourite, by the sound of it.'

Lloyd was draining the teapot into his own cup. 'For a man of his calling,' he said, 'the Reverend Treace isn't all that hot on human relations, is he?'

'You mean the way he announced his intentions to his family? I agree. He certainly wanted to bulldoze everybody into accepting everything, and that included the parishioners. Very self-centred man. To the point of . . . megalomania, almost. I'd say his believing he was going to get a new young wife and hold on to his job was just wishful thinking.'

'Except he'd spoken to his bosses.'

'Who'd given him a very iffy kind of response, Gomer, even if he'd kidded himself it was better than that.' The chief inspector paused for a second. 'What would his reaction have been, I wonder, if Dr Bewen had pulled out of their wedding arrangements after all.'

'Why would she have done that, boss?'

'All kinds of reasons. Sounds as if it was a pretty unlikely kind of romance in the first place. The kind that can end as abruptly as it starts. It was very probably going to cost him his job, which I guess she knew, deep down. That could have bothered her a lot. Bound to have, really, even if she didn't admit it. And she was an especially caring kind of medic, according to him. So what if she was suddenly conscience-stricken by his wife's reaction last night, feeling she was responsible for making a sick woman worse.'

'The exhibition in the church hall, you mean, boss? Being drunk and all that.'

'Being driven back to drink by a callous husband, and Dr Bewen knowing she was the cause,' Parry progressed the point while fingering his saucer. 'Maybe Treace really had misled the lovely doctor.'

'Told her his wife would go quietly, like,' said Lloyd. 'So once she knew he'd been lying to her, she tells him she doesn't want anything more to do with him. That would make him mad, wouldn't it? After all he'd been through.'

'Mad enough to kill her, between finishing his Lent lecture and getting home for a quiet cuppa and a chat with his daughter?' Parry chuckled, then shook his head. 'It's late, and we're getting over-imaginative, Gomer. Must be the effect of what Gracie puts in her Welsh cakes.'

Lloyd was looking less dismissive. 'But if there wasn't any other man in her life, like Mr Treace told you,' he pressed, 'it just could be him who killed her.'

'Except he's a clergyman, which must count for something positive. And we don't know if Dr Bewen really was upset about his wife, and . . . and, anyway, he didn't have blood on him when he got home, or not that his daughter noticed. Always assuming she would have reported it to Mary Norris if she had noticed it.' Parry stood up to leave. He stretched his arms above his head, then clasped his hands behind his neck, while failing to dismiss the last thought that had come into his mind. 'We'll have a lot more information in the morning, perhaps on whether Delia Bewen was telling him the truth.'

'About what, boss?'

'About there being no other man in her life.' His lips

pouted. 'Remembering, Gomer, that piece of possibly mis-leading information must have originated with her, not him.'

Olaf Lewis ran the Jaguar into the three-car garage, switched off the engine, then sat in the driving seat for a minute, breathing deeply, marshalling his thoughts, going over what he intended to say at breakfast about his move-ments during the evening.

He was surprised that his hands were shaking a little still, that his heart was bumping slightly and beating faster than was normal for him. He put it all down to the excite-ment, to the whisky he had taken afterwards to settle his nerves, plus the fast driving. In his own opinion, he had always been audacious – daring by nature, even as a schoolboy. Doing something over the top again had given him a lift, a terrific sense of exhilaration: and he was going to get away with it, too, of that he had no doubt. The risk had still been an enduring part of the satisfaction.

Content with his concocted story, he got out of the car, and pressed the wall button to close the up-and-over metal door electrically. He looked at the time. It was five past two, later than he'd intended, but timing wasn't that criti-cal. Sheila would have gone to bed two hours ago at least. She'd be asleep, and nothing much ever woke her. He let himself into the house through the connecting corridor they had built from the garage, which involved passing through two doors. The main house was thatch-roofed and, according to the estate agents who had sold it to him, over three hundred years old. It was in the pretty rural hamlet of Penmaes, not far from Cowbridge. The local authority had insisted on the extra lobby from the new garage as a fire precaution. The house was called Earl's Lodge. He felt it lived up to its name, too, every time he passed the inscription on the gate and fancied himself as the earl.

He commuted the dozen or so miles into Cardiff every day. The last part of the journey was usually slow, but he preferred living away from the city. Their last house had been in Radyr, which had been nice enough, but too close for total comfort. Lewis preferred not to have his wife and family living near enough to his work to be metaphorically, and often truly, breathing down his neck: it restricted his activities, especially what he dubbed his extramural activities.

Sheila Lewis was a keen horsewoman. Living where they did now, she could stable her horse at home, and there was a good-sized paddock beyond the garden. Their two daughters, Christine and Arabella, were as crazy about riding as Sheila was, and although they were away at school, Lewis had bought them both ponies. In term time, the ponies were boarded at the local livery stables and hired out by the liverymaster to other children. This reduced what Lewis had to pay for their keep, but the girls had the animals entirely to themselves in the holidays.

Altogether Lewis felt that he had firmly underwritten his relative freedom to lead the kind of life he enjoyed – underwritten it at a formidable price too, what with the new house, the horses, the school fees, and Sheila's new Merc: he just wished his wife was more appreciative. Being honest with himself, though, he had to admit that the accountancy practice was flourishing, and while outwardly he pretended he was making personal financial sacrifices for the sake of his family, in fact he was doing nothing of the sort.

Olaf Lewis fantasized a very great deal. His relationship with Delia had been almost all fantasy – because she had never allowed it to develop into anything more. In his imagination he had adored her, yearned for her, aspired to her even, because in truth he had been in awe of her. She represented the ultimate in the kind of woman he was always compelling himself to conquer in heart and mind – and he had certainly enjoyed some success with previous efforts to captivate lesser paragons. From the start, he had seen Delia as a beautiful, professional achiever, with a marvellous, sexy body – and very vulnerable in widowhood. He had wanted to possess her, but not, to be perfectly accurate, to marry her – or anybody else. His present marital arrangements suited him admirably.

The line he had shot Delia about their future together had been a failure. This had surprised him, because it was a devious approach that had worked on several other women, notably on two of his wife's closest friends. As with these others, he had never believed that Delia would have allowed him to leave Sheila and the girls for her, only that she would be flattered by his expressed, determined intention to do so. Equally he had counted on her loneliness to make her accessible to him, wholly accessible. The arrival of Peter Treace in her life had astonished him – astonished and mystified him. Her plan to marry this nobody had made him very sore indeed. If she'd been ready to steal Treace from his wife, then, to Lewis's tortuous way of thinking, it showed that Delia had actually cared for Sheila more than she had for him. And that had been the irredeemable insult.

He dropped his briefcase on a chair in the white-walled, oak-beamed kitchen, glancing about as he went through to the hall. He was glad that Sheila had kept the place looking reasonably rustic, despite the money he had put into modernizing everything. She had left the lights on for him on the stairs – and one of his big A4 envelopes propped against the first carpeted step beyond the first landing. It had 'OLAF – READ THIS BEFORE YOU COME UP' written across it in big, red-inked capitals. It would be an urgent, phoned message from a client, no doubt: she was good at things like that. He picked up the envelope and opened the flap. Inside was a sheet of their home letterhead with typing on it. Sheila was an adequate typist, which was another way of saying her typing was better than her handwriting. The text read:

Bastard Olaf,
Carrie saw you tonight with a smashing blonde in Henry's

Bar. She says you left together as well. She couldn't wait to ring me, of course, to tell me you were at it again.

Well, here's some news for you for a change.

I've had as much as I can take of you screwing all over Cardiff, humiliating me with your whoring in public, because that's what gives you your kicks, because you enjoy explaining it all away to me after, or thinking you do, with stories about late meetings with impossible clients.

So here's a story from me to you for once, only – unlike any of yours – it's true.

When you come to bed tonight I'll be dead – yes, dead. And it'll be your fault.

Look after our children.

There had been no sad, endearing farewell. Her name was scribbled at the bottom in the red ink, only he didn't stop to take in that, or the omission.

On the instant, he didn't believe what she'd typed, then he did. Taking the remaining steps two at a time, he hurled himself on to the landing, then through their bedroom door crying irrationally: 'Sheila, Sheila, I'm here. Don't do it, darling. I can explain. I can explain.'

She was lying on top of the bed looking very peaceful in a pink nightdress – very peaceful, and very dead. There was a book fallen open against her stomach, a glass on the bedside table, with a bottle of gin, a bottle of tonic, and a pill bottle there too. The gin bottle was half-full, but the glass and the other two bottles were empty.

'Oh, God. Don't let her be dead. Sheila, wake up, love,' he anguished aloud, shaking her by the shoulders, then searching feverishly for a pulse in her wrist. 'Sheila, don't do this to me. Think of the girls. Wake up. Wake up, you stupid bitch.'

Then he grasped the telephone from its cradle and started to punch 999, stopped after the second 9, snatched their leatherbound address book from the table drawer, and scrambled through the pages searching feverishly for the telephone number of their doctor.

The doctor was local, in the village, a lot closer than the hospital, and – since he was retained privately – hopefully he would be a lot more malleable. Lewis was thinking ahead now a little more coolly. As he started dialling again, he was thinking of the suicide note in particular – and the best and quickest way of destroying it.

Although he had been the second child of respectable, married parents, Sheila had been right in the way she had addressed him. Olaf Lewis was truly a very special kind of bastard, in the colloquial sense of the word.

9

'So you left your mother alone, Simon, at Mrs Hughes's house. That was at approximately 8.20 last night. Then you drove about, by yourself, for two and a half hours, without seeing anyone you knew. Or anyone you can remember,' said Parry. He was seated on the same side of the desk in Peter Treace's study as the young man he was questioning. Lloyd was taking notes in a chair near the door.

The policemen had learned, first thing, that Simon Treace had returned to the vicarage at 1.20 in the morning. His father, who had still been awake, had told him to telephone the police immediately. He had done this, and a detective constable had come from Fairwater police station to question him about where he had been since leaving his mother. Parry had already received a transcript of the interview.

Simon shifted in his seat. 'Like I said, I was killing time till Harry Snelling got home. Except he didn't get home. He must be away. And his parents.' He was unshaven, and uncombed, though his hair was short enough for the deficiency to be ignorable. His eyes, behind the spectacles, looked as bleary still as they must have been when his sister had woken him to say the police were downstairs to see them both. That had been ten minutes earlier. He was dressed in the things that probably had been handiest – a T-shirt, blue jeans, and a soiled pair of canvas shoes, but no socks.

Janet and the two officers had already gone over the

account she had given to Mary Norris of her own movements the evening before. She hadn't been sure that her
brother had returned home, she said, until she'd gone to
wake him a few minutes before this. She had been leaving
as he had arrived at the study door.

'And Mr Snelling, who lives in Roath, he's secretary of
this Seconds Rugby Club you belong to?'

'That's right. Well, it's not really a club. Well it is, except
we don't get many advance fixtures. Only fillers, like,
when other clubs cancel, or want a game for their reserve
teams. It's why we're called –'

'The Seconds. I understand,' Parry put in helpfully. 'So
around nine o'clock, you remember driving to the Golden
Lion in Penarth. You don't drink locally?' Penarth is on
the coast, slightly to the west of Cardiff, and six miles
south of Bryntaf.

'I drink where my friends drink. Where we like the ale.
No law against that, is there?' Simon's accent was more
recognizably Welsh than his sister's. Sergeant Lloyd, for
one, construed that her speech had been more altered
than her brother's during the time each had spent at English universities – and not for the better either, was the
sergeant's unabashed and patriotic view.

'No law against it at all,' the chief inspector countered
the challenge with equanimity. 'And you hoped to meet
two other friends at the Golden Lion?'

'That's right. Bernie Janes and his brother. Bernie's captain of the club. He and Harry Snelling usually meet there
on Wednesdays to sort out a team. If they'd got a fixture
for the Saturday.'

'But they weren't there last night?'

'No, well, they've changed pubs, most likely. I've been
away for two months.' He adjusted the transparent framed
spectacles on his nose once again – an often repeated
action, conducted with the minimum of arm movement,
his head bending each time in an almost deferential way
to meet the upraised hand. The lenses in the frames were
unusually thick. Parry wondered how someone with sight

requiring so much correction coped on the sports field.

'And you didn't see anyone else you knew at the Golden Lion?'

The student shrugged. 'Probably people I knew by sight. I've been in there a fair amount over the last couple of years.'

'Can you give us the names of any you knew who were there last night?'

'No, I . . . I only said I probably saw them.' The reply had been a stumbling one.

'And you didn't actually speak to anyone?'

'Not really, no. When Bernie and his brother weren't there, I left.'

'You didn't buy a drink, even?'

'No.'

'So no one behind the bar would remember seeing you?'

Simon considered for a moment. 'The barmaid might,' he said. 'She knows me. I . . . I gave her a sort of wave from by the door. I'm not sure she saw me, though.'

Parry glanced at Lloyd. He had already concluded that although Simon Treace was heavy and tallish, he was not someone who would stand out in a crowd. His manner was as withdrawn and self-effacing as his general appearance was unremarkable. The wave to the barmaid had probably been a constricted, half-hearted gesture, like his movements generally. He was occasionally belligerent in his response to questions – but that wouldn't single him out except during verbal exchanges. In any case, the belligerence might have been reserved for policemen.

'Can you tell us why you decided to leave your mother by herself in the first place, Simon? It was quite early, wasn't it?' the chief inspector continued.

There was another silence, this time long enough to make the questioner wonder whether an answer would be forthcoming at all. 'Well . . .' Simon began at last, haltingly. 'Well . . . I'd spent half the day with her already. We'd talked through what my father was . . . what he was

93

doing to her. There didn't seem to be anything left to say. Not about that. Not for the time being, anyway. She looked tired. I think she'd said she wanted to go to bed early.'

The allusion to what his father 'was doing' to his mother had been redolent with meaning, although it had been voiced without emphasis or venom. Lloyd had looked up quickly from his notebook to see if Simon's facial expression had hardened to match the implication of the words: it hadn't. The dour young Mr Treace was not much given to changes of expression.

Parry rubbed his chin as he glanced again at the transcript. 'So you arrived in Llandaff, at the home of your other friend, Arnold Grunnow, at 10.50 – '

'No. It was more like 10.30,' Simon interrupted.

'I see. You told the detective constable who interviewed you earlier it was 10.50.'

'So I made a mistake. It was late when I was questioned. I wasn't thinking properly.'

Parry smiled. 'Well, the mistake's easily corrected, provided you're sure you've got it right this time.'

'I'm sure.'

'Good.' Parry wasn't much interested in the young man's whereabouts beyond 10.30 in any case. 'And you stayed with Mr Grunnow for the next two hours? Till you drove back here.'

'That's right.'

'And he's the only person who can confirm your whereabouts at any time from 8.20 onwards?'

'Suppose so. I didn't think of Arnold till late on. Otherwise, I might have gone to see him first. He belongs to the club too. But, like me, he ... he only plays in the vacations. We're both still hoping to get a game this Saturday.'

'What position do you play, Simon?' The cheerful, personal question had come from Lloyd. 'Front row forward, is it? Big chap like you?'

'That's right. Well, anywhere in the pack, really.' A

flicker of an appreciative smile came with the reply.

'And do you know yet if the Seconds have got a match Saturday?' asked Parry.

'Yes. Arnold's playing. But he thinks the team's made up. I may get in as first substitute though. I, er . . . I'd meant to do something about it yesterday morning, when I got home. But that was before my father broke the news.' The hand had gone to the glasses again. 'After that, I was too involved with my mother. I took her round to Mrs Hughes, too.'

'Do you mind telling us what your feelings were toward Dr Bewen, after you'd heard your father was leaving your mother?' asked Parry.

'Feelings?' He swallowed. 'I didn't have any. Not about her. I didn't know her.' The speaker's eyes had become briefly more alert as he went on. 'If you need to know my movements last night because you think I killed her, you can save yourselves the effort. I didn't have anything to do with it. Didn't know where she lived, or what she looked like, even. And I wouldn't commit murder. It's my mother I'm concerned about.'

The last two short sentences were pronounced with heavy conviction, even though, in a sense, they cancelled each other out, Parry thought.

'Well there's a lacklustre boy, if ever there was one,' said Lloyd, as Parry moved the car off. They were on their way to Bronwyn Hughes's house. 'Not a patch on his sister, is he?'

'She's better looking, certainly,' Parry replied with a grin.

'I meant in . . . in what's it? .. acuity, boss. Very switched on, the girl is. And yes, I agree, a fragile beauty with it. Whereas the brother's too slow to get out of his own way.' Lloyd absently levered a peppermint out of the roll in his hand, put it in his mouth, and the roll back in his pocket.

'So you think he wouldn't have the wit to do a murder, Gomer? And his sister's too delicate and refined?'

'I wouldn't say that, no. Very defensive of her father, Janet was. Whether she'd manage a murder's a different matter. No witnesses to where she was between 7.30 and 9.20, nor where her brother was between 8.20 and 10.30. Time enough for either of them to have done it.'

'Or done it together, Gomer? As a team?' Parry ruminated as the car passed the end of Picton Grove.

'Oh, I didn't mean that, boss.' Lloyd started chewing instead of sucking the mint – in his case, always a sign of mounting cerebral activity.

'I know, but it's worth thinking about,' the other man countered. 'We agreed before they could both have had it in for Delia Bewen. For different reasons. It wouldn't be the first time a brother and sister have –' Parry broke off as he braked sharply and swung the car into Helgarth Road. 'Sorry about that, nearly missed the turning. As Mary Norris said, it's pretty close to Kingfishers, isn't it? And this must be the place. She said it's the only bungalow on the left. Number twenty-three.'

The houses in Helgarth Road were smaller than those in Picton Grove, but they were newer, and more varied in design. Although also all detached, they were built very close to each other, and were identified by numbers, or occasionally by names as well, but always by numbers. The obligatory numbers had a social significance perceived by those residents who had still added names to their properties. The Post Office and the local authority insisted on house numbers in streets with high building density – high density not being an easily acknowledged feature of Bryntaf.

Number twenty-three was a brick-built bungalow with green pantile roofing. There were gables at both ends of the building, facing forward towards the street, with timber cladding under them. Rose bushes edged the half-moon of lawn at the front. The semicircular drive behind the bushes was served by openings at both ends on to the road. There were no gates to the house – and no name, only the house number above the red-painted, iron-studded door: the owner evidently didn't go in for non-statutory embellishment.

'Mr Parry and Mr Lloyd, is it? I'm Bronwyn Hughes. I saw the car from the kitchen. We've been expecting you,' said the neat, dark-haired woman with the grave, intelligent eyes a minute later. Her voice was quiet and well modulated. She had opened the door before the two policemen had quite reached it.

'How do you do, Mrs Hughes. Sorry you were disturbed so late last night,' said the chief inspector. 'We try not to waste any time at the start of a murder inquiry.'

'No, no. That was understood. Tragic thing to happen, I'm sure. Come in, won't you? Mrs Treace is through there in the lounge. You said you'd want to see both of us.' The speaker lowered her voice. 'I should warn you, she's not herself yet. Very upset still about her husband announcing he was leaving her. The death of Dr Bewen hasn't really sunk in, I'm afraid.'

Bronwyn Hughes was younger than Parry had been led to expect. From her appearance, he guessed she was in her late thirties. It was her being a divorcée, with a grown-up daughter, that had suggested she might be a good deal older. That she was a devout churchgoer, who had befriended the vicar's troubled wife, and taken her into her home, had further contributed to the image of a comforting, motherly person in her fifties, not someone who was crisp in both looks and manner.

The entrance to the wide room the visitors were shown into was through an open archway across the hall, and nearly opposite the front door. The room was south-facing, with long picture windows on to a paved terrace, and a small, manicured garden beyond. The furnishings inside were neat and pristine, if unimaginative.

Sybil Treace was in an armchair covered in a William Morris-type chintz and set near the windows. She had an unopened newspaper in her lap, which she didn't appear to have been reading. When she turned her head to acknowledge the newcomers, both were struck with how closely her features resembled those of her son, something which included the bland stare from behind thick lenses. In comparison to her hostess, Mrs Treace was the epitome of motherliness, though, right now, she also seemed wan and dejected.

'We won't keep you long, ladies,' said Parry. 'I expect you'll need to get to your boutique, Mrs Hughes.'

'Oh, I'm all right for a bit. I open at ten on ordinary weekdays, earlier on Saturdays,' the lady answered. 'Won't you sit down, both of you?' She sat herself on a window seat close to her house guest.

The two men settled themselves on the sofa as Parry continued. 'We really just want to confirm the movements of both of you between 8.30 and 10.30 last evening. Just for the record, you understand?'

'Is that when Delia Bewen was killed?' asked Mrs Treace unexpectedly, since she hadn't uttered to this point – only nodded an acknowledgement when the policemen had been introduced.

'So far as we can calculate at the moment, ma'am, yes,' Lloyd replied, while both policemen noted that if Mrs Treace hadn't taken in the doctor's death before their arrival, she had done so now. 'We understand from what you told Detective Sergeant Norris, you were both here with Mr Simon Treace up to around twenty past eight, which was when you left for your shop, Mrs Hughes.'

'That's right. I wouldn't have gone out, leaving Mrs Treace by herself, not if Simon hadn't been here. As it was, it gave me the chance to nip down there and finish some jobs. I wasn't long.'

'But by the time you got back, we gather Simon had left. Have you remembered exactly when he left, Mrs Treace?' the sergeant enquired, turning back to the other woman.

Sybil frowned, and rubbed the front of her right wrist with the fingertips of her left hand. 'I've tried to. I think it was only a minute or so after Bronwyn. Simon himself would know. Why don't you ask him? Except I'm sure I don't know why it's important to you.'

Parry cleared his throat. 'It's just that we need to check on the movements of everyone involved with Dr Bewen, directly or indirectly,' he said. 'What they were doing between the times mentioned, Mrs Treace.'

She had stiffened at the words. 'Well, I wasn't involved with her, and neither was my son,' she said, rallying sharply, despite her forlorn appearance.

'We know that, ma'am,' put in the sergeant tactfully. 'It's just routine inquiries, like Mr Parry said. Can you tell us, for instance, if you went out, at all, after your son left?'

'Why would I have gone out? Sitting here thinking, I was. Then I went to bed.'

'You didn't take a short walk? To get some air, perhaps? At about twenty-five past eight? It was quite a warm evening, and a neighbour says she thought she might have seen someone leave the house on foot about then.'

Sybil looked confused. 'Tell you the truth, I don't really remember.' She paused, straightening the newspaper that was still in her lap. 'Yesterday was a terrible day for me. Someone saw me, you say?'

'No ma'am, nothing so definite. It was a neighbour who thinks she may have seen –'

'Yes, I may have gone out,' Sybil interrupted suddenly. 'Just for a minute it was. Down the road. To stretch my legs before bed. Yes, I think I did.'

'And what time did you go to bed, ma'am?' asked Lloyd.

'Oh dear, I don't really know that either. You don't time things usually, do you? It was ... oh, about twenty to nine, I should think?' Her answer had come as a question directed at Mrs Hughes.

'I'd say before that, Sybil,' Her friend volunteered. 'Your room was dead quiet when I got back at quarter to nine. You were fast asleep, I thought. She really was worn out,' she added for the benefit of the policemen.

'Thank you, ma'am.' Lloyd made a note, then turned his

gaze again on Sybil. 'Before he left, did your son happen to mention where he was going, ma'am?'

'No, he didn't. I think he wanted to arrange a game for Saturday. He's mad about rugby.'

'So he didn't say he was going to see Dr Bewen?' asked Parry.

'Dr Bewen? Of course he didn't. He wouldn't have gone near the woman.'

'Because he strongly disapproved of her relationship with your husband?'

'Yes, Mr . . . I'm so sorry, I've forgotten your name.'

'Parry, ma'am.'

Sybil nodded. 'Mr Parry, my son was brought up to be a God-fearing boy. He knows the sacredness of holy vows, marriage vows. His father's the same, of course. Well, as a clergymen he would be, wouldn't he? In the ordinary course. Only Dr Bewen was trying to blow him off that course, wasn't she?' Earlier she had been slumped in her chair, but she was sitting more upright as she went on. 'She was a misguided woman. My husband had the Lord's work to do in this parish. Work he'd never have finished if he'd left me and his children, and gone off with a . . . with a painted Jezebel. But the Lord has intervened, hasn't he, as the Lord often does in answer to the prayers of His faithful.'

10

'We've talked to Dr Bewen's secretary at the infirmary, sir. She got in just after eight this morning,' Sergeant Mary Norris was reporting, seated on the edge of a desk with her legs crossed, a clipboard resting on her short, but not too short, tweed skirt. 'Her name's Durrant, Mrs Betty Durrant, and she's very upset at the news. She says Dr Bewen was meeting a Mr Olaf Lewis last night at Henry's Café Bar, Park Place. That was at 6.45, for a drink. Mr Lewis is her tax accountant.' The speaker paused to check her own writing, leaning a little to one side, while she gave a tug to the hem at the back of her skirt – this for reasons of comfort not decorum. 'The doctor was probably a bit late getting there. We've since been on to the head barman at his home. He knows Mr Lewis, and confirms he was there with a blonde woman fitting the doctor's description. He's not exactly sure when either of them arrived, except it was after 6.30 and before 7 p.m. They had two drinks each, and left together at around 7.40. Mr Lewis is married, in his mid forties, and lives in Penmaes.'

'Anyone spoken to him yet?' asked Parry. They were in the crowded incident room at Fairwater, where a dozen operatives, police and civilian, were busy working at telephones or desk computers. There had been very little fresh intelligence of the calibre just reported when he had checked here by telephone earlier. That was before he and Lloyd had seen Janet and Simon Treace, and the two ladies. The two officers had also paid a brief visit to King-fishers before coming to the police station.

'We've tried to reach him, sir, but there's no one at his house. He's probably on the way to his office, but there's no one there either yet. It's in Park Crescent.'

'And his wife isn't home?'

'If she is, she's not answering the door bell or the telephone.'

'Taking the kids to school, probably.'

'No, sir. They have children, but they're away at boarding school till tomorrow, when the Easter holidays start. We got that from a neighbour. We're making more enquiries in the area now.' The woman sergeant hesitated, glancing at her notes again before going on. 'The officers who saw Mrs Durrant are talking to other people in Dr Bewen's department as well, and anyone in the hospital she had close contact with.'

'Good. Have we got enough people on the ground in Bryntaf?'

'There's four DCs and six constables lent from uniform doing more neighbourhood interviews now, sir.'

'We saw some of them at it, yes.'

'And they'll be covering the list of regular churchgoers you asked us to get. Also, they'll be talking to local shopkeepers as soon as the shops open.'

'Did Mrs Durrant say if the Olaf Lewis meeting was social or business?' Parry was sitting on a desktop opposite Sergeant Norris, sipping coffee from a polystyrene cup. Lloyd was beside him doing the same, except he had a doughnut as a well as coffee.

'She says it was probably social, sir. Dr Bewen was a friend as well as a client of Mr Lewis. She was a friend of his wife's too.'

'OK. Keep after them both. And did the secretary know anything about Audrey S.? The one with the appointment at nine?'

'Yes, sir. That appointment was cancelled. She's a Mrs Audrey Slattery from Newport. Director of a construction company. Private patient of Dr Bewen's. High-powered lady, according to Mrs Durrant. She rang from London yesterday at six, full of apologies. A meeting she was at there was running late, and she wouldn't have been able to get to Bryntaf in time. The doctor didn't mind, apparently. Mrs Slattery was a friend as well as a patient.'

'Was it after her call that Dr Bewen arranged to meet Lewis?'

'No, sir. That was fixed mid morning on the telephone. He wanted to give her lunch at Quayles, but she couldn't manage it.'

'Sounds as if she pays him plenty for tax advice,' Parry commented. Quayles was his girlfriend Perdita's favourite restaurant, pricey by a policeman's standards, but worth it. 'Did she make any other plans for the evening?'

'None that Mrs Durrant knew about, sir.'

'And she hadn't arranged to have dinner with Lewis?'

'Definitely not, sir. Dr Bewen told her to tell Mr Lewis she'd only have time for a drink. The arrangements were all made through Mrs Durrant.'

'But Dr Bewen could have changed her mind, especially since the nine o'clock appointment was cancelled. She could have gone on somewhere with him for dinner. Except, if Dr Maltravers was right about the time of death, would there have been time for that?' Parry debated.

'Dr Maltravers was only making an intelligent guess about the time, boss,' Lloyd put in, wiping his mouth with the back of his hand. 'And if Dr Bewen said she'd only have time for a drink, maybe she had someone else to see before nine o'clock.'

'Possibly, yes,' said Parry. 'But if they'd decided on an early dinner, they could have had it at Henry's Bar.'

'Or she could have invited him home for a meal, boss.'

'Mm, or what if she did have someone else to see and ... and arranged for Lewis to pick her up at home later,' Parry countered. 'After she'd been back to shower and change. That would account for the way she was dressed. Half-dressed. Ready for going out, not for going to bed. At least that's the most conventional explanation.'

Mary Norris, who had been drawing doodles on the top

sheet in her clipboard, looked up quizzically and offered: 'Another one would be that she hadn't put a dress on because she wasn't sure if she'd need to take it off again, when Mr Lewis arrived, sir.'

'That had occurred to me as well,' said Parry soberly. 'But is it likely a responsible, mature woman like her would have asked a man to her house to make love the day after it was announced she was going to marry the local vicar? Morality aside, it's not really in character, is it?'

'No, it's not, sir. And like we said before, if she'd definitely intended they were going to make love, she'd probably have been naked under the dressing gown.'

Parry didn't trouble to make the point that it had been Sergeant Norris who'd drawn that conclusion on her own. 'You mean the bra and panties made it kind of optional, Mary?' he asked.

'Only just optional, and still very debatable, sir, don't you think?' The query had a serious, academic, seeker-after-truth quality to it.

Lloyd put down his coffee. 'We don't know if they'd been lovers in the past, do we, boss?' he said. 'If they had been, last night's meeting might have been the fond farewell, with special favours to match, like. Or maybe she really was in two minds about what would happen when he arrived. What she was going to allow to happen. Only he opted for serious sex, and she didn't want it. She resisted, he got angry, and bashed her over the head.' Gomer Lloyd was given to simple, well-tried scenarios, wholly lacking in academic niceties.

'That could be right, sir,' Mary Norris agreed. 'Only I think it's most likely she asked him back to her house just to eat. Mr Treace was ringing her at ten. There wasn't all that much time to eat out and be back for that. A commitment to Mr Treace would have . . . well, sort of got priority, I think. Also she might have meant to ask him over later.'

'And the dressing gown was for wearing while she did the cooking. To save spoiling her dress,' Lloyd suggested, but without much conviction, except he added grudgingly: 'Gracie does that sometimes.'

'Isn't it still unlikely she'd have set up a cosy dinner at home with her friendly accountant?' said Parry. 'Unless they had unfinished business to discuss. Professional or personal, despite what Mrs Durrant thought.' He frowned. 'Of course, there were no signs of food being prepared in that kitchen.'

'She could have phoned for pizzas, boss.' Lloyd was a keen pizza consumer, but preferably of the ones made at home by his wife.

'Possible, Gomer. If she did, the call will be logged by BT. We'd still need to know what happened to the pizzas, though. With any luck we should hear today what the autopsy showed about when she last ate, and what. Incidentally, anything from BT yet, Mary?'

'No, sir. They'll be faxing us any minute with a print-out of her calls yesterday, inward as well as outward. We've asked for the same from her mobile phone company.'

'Good. Anything else?'

'Yes, sir. Dr Bewen's daily cleaner turned up at the house this morning, just after you left. Name of Myfanwy Evans. Age eighteen. Single mother with a daughter of fourteen months. Ms Evans broke down when told about the doctor, and she's been weeping buckets ever since. Dr Bewen was her best friend, she says, as well as her employer – oh, and her gynaecologist. She's not been much use yet as a –'

'Urgent call from Cardiff Infirmary for you, sir,' interrupted a male civilian member of the unit who was seated behind the desk Parry was perched on.

The chief inspector took the receiver. After a few seconds listening to the caller he broke in with: 'Right. Keep him there. Not that he's likely to leave, is he? I'll be over right away with DS Lloyd.' Passing the phone back, he got to his feet. 'Sorry, Mary, but Myfanwy Evans will have to keep for a bit. Tell them at Kingfishers that

I'll want to see her before she leaves, but we may be some time getting back to Bryntaf.'

'We'll keep her there, sir. She came intending to work this morning in any case. Going to the RCI, are you?'

'Yes. Olaf Lewis is there. He's all right, but his wife's been admitted in a coma. She's in intensive care.'

'Accident, boss?' asked Lloyd, who had also stood up.

'No. They think barbiturate poisoning. Bright Mrs Durrant heard about it by chance, and told the detective constable who talked to her earlier. He was still interviewing other people at the hospital. Looks as though Mrs Lewis tried to commit suicide last night. We need to know if her husband was the reason, and why.'

'Not for us to say, is it, officer?' said Mrs Craig-Owen, with a shrug of her shoulders, her folded arms at the same time inadvertently giving a sympathetic lift to her rampant bosoms, shrouded today under a lamb's-wool twinset – her cashmeres were kept for best. She was standing opposite her husband, and talking to Detective Constable Alf Vaughan in the small, and only half-partitioned area that did service as an office at the rear of the stockroom in Bryntaf's single grocery store. 'I only mentioned it because it's never happened before. We were flabbergasted, weren't we, Roland?' she sternly demanded rather than questioned, her knees a fraction bent, her solid legs set well apart, her brogue-shod feet pointing slightly outwards – like a sumo wrestler preparing to engage. Or that's what the imaginative, forty-eight-year-old, bronzed DC Vaughan had concluded. Apart from being something of an amateur authority on rhododendrons and bonsai trees, Vaughan was currently studying Oriental martial arts – because, with him, one interest tended to lead on to another.

'Yes, dear. Flabbergasted,' said Roland Craig-Owen, who was in a long white cotton coat and holding a shrink-wrapped pack of twelve boxes of Kellogg's All-Bran in front of him. He had been about to take the pack into the self-service shop when the detective had appeared at the back delivery door some minutes before this. The Craig-Owens had by that time known about the murder, like everyone else in the village.

'Miss Davies was on my list of people to see, in any case,' said Vaughan. 'I understand she's a member of the Parochial Church Council, like yourself, Mrs Craig-Owen, and a frequent attender at worship.' They had just been discussing Maud Davies's failure to appear at the vicar's Lent lecture the night before.

'She'd attend a cockfight or a trip to the moon if Peter Treace was going,' replied Mrs Craig-Owen with conviction. 'Dotty about him, she is. Sad really, when you think of it. But pious spinsters get like that, don't they?'

DC Vaughan wasn't prepared to volunteer an opinion on the predilections of pious spinsters, mainly because he personally knew very few of them, not being at all religious himself, and being married into the bargain, which considerations together limited the likelihood of his acquaintance with the group or species ever being enlarged very much. In any case, he divined that Mrs Craig-Owen's comment lacked common charity, especially coming from a member of a PCC. 'And that's what really struck you as unusual, was it, that she wasn't at the lecture?' he questioned, without commitment.

'Couldn't get over it, could we, Roland? Never missed one before, and that goes back years. And she wasn't ill, I know that. She was working in the library just before they closed at six. I saw her through the window when I went past. She was looking well enough then.'

'And you think she strongly disapproved of the vicar's involvement with Dr Bewen, ma'am?'

'As I said before, that's something you'll have to ask her yourself. We're just giving you candid answers to questions. Candid and confidential, like you said,' she added pointedly, though the subject of Maud Davies had first been broached by Mrs Craig-Owen herself, not brought up in any question from the policeman. Roland

Craig-Owen had swallowed at the declaration that answers had been emanating from both of them, since he had so far had no chance to furnish one, candid or otherwise. 'You see, we both said when we came from the parish meeting the previous night,' his wife continued, 'the vicar's announcement must have broken her heart.'

'Any history of irrational behaviour there that you know of?'

Mrs Craig-Owen sniffed and gave a questioning glance at the All-Bran. 'Well, I wouldn't go so far as to say irrational. But people do funny things where deep emotions are involved, don't they? Of course, she's not the only member of the congregation who wouldn't have approved of him getting a divorce, let alone the other.' The last phrase was accompanied by a meaningful nod.

'And how do you feel yourself about that, Mrs Craig-Owen?'

'That it's all very sad, but something you could see coming a mile off.'

'The marriage to Dr Bewen included?'

'Not to her in particular, but to someone. Attractive man like him.' Mrs Craig-Owen was now absently regarding her own husband and not, it seemed, with approval, as she continued. 'Anyway, remarriage to someone like Dr Bewen wasn't something that should have meant him having to give up his job. My husband was going to write to the archdeacon saying just that, weren't you, Roland?'

'Well, I –'

'No point now, of course,' the lady interrupted her spouse's hesitant response, in case he meant to offer unsuitable, demeaning reasons for his not wanting to address higher church authority. 'Poor Sybil Treace, she's her own worst enemy. Drink, as I'm sure you know. And, by the way, there's plenty of evidence there of irrational behaviour.'

'But you've never known her to physically attack anyone, ma'am? Her husband, for instance?'

'No.' The word had been made to develop slowly. 'But

who knows what goes on behind closed doors between husband and wife? Terrible dance she's led him all these years. That's common knowledge.' The bosoms were uplifted once more, and a deepening look of abject despair appeared now to be fixed on the still encumbered Roland, as if it had been his own private and despicable conduct that had been brought into question. 'But if you're asking frankly do we think she was capable of murdering Dr Bewen, we can't tell you, and that's candid enough, isn't it? Strong drink does funny things to people, of course. There's too much of it being consumed by the public today, no doubt.'

'Indeed, Mrs Craig-Owen,' Vaughan commented, while his eyes lingered on the cases of sherry, gin, and whisky stacked on the shelving closest to the office area. 'Well, thank you again for your time.' He glanced at his notes. 'I expect you know Mrs Bronwyn Hughes, do you? Her –'

'Of course I know Bronwyn. She's next door but two. The Top Notch boutique. She's one of my shop tenants,' Mrs Craig-Owen had broken in with confidence. 'Wonderful woman. Keeps herself to herself, mind. That's in her private life, like. She's also on the PCC with me. It's Bronwyn who's given Sybil Treace a roof for the time being. There's charitable of her. Well, Sybil couldn't very well stay on at the vicarage, could she? Although the vicar suggested it, or so we're told. Only a temporary measure, of course. Whether it's needed now, I don't know. Not with Dr Bewen gone.' She made a tutting noise.

'Mrs Hughes wouldn't be one of the ladies who'd be jealous of Dr Bewen in any way?' It was the standard question he had been instructed to ask about all unattached females in the village.

'Like Maud Davies, you mean? Oh, no. Wouldn't have an unkind thought in her mind. Committed to religion, she is. A paragon, though that daughter of hers doesn't appreciate it.' Mrs Craig-Owen was naturally zealous in lauding the virtues of those tenants who paid their shop rents regularly, and who wouldn't be forced out of

109

business if disaster struck in the shape of a giant super-market: supermarkets didn't sell dresses, after all.

The policeman looked at his list again. 'The daughter doesn't live at home? With Mrs Hughes?'

'Not any more, she doesn't. More fool her. Her name's Dilys. We heard she went off with a boy. Tearaway, I expect. Living together somewhere, they are. She's only nineteen.'

'So Dilys Hughes wouldn't have been involved in church affairs? Not recently, ma'am?'

'No.' Mrs Craig-Owen, gave a cynical smile. 'Too many affairs of her own to contend with. Anyway, she hasn't lived at home for a long time.' She plucked at a middle button on her cardigan. 'No, officer, if you're looking for the one who'd have felt most bitter about it all, it's Maud Davies you should talk to,' she completed.

'Yes, I've made a note of that, ma'am.' Vaughan won-dered whether Mrs Craig-Owen's jaundiced view of Miss Davies was too subjective to be worth anything at all, and also what had given rise to the enmity underlying it. 'And you did say Dr Bewen didn't do much shopping in the village?' he asked, changing the subject.

'That's right. Well, it seemed she was never in Bryntaf in shopping hours. Her cleaner used to get a lot of her groceries from us though. Other things she'd have got herself in Cardiff, I expect, from nearer the Infirmary. Pity. There's plenty of other good shops in the village.'

11

'And there's no reason why your wife might have wanted to take her own life, sir? Or not one that you know of?' Parry's questions to Olaf Lewis were sympathetic not confrontational – delivered in a friendly tone, commiserative even. It wasn't Mrs Lewis who was his prime concern.

'That's right. Absolutely right. It's why I'm quite sure it was an accident. Silly girl took her sleeping pills twice, probably. She's such a scatterbrain sometimes.' Lewis's response was equally easy and man to man, trusting to a degree, and indulgent about a cherished spouse's foolish peccadilloes. Despite his tired, dishevelled appearance – stubbled chin, white shirt soiled at the collar and cuffs, suit crumpled – mentally he seemed to be firmly in control of himself.

'She took more than twice the dose, wouldn't you think, sir? To get in a coma,' commented Gomer Lloyd – also with measured understanding, but mixed, in his case, with honest-sounding if calculating curiosity.

Lewis bit his teeth into his lower lip before he spoke. 'I don't know enough about these things to answer that. All I do know is, I left her happy enough at breakfast, and came back to find her at death's door. Well, literally, according to our doctor. Thank God she's coming round all right, even though she's pretty groggy still, and not speaking yet.'

The three men were in a side ward at the Royal Cardiff Infirmary, on Newport Road, half a mile to the east of the city centre. Being next to the hospital's intensive care unit,

the space was normally used as a high-dependency ward
– as an intermediary stop for patients discharged from the
main unit. Today, though, it was not in use at all, which
was why Parry had been able to borrow it. The four beds
in the room had been shorn of everything save mattresses.
Each white-painted bed frame was coldly skeletal, the
adjusting mechanism exposed underneath like some stark
kind of entrail. Wall-mounted equipment was arranged
behind the beds – jumbles of tubes, wires and jointed
metal extensions, plus the inevitable video monitors. The
hollow emptiness of the place, to the suggestible, begged
the question, that perhaps all these aids to succour had
proved to be in vain to the last four hapless inmates – or
it did to Lloyd, who hated hospitals.

A wooden-armed, upholstered chair, with washable
covers in cheerful, long-wearing materials, their ribbon
fastenings unknotted and hanging down limply, belonged
beside each bed – a reminder of familiar comforts from
the world outside.

The three men had each drawn one of the chairs into
what was roughly, but not precisely, the centre space, and
were seated there at different angles to one another. This
had created what to Parry seemed a Pinteresque kind of
tableau – awkward, irregular, exploitable, and strangely
threatening.

'And there was no note, sir? People about to take their
lives on purpose, like, they usually leave notes,' said Lloyd,
the depth of his voice perfectly matching the morbid
comment.

'Exactly what I said to your colleague earlier. If Sheila
had been going to commit suicide, she'd have left a note.
A letter. No question.'

'So you didn't see any note, sir?'

'No. Of course I didn't. Mark you, it never occurred to
me to look. All I knew was she'd been taken ill. So if there
was a note it'll still be there, won't it? But I'm sure there
wasn't. I'd have seen it eventually, or the doctor would
have.'

'Quite so,' said Lloyd. 'So how exactly did you know she was ill, sir, not just asleep?'

'Oh, the light being on still. The empty pill bottle. The book open on the bed. It isn't like Sheila to fall asleep on her book. Yes, it was the empty pill bottle that really got me worried. How was I to know how much phenobarb she'd taken? I was scared, I can tell you. That's why I shook her.'

'Good thing you did, sir. And we're glad they're saying she's going to be all right.'

'Thank you. I'm sure she will be, and no er . . . no silly complications. Straightforward enough accident, of course.' There was a strong hint of question as well as wishful thinking in the tone.

'Of course, Mr Lewis,' Parry put in, repeating the other's last words, but without quite the same assurance. Then he paused before asking. 'Your wife takes phenobarbital for sleep, does she?'

'Yes, we both do. Not frequently, either of us.'

'Not so many doctors prescribe it for that any more. Because of the risk of . . . of accident, sir.'

'I know. Our own doctor's not keen, but none of the latest sleeping pills seem to work for us.'

'Matter of getting used to, perhaps, sir. Anyway, all's well that ends well this time,' Parry commented cheerfully, then adopted a more serious expression. 'In fact, what we really wanted to talk to you about was Dr Bewen.'

'Oh, yes, of course. Fire away. Glad to help you in any way I can.'

'Thank you, sir. Can you tell us when you heard about her death?'

'Too soon after we'd dealt with Sheila's situation, I can tell you.' Lewis had been leaning forward, head bent, eyes studying his hands which were clenched between his knees. He looked up now, still blearily, from lack of sleep. 'Must have been about five this morning, I suppose.'

'Here, in the hospital, sir?'

'Yes. I've been here all night. I'd given up trying to sleep in the visitors' area. That's just along the corridor. They'd suggested I went home. But, I ask you, how could I? Anyway, I heard two of the night nurses talking about Delia. They were making tea. One of them brought me some. I couldn't believe it when she said Delia Bewen was dead. Mark you, she said she thought it was an accident. It was your colleague who told me it was suspected murder. That was later. He came up to me in the café when I was getting some breakfast. You know I was with Delia quite early last evening?'

'Yes, we did know that, sir. At Henry's in Park Place wasn't it?' said Parry.

'That's right. We had a drink. It was to congratulate her on her wedding plans.'

'And she was a client of yours, I believe.'

'Oh yes, but much more than that. A dear friend – of my wife's, as well as me.'

It registered with Parry that this assertion was being put to him too often. 'Did you know her before she came to live in the area, sir?'

'No, but we met professionally soon after. That'd be more than three years ago, I suppose. She and her husband needed an accountant, and one of the other consultants here recommended me. We hit it off pretty well from the start. All four of us, I mean. After her husband's tragic death, I'd like to think Sheila and I were friends she relied on deeply. I have to admit, though, we hadn't seen quite so much of her in recent months.'

'Except presumably you went on seeing her in your capacity as her accountant, sir?'

'Oh, yes. But most of that's telephone calls, not meetings.'

'And did you approve of her relationship with the Reverend Peter Treace, sir?'

Lewis shifted his focus slightly, staring thoughtfully over Parry's shoulder at the window and the blue sky outside. 'It was hardly for us to approve or disapprove, was it?

To be honest, we've never even met the man.' His eyes returned to meet Parry's. 'It was quite a surprise to us to read they were planning to marry.'

'So you didn't know they were close?'

'We knew she was seeing him for . . . for what I suppose you'd call counselling. That was some time back, though. We didn't know their relations had developed into anything deeper. Still, in answer to your question, if he was bringing happiness to her life again, we were all for him, naturally.'

'Your wife wasn't with you when you met Dr Bewen last evening, sir?'

There was hesitation before the answer. 'No. Not enough notice. If Delia had been free for dinner, Sheila might have made the effort. But Delia had to get home for something at nine. A patient. When I rang her at the Infirmary, her secretary said she'd only have time for a drink.'

'If it was the patient we know about, sir, the appointment was cancelled.'

'Was it? She didn't tell me that.'

'And Dr Bewen didn't mention anyone else she was expecting to see, sir?'

'No. I'd assumed it was just one patient.'

'So you didn't have dinner with her, sir?'

'No. I've just said.'

'You left Henry's together, though, at 7.40?'

'About then, yes. And we parted soon after. My car was parked behind my office. Hers was closer. Only a few yards up Park Place.'

'So you saw her to her car, sir?'

'Yes.'

'But you didn't go back to her house?'

'Good heavens, no.' Lewis frowned. 'Look, you're not suggesting I had anything remotely to do with her death, are you? That would be just, just . . . preposterous.'

'Certainly not, sir,' said Parry, though Lloyd's stony expression did nothing to affirm the sentiment. 'We just need to check on the whereabouts of anyone who was with her last evening. So, just for the record, would you mind telling us where you went when you left Dr Bewen? I believe you told the other officer you got home at 2.05 this morning.'

'That's right. As a matter of fact, I went back to the office for a bit, then to Bristol for the rest of the evening.'

'I see, sir. That's quite a distance. Did you have any particular reason for going to Bristol?'

'No. Except it was a fine night, and I'm running in a new car. Getting the feel of it. The roads were pretty empty, especially the motorways.'

'Your wife knew you wouldn't be home for dinner, sir?'

'Yes. I often take an evening off from home. Sheila does the same. Has supper with a girlfriend. We think it's one of the things that helps keep our marriage so fresh.'

'And did you go right into Bristol, sir?'

'I did, yes. Had some food at a pub I know.'

'Which one, sir?'

'The Cape Cod.'

'In Grant Street, is that, sir?' asked Gomer Lloyd, who knew Bristol well.

'I think so.'

'And what time did you get to the Cape Cod, sir?' Parry questioned next.

'Mm . . . nine-ish, I'd say.'

'And did you meet anyone you knew there?'

'One or two I might have known by sight. I've been there a couple of times before.'

'No one you know better than that, sir?'

Lewis sighed and dropped his shoulders, then gave a jokingly guilty kind of grimace. 'How did you guess?' His eyes narrowed. 'I assume, in the circumstances, this needn't go any further, but, yes, I ran into a bird I know there. Name's Fiona. Don't know her surname.' The tone had become jauntily conspiratorial.

Funny way of keeping a marriage fresh, Lloyd was

thinking, while Parry was deciding they would need more corroboration on the story – a lot more.

'It was the lady from the library. Everybody knows her. Big in the church, so they tell me. We're chapel.'

The speaker, eighty-five-year-old retired railway stoker Ianto Price, was being interviewed by an energetic, angular young woman detective constable on the doorstep of 3 Valley Lane, Bryntaf, where he lived with his married daughter and her family. Valley Lane was part of old Bryntaf, on the west side of the main Valley Road, and not far from the church. At this near end, Valley Lane consisted of facing rows of small, stone-faced terrace houses erected in the 1890s. The minute front gardens were now mostly concreted over and used for parking householders' cars – a practice that effectively, if insensitively, blocked the view from the single ground-floor windows. Further along, the houses were semi-detached, and built in the late 1930s. Beyond these, the road rose quite steeply, like the prices of the modern homes there.

'Would the name be Miss Maud Davies, sir?' asked the constable, whose name was Alison Pope. She smiled encouragingly, while moving her weight expectantly, and over-actively, from one side to the other, then back again, lifting the unweighted foot halfway off the ground each time. It was a habit she'd got into through playing hockey, to keep herself mobile.

'What's that again?' Mr Price cupped his hand to his ear and leaned forward. 'I told you, love, you'll have to speak up, the battery's gone in my aid, again.'

'Was her name Maud Davies, sir? Miss Davies?' DC Pope repeated with gusto, making things worse since she had a shrill voice to begin with, and it was the higher registers he missed.

'Davies you said? Yes, that's right.' His brow furrowed before he added in a confiding tone. 'And I think you'll find it's Maud Davies. I remember because my mother was a Maud. Very nice lady. Maud Davies, I mean. But my mother was as well.' He smiled wanly. 'Miss Davies is very helpful with the big-print books. I read a lot of them. The light in my room isn't very good. But it doesn't do to complain,' he continued, with the stoicism of the lone aged parent, conscious that there were limits to the sufferance he enjoyed. 'Yes, romances I like. My daughter says I ought to act my age, but where's the harm, I ask you?' He gave a bronchitic cackle while smoothing down the wisp of hair that lay across his otherwise bald dome, and trying to fathom why his interviewer couldn't keep still. 'My daughter, she's a school cook. St Gregory's. It's a private school,' he added, in a proud afterthought. 'She doesn't leave for a bit. Did you want to see her? She's in the kitchen doing the breakfast washing-up.'

'Not for the minute, sir. Later perhaps. So where exactly was it you saw Miss Davies?'

'I told you. Last night. Wednesday. Ten past nine.' As if to confirm the point, he withdrew a typical railwayman's heavy silver pocket watch from the waistcoat he was wearing over an open shirt with the sleeves rolled up. The watch was attached to an impressive silver chain. After appearing to study both objects keenly, he put the watch away again with care, first rubbing its glass on his shirt front.

'I meant, where did you see her, sir?' This time the questioner accentuated the word 'where' by doing an exaggerated pursing of her lips at the start of it, opening her mouth very wide as the sound developed, then baring her teeth savagely over the last bit.

'You all right, are you?' asked Mr Price with some concern. 'Oh . . . you mean, *where* was it? On the corner of Valley Lane and Picton Grove. Long way up from here, of course. She turned into Picton Grove before we got there, Ida and me. Only we was coming the other way. Coming back, see? And we're a bit slow, even downhill, aren't we, old girl?' He cackled again. 'There's a lovely smell a bit the other side of Picton Grove. Ida likes to . . . to savour that. Isn't that right, you old sniffer?' He bent

118

down slowly, as far as he was able, to ruffle the fur of an obese and fairly ugly, short-haired, black and white mongrel bitch that was flopped beside his feet in the hallway.

'So you didn't see which house she went to, sir?' Because she seemed to have been interviewing nothing but hard of hearing pensioners all morning so far, the constable was getting hoarse. In consequence, at this point her voice had lowered half a tone, just as, perforce, the volume of it was reduced. This made her words a good deal more decipherable – except, as it happened, to the unseen neighbour two doors down who had been listening with interest through an open upper storey window.

'I didn't see where she went, no. It was dark up the Grove. The council's always saying they'll put more lights in, but they never do. There's only the one on the corner there. Anyway, the car had headlights on. Nearly blinded us that did.' He'd been watching the policewoman carefully as he'd been speaking. 'You don't want to use the lav, do you?' He thought he'd found the reason for her perpetual rocking from foot to foot.

'No, thank you,' DC Pope replied, primly. 'So what car was that, sir?'

'The one that came out of Picton Grove. Turned down this way, it did. Turned left, away from us. That was a bit after Miss Davies went in. Didn't I say?'

'No, sir. Never mind. How soon was that after Miss Davies went into Picton Grove?'

He rubbed the end of his nose vigorously with the flat of his palm. 'How soon? Hard to say. Two minutes?'

'Did you notice what make of car it was?'

''Course not.' His gaze had moved coldly to consider the battered and now only patchily red Morris Mini on the tiny forecourt: his grandson was rebuilding and repainting the car at weekends. 'Not with the headlights, and the speed it was going, I didn't.' Once his eyes had left the Mini, some sparkle reappeared in them. 'Too much action altogether it was for a bit, see,' he explained. 'Miss

Davies going in, and the car coming out.' His brow furrowed, making his face seem a good deal older even than it was. 'Come to think, it was a little car.'

'Like this Mini, sir?'

'God help whoever was driving if it was. No, not like this old heap. Bit bigger, I'd say.' He shook his head, looking again briefly at the object of his disdain. 'Most nights there isn't a soul about at that time. Everybody watching the telly, see? Usually we get the street to our ownselves, don't we, Ida?' He directed his voice at the animal, which lifted its heavy head a fraction in response, then dropped it again, but in what might easily have been taken for a canine signal of solid agreement.

'And you didn't see who was in the car, sir?'

'Only one person.' He paused, before adding with solemn conviction. 'The driver. Yes. But I never saw who it was.'

'Would it have been a man or a woman, sir?'

'No idea.'

'What about the colour of the car, sir?'

He glanced at the mottled Mini again, with even less favour than before. 'A light colour, I think. But I couldn't be sure.'

She debated about asking him if he'd noted the car's number, and decided it wasn't worth the effort.

This was just before Mr Price added innocently: 'I was looking for the number, see?'

12

'Could you tell us where you live, Miss Evans?' asked Parry.

'Isabella Street. Number eight.'

'That's in Grangetown is it, Miss Evans?' This was Sergeant Lloyd, with pencil poised over notebook.

'That's right. Call me Mif if you like. Everybody else does.' The comment was resigned rather than friendly, as though everybody else had been taking advantage.

Grangetown is an old dockland district in southwest Cardiff, on the left bank of the Taff River estuary. 'Well that's nice of you, Mif,' the sergeant continued, affably, and getting a half-smile for his pains. 'So it's a flat you've got there, is it?'

'Sort of flat, yes. Not very big. But we got our own bathroom. All right for us. Better than bed and breakfast on the council, I can tell you. I couldn't stand that any longer.' She blew her nose on a crumpled tissue.

Myfanwy Evans, daily 'cleaning lady' to the late Dr Bewen, was an undernourished-looking eighteen-year-old waif, dressed now in a tight white singlet, even tighter bleached blue jeans, and pull-on pumps. Her dark hair was cut very short, accentuating the stark, thinly fleshed outline of the head and face – the deep arches under the eyebrows, the high cheekbones, and the sharply sculpted chin. She wasn't pretty, but there was a striking quality in her appearance all the same. She was fairly tall, and it had already gone through Parry's mind that, with the right training, she might have done fashion modelling:

her boyish figure was skinny enough, but, more to the point, her movements were naturally graceful, and very deliberate, while her posture was instinctively erect. Only the nervous slate-grey eyes were still too reddened from recent weeping for her to be making the best of herself this morning.

It was just after eleven. The two policemen had come to Kingfishers from the Infirmary, making brief stops on the way at Dr Bewen's bank in Queen Street, and at the Fairwater police station. They were seated, with the girl, at the little alcove table set under one of the two windows in the kitchen.

Compared to the eccentrically outmoded décor and furnishings of the Kingfishers sitting room, the burnished kitchen made a surprising contrast. It was well equipped, even luxuriously so, with state-of-the-art gadgetry, gleaming copper cookware, and light oak facings to the drawers and cupboards. Hanging bunches of herbs contributed aroma as well as conviction, with fresh vegetables and fruit in handy open containers accentuating the sense that this was the practical domain of a very keen cook.

'Your parents aren't from Cardiff, then, Mif?' Parry took up the questioning again, putting this one tentatively.

'I don't have parents. Not to speak of.' Her tone was cool and indifferent. 'The ones I did have split up. I don't know what's happened to him, and I don't care. My Mum lives in Neath now. But she got a new bloke. When he started making passes, I left.' She shrugged.

'How long ago was that?'

'About two years, I suppose.'

'And that's when you came to Cardiff. Did you get a job straight away?'

'Jobs. This and that. Part-time stuff, mostly. Plus some escort agency work, as well. But I went off that.' She wiped her nose again, then, because she had seen the change of expression in Lloyd's eyes she added quickly: 'But I wasn't on the game. Not ever.'

'But you were once cautioned because you were suspected of soliciting. In Western Lane wasn't it?'

'Ah, you would know about that, wouldn't you? It was ages ago. A mistake. I was waiting for a friend. She was late. Bloody copper was frantic to make his quota, that's all.' The response had been rapid and stridently defensive.

'I'll believe you, Mif.' It wasn't what the record said, all the same: according to the police file, the only reason she hadn't been arrested was because the evidence had been wrongly worded. Still, that had been well over a year ago. 'And you've been working for Dr Bewen every weekday for how long?'

'A twelve-month. I come Saturdays as well, most weeks, that's if Delia wanted, and usually she did. She worked terrible hours herself, including weekends. I did her shopping, as well as the house. And cleaning veg and things, ready for the evenings, specially if she had anyone coming round. She liked fresh stuff. No frozen. She was ever so particular about that.'

'Good cook, was she, Mif?' asked Lloyd, looking around the kitchen.

'The best. Really, she was. She said she'd rather do cooking than anything. Some of the things she made, you wouldn't believe. She designed this kitchen, too. It was her present to her husband, she told me. Her late husband.' There was a pause. 'She was ever so kind to me and Sandra. Knew we needed the money. We owe her like . . . well, everything. Now she's gone, I don't know what we'll do.' The eyes were glistening with fresh tears as she stopped speaking again, before she leaned behind her to see to the baby girl asleep in a pushchair there.

'It's quite a long way for you and . . . and Sandra to travel,' commented Lloyd, smiling in the child's direction.

Mif turned round again, her eyes less watery. 'Yeah, but we come just after the rush hour. The bus is OK then. Quick, I mean. We go at four. We have our lunch here. Delia used to leave special things for us some days, things she'd made. Fab they were. Otherwise, she'd say to help

123

ourselves to what there was. In the fridge, like. She was ever so generous.'

'So you always bring Sandra with you?'

'Always.' The firm response indicated the question could have produced only one answer.

'So how did you meet Dr Bewen?'

'Through the Infirmary. I got pregnant again. She did the abortion. Said it was best for me. Then, after, she said she needed someone regular for here. Her old daily had to give up. And I could bring Sandra. I don't hold with minders. It was great for us.'

'And your boyfriend –'

'I don't have a boyfriend. Not any more.' The words had a defiant flavour to them.

Lloyd nodded and decided not to press the point further. 'I see. And you always called the doctor by her first name, did you, Mif?'

'Yeah, she said to. She was like that. Friendly. Nothing stuck-up about her. Not like some.'

'Like whom, for instance?'

She shrugged. 'Just other people I worked for.'

'I see. And did the doctor ever ask you to live here?'

'To live in, you mean? No. I think she wanted the place to herself at night. Couldn't blame her, neither. But it was through her that Dilys and me got friendly. Dilys and her boyfriend own number eight, where I got the flat. So that was thanks to Delia as well, see.'

'You share the Grangetown house with them?'

'No. It's their house. I just rent the basement. Dilys is from here. From Bryntaf.'

'And that was where you were last night, was it? At the flat, Mif?' The question had been put lightly, and in the hope that it wouldn't upset the girl, or prompt her to analyse the motive behind it.

'Yeah. From after we got home at five. I was painting the kitchen. Alex, that's Dilys's boyfriend, he was helping.'

Which, to Lloyd, seemed a sufficient answer.

'By the way, what's Dilys's other name, Mif?' Parry put in.

'Hughes. Her mum owns the dress shop in the village. But they've er . . . they've fallen out, like.'

'Did Dilys meet the doctor professionally, like you?'

'How d'you mean? . . . Oh, yeah. Only not in the Infirmary. It was at the cottage hospital. In Bryntaf. That was before she left home, see? Delia was great with her as well. A really great doctor. She helped hundreds like us.'

'She was a specialist, of course, Mif. Not an ordinary doctor. I mean you only went to her for –'

'Women's things, yeah, that's what I meant,' the girl interrupted. 'She was . . . she was really, really great. Fantastic.'

Parry leaned back a little from the table. 'Can you tell us who she used to invite here for the evening? Was it always the same person or the same people?'

'I dunno.'

'You must know how many, at least, since you did the clearing up in the mornings.'

'Suppose so, yeah. Er . . . well it was mostly one other person. Sometimes more. I dunno if it was the same people.'

'I see. You know she got engaged to Mr Treace this week?'

'He's the vicar. Yeah, Dilys told me about that yesterday. She read it in the paper.'

'Had you ever met him?'

'The vicar? No.' She seemed to find the question briefly comical.

Lloyd shifted on the cushion of the bench seat as he searched for peppermints in his pocket. 'When you cleared up the place in the mornings,' he asked, 'had anyone ever stayed the night?'

'Not very often they hadn't, no. The guests was usually just for dinner. Only her mum, Mrs Elliott, from Chester, she stayed. Used the guest bedroom. I know her. She'd stay on in the day sometimes, as well. After Delia went to work. We talked then. A lot sometimes. She's nice, as well. Like Delia. More old-fashioned though. Well, you'd expect that. She'll be coming down then, will she?'

'Probably. She was the next of kin we had to inform about the death. I expect she'll be here to identify the body.'

'Oh lor.' Then the girl's eyes brightened. 'I could do that, couldn't I? To save her? I wouldn't mind.'

'Well, that's a kind thought, Mif, but we need a relative, so long as there's one available.'

Mif looked disappointed. 'Mrs Elliott, she'll want the guest room, won't she? I'd better get it ready then.'

'That sounds like a good idea. The doctor slept in a double bed, Mif. Do you know if anyone ever slept with her? I mean, was the bed rumpled on both sides ever? Extra number of towels used in the bathroom, that kind of thing?'

'Why d'you want to know a thing like that?'

The answer did her credit, Parry thought. It was he who now put in firmly: 'Because we all want to catch your friend's murderer, Mif. Especially you, I'd have thought, because, as you said, you owe Delia. We need to know about all the people who were close to her. Especially the men, and there were possibly more of those than we know about yet. So please answer Sergeant Lloyd's question.'

She was still a little diffident in her response. 'I don't think anyone slept the night with her. Not all night. I think the bed could have been used for sex though. Sometimes. Not very often. You could tell, sort of, from the sheets, like.' The answer had embarrassed her a lot less than the question had peeved her.

'And would that always have been after she'd had one person to dinner, Mif?' Lloyd pressed. 'When there was just the table for two for you to clear in the morning?'

'Not usually, no.'

'I see. But when it was after she'd had only the one

126

dinner guest, and the guest stayed the night, did you ever find out who the guest was?'

'No. How could I? Whoever it was'd be gone by the time we got here. Anyway, it wasn't my business to know, was it?'

'Except it is now, Mif. Your business to help us in any way you can, remember?' said Parry pointedly.

'Yeah, yeah. OK. And I didn't ever know who . . . who was in the bedroom with her. And anyway, like I said, I don't know if they did stay all night. Like there weren't extra breakfast things to clear up in here. Not ever. Only extra dinner stuff in the dining room. She always used the dining room when she had guests, even her mother.'

Lloyd nodded. 'So going back to the mornings when you noticed what you said about . . . about the sheets, Mif, were any of those mornings very recent?'

She shrugged. 'Not this week, I don't think. Last week though, once.'

'Which morning?'

'Thursday.'

'We'd like you to be sure.'

She thought for a moment. 'Yeah, it was Thursday.'

'And on previous times? Was it always Thursday?'

'For the last three times, yes.'

'And was there always someone to dinner on the Wednesday evening before?'

'No. Dinner guests was usually Fridays. Maybe Saturdays too, but I never come Sundays, so I wouldn't know. She had people in for dinner on Tuesdays, sometimes. She was supposed to be home early then, because of her Tuesday clinic in Bryntaf. But she wasn't ever back on Tuesdays before Sandra and me left, except she'd maybe pop in earlier, on her way to the clinic.'

'Thanks, Mif, that should be very helpful,' said Parry warmly. 'Tell me, you were here yesterday, I expect?'

'Like every day, yeah.'

'Did you clean any particular rooms?'

'Her bedroom and bathroom, as usual. And the lounge,

127

what Delia called the sitting room. And in here. Then the rest of the downstairs. Like today, I ought to be doing the rest of the upstairs, except I'm not allowed.'

'Well, that was for a good reason, Mif. And you'll be allowed by lunchtime. But tell me something else, you know the miner's lamp on the table in the sitting room?'

'Yeah. My granda was a miner. He used a lamp like that. It's not there today, though.'

'That's right. We've taken it away to look at. Now, please think carefully before you answer the next question. Did you pick up the lamp and dust it with your bare hands yesterday?'

She hesitated. 'Why? – I mean, no,' she added quickly, because she had remembered the previous admonition about co-operating. 'It's heavy. I do things like that with a feather duster most days.'

'So you're sure you didn't pick it up, and then, perhaps, not put it back in its usual place on the table? Think hard again now. It's important,' the chief inspector pressed.

'Not yesterday, no. Once a week, Fridays, I bring it in here and give it a real polish, like Delia told me when I first come. I do some of the other metal things in there the same, and the silver. But I had to put everything back in the same place after. She didn't like things being moved round. That room's a sod, mind, with all that stuff to keep clean. Not that I minded. Not really.'

'And you've had a good look round in there today. I'm afraid plenty of things have been moved by us. Is there anything missing besides the lamp? Anything at all you haven't already mentioned to the other police officers?'

'There's nothing else missing in the sitting room. I said the only things was in the kitchen.'

'That's the plastic bowl in the sink, which we've taken away ourselves, and the pair of yellow rubber gloves you say you kept under the sink.'

'Yeah.'

'The gloves aren't on the list of things we've taken, Mif. You're sure they were there when you left yesterday?'

'Positive.' She was jamming the loosened hem of the singlet back into the top of her jeans.

Parry leaned forward. 'Did Delia use those gloves too?'

'No. She had her own. Particular about stuff like that, she was. Gloves specially. Hers were green. They're in the drawer next to the sink.'

'And they're still there?'

'Yeah, I looked first thing. She never used them much. But she got new ones regular. And for me.'

'Well, we're looking very hard for your gloves, Mif. And it could be important we find them. If you come across them, you'll let us know, won't you?'

She shrugged. 'Yeah. 'Cept how could I come across them?'

'Probably you won't, but they could turn up somewhere here where we haven't looked, or you might have taken them home by mistake.'

'Never.' She had bridled at the last suggestion. 'I've never took anything from here.'

'I said "by mistake", Mif. Such things are easily done.'

During Parry's last comment, Lloyd had been turning back pages in his notebook. Now he put in: 'Did you make any phone calls when you were here yesterday, Mif?'

'No. But Delia let me use the phone, any time.' Again the words were defensive. 'If I made a call, I always left her a note to say. But she never let me pay.' Her forehead wrinkled a little. 'She phoned me yesterday, though. From the Infirmary.' She paused. 'It'll be the last time I'll ever speak to her, won't it? Funny you can't know something like that. Not when it's happening.' Her voice had broken on the words, and, quite suddenly, she began to weep again, but not for very long. Afterwards, she dried her eyes on the ball of tissue. 'Sorry,' she said.

'That's all right, Mif. Can you tell us what the phone call was about?'

'Yeah, about shopping she wanted done. There wasn't much to get.'

'Was she expecting anyone to a meal, did she say?'

Parry kept any hopeful expectancy out of his voice.

'No. It was stuff she needed for today. Just for her, I think. Them oranges and apples over there. She said she'd be going out last night, probably, after she'd seen a patient, or she'd be having an omelette.'

'What time did she ring you?'

'About ten. I hadn't been here long.'

'One last question, Mif,' said Parry. 'Do you know Miss Maud Davies? She runs the Bryntaf public library.'

It was the first time she had smiled properly. 'No, I don't know her.' She scratched her midriff. 'Well, I wouldn't, would I? Sandra and me, we don't do a lot of reading, like.'

13

Lloyd wiped his lips, and considered the inch of beer left in his glass. 'Ready for the other half, boss?' he asked, preparing to push his chair back.

'No, this'll do me.' Parry's glass was still a third full. They were sitting in the partly stone-flagged garden at the back of the Waggoner, the whitewashed Bryntaf pub, which most people agreed was the oldest building in the village apart from the church. Some of the structure probably was very old indeed, but it had been extended several times over the previous sixty years, and all of it had been refurbished during the last ten. Still, it had atmosphere, and the beers were good. The policemen were the only customers outside. Although it wasn't particularly warm, the sun was shining fitfully. They had brought their drinks and sandwiches out here partly for the air, but mostly for privacy.

While Lloyd had been setting up their order at the bar earlier, Parry had stayed in the car, listening to the latest situation report from the incident room collator on his cellphone. There had been important information from the pathologist in Cardiff and from the forensic laboratory in Chepstow establishing the identity of the weapons used by the murderer. There were also reports on the interviews with householders that had not been to hand before the two policemen had left to see Myfanwy Evans.

'Would Mr Treace have lied about him and Dr Bewen not having sex, boss?' the sergeant questioned, after deciding not to order another half-pint for himself. He wasn't expecting to drive, but he'd promised Gracie he'd limit himself at lunchtimes for weight reasons.

'He only implied that to me,' said Parry. 'It was just as he was leaving last night. Better if he had been lying, in a way. If he wasn't, it looks as if she was being unfaithful to him. That's if Mif's got it right about the bedclothes.'

'Do clergymen lie, boss?' It was the kind of subject on which Lloyd was given to affecting ignorance, deferring to the other's judgement out of politeness – because Parry went to church and he didn't.

The chief inspector grinned. 'Some would lie. About a thing like that, anyway. Wouldn't you, in the circumstances? If your job depended on your being without sin? Especially that particular sin.' Parry's attitudes on such issues were practical rather than liberal – even if they often seemed to be both. 'Anyway,' he completed, 'as I said, he didn't absolutely deny they were at it.'

'But it's not likely he was one of the people invited to supper on Tuesdays, Fridays or Saturdays, is it, boss? Too formal, I'd have thought. Or if he was, his wife would have been invited as well, wouldn't she?'

Parry nodded. 'Probably. A cup of tea at Kingfishers on a Wednesday evening, after the Lent lecture, would have been more likely in his case. When he wouldn't have been expected home at any special time, perhaps.'

'But as her moral counsellor, he had the excuse to show up there when he pleased, didn't he?'

'Broadly, I suppose, yes. But bear in mind, she was hardly ever there in the daytime. And for counselling, it's quite likely she'd have gone to see him at the church or the vicarage, by appointment.'

'Well if he's been sneaking up on Wednesday evenings, it probably is him whose been rumpling the sheets, like Mif said, boss. But if it wasn't him, we could be looking at a jealousy killing, couldn't we?'

'If there was another man,' Parry agreed, 'and after it was known Treace was going to marry her.'

'And in that case, I know who gets my nomination as well,' said Lloyd heavily. 'Mr Olaf Lewis.'

'Who says he was at the Cape Cod in Bristol by nine.'

'Nine-ish, was what he said, boss, which could mean half past, or quarter to ten even, with no one to deny it. I mean, he's probably squared this Fiona he says he was with. That's if she exists, of course, and I'll be finding that out later today.'

'I think you'll find she does exist, Gomer. And she'll be quite a dish, too. It's pretty certain Lewis likes making conquests he can brag about. I imagine they're important to his self-esteem, even if the bragging means risk. Like his wife finding out what he does on his evenings off.'

'Agreed, boss. Full of himself, wasn't he? Anyway, with clear roads, he could have got to Bristol in forty minutes, easy. This Ianto Price, he said the car came out of Picton Grove at ten past nine, did he?'

One of the reports Parry had listened to had covered DC Alison Pope's interview with the old man. 'Except Lewis was driving a new Jaguar coupé,' said the chief inspector, opening his sandwich to examine the ham in it. 'And Price thought it was a small car, with blinding headlights.'

'Jaguars are low on the ground, boss. It might just have seemed small to him. And probably the headlights would have blinded him anyway, specially if they were meant to blind anyone there at the time.'

'Except there are holes in Price's story. The lights couldn't have blinded him, because he said the car turned left out of Picton Grove. That's away from where he and his dog were in Valley Lane. I've told the collator to have that checked.' Parry scooped up a piece of tomato on his plate. 'And while he looked for the number, he only got one letter, which he thinks was either P or B, and he's not even sure of that.' He shook his head as he chewed the tomato.

Lloyd reached for his notebook. 'There's a P in the Jaguar number, boss, but no B.'

'Yes, so they told me.'

'Was there any reason why Mr Price should have been noting car numbers?' the sergeant questioned. 'An old chap walking his dog?'

'Yes, there was. Seems they have a neighbourhood watch scheme in Valley Lane. Price isn't one of their street wardens. He volunteered for it, but they said he was too old.'

'Ah, so he memorizes car numbers, and the rest', Lloyd offered, 'to show he isn't past it. Only his eyesight's not up to the job for a start.'

'That's about it, I expect.' Parry drank some beer. 'And we've only got Lewis's word for it that Dr Bewen never told him her patient had cancelled the nine o'clock appointment,' he said. 'That was Mrs Audrey Slattery, wasn't it? And wasn't someone contacting her this morning?'

'Yes, boss. DS Norris.'

'And the lady's in the clear?'

'Pretty well. Seems she had regular consultations with the doctor for a . . . for an ongoing condition. She didn't say what it was. Well, you wouldn't expect, would you?' Lloyd pursed his lips and gave an understanding nod before he continued. 'She did say she always came to the house, and the two of them often went out after for a Chinese meal. In Bryntaf. To a place called the Jade Tower.'

'Which explains why I've just been told the doctor hadn't made a reservation there last night,' said Parry, throwing a piece of bread to a predatory house sparrow.

'That's right, boss. I'd asked for that to be checked. Seems that whether they went out to eat or not depended on how long a consultation took. Mrs Slattery said her other appointments had always been earlier than the one last night. Seven o'clock, usually. She'd asked for a later one this time because of her London meeting. She wasn't sure if they'd have gone out together if she'd got there last night. Anyway, she didn't get there. Worse luck.'

134

'Were her appointments always on a Wednesday?' Parry asked slowly.

'Usually, boss.' The sergeant cleared his throat. 'And Mary Norris says Mrs Slattery is happily married with two teenage children, and as heterosexual as we think Dr Bewen was. Not much chance it was the two of them went to bed together on Wednesday evenings, after they'd been to the Chinese.'

Parry gave a wan smile. 'It was only a passing thought, Gomer, that's all. Did we find out what time Mrs Slattery left the London meeting?' he added, possibly because a vestige of the same thought still lingered.

'Yes. It was just before nine, and her assistant travelled back with her to Newport.'

'Well, I suppose that settles it. Good.' Parry pondered for a moment, while finishing his sandwich. 'So if the doctor had told Lewis she was going to be free after all, he could have driven up to Kingfishers any time after they parted in Cardiff. But, except for old Mr Price, no one's reported seeing a car arrive or leave Picton Grove between eight and ten last night, have they?'

'No, boss. Not even the doctor's own car, which we know she must have come home in.' Lloyd drank the last drop of beer, then studied the bottom of the glass with a look of regret that overmatched his decision not to replenish the contents – until it was clear his face was actually mirroring his opinion of Olaf Lewis. 'Mr Lewis could also be lying about what happened to his wife, couldn't he?' he observed, looking up. 'If it was attempted suicide, say, because she knew he was having an affair with someone. And he's got rid of the note, if there was one.' On top of which, the speaker's dark expression suggested, he believed that there had been.

'Well, she's still too ill to be interviewed,' Parry replied. 'When she does talk to us, if she took the pills intentionally, it's quite possible she's not going to admit it.'

'Because she'd be ashamed of what she did, like?'

'Yes, but if you're right, it's more likely the whole thing

135

was a cry for attention, not a real suicide attempt.' Parry folded his arms in front of him while his eyes went to study the heavily budding cherry tree in the centre of the pub garden. 'And if this Ianto Price's eyesight can be trusted on anything,' he went on, 'Maud Davies is another liar, even if she's a particularly pious one. By all accounts, she's almost an unpaid curate in this parish. Fact remains though, she told DC Vaughan this morning that she was home all evening with a headache.'

'With no witnesses, boss?'

Parry shrugged. 'Her father lives with her, but he was here all evening, in the Waggoner, playing in a darts match. Came home at ten thirty. All we can be certain of is she was there when he left, and again when he got back. That's what he told Vaughan when they were both interviewed at home.'

'But with Ianto Price just as certain she was in Picton Grove at ten past nine,' said Lloyd.

'And Mrs Craig-Owen, who owns the grocery store, is adamant that Miss Davies is besotted with the Reverend Treace.'

'Is that a fact, boss?'

'No, it's what Mrs Craig-Owen alleges,' the grinning Parry responded pedantically. 'But what she said is supported by her husband.'

'Still, you could say we got a motive there, all right,' the sergeant observed.

Parry did not appear as convinced. 'I didn't ask whether Mrs Craig-Owen came forward with her information voluntarily.'

'Shouldn't think so, boss. She and her husband's names were on DC Vaughan's special interview list for this morning. Of people involved with the church.'

'Hm. And also people not too charitably inclined toward one another, judging by what Mrs Craig-Owen has said about Maud Davies. Anyway, we'll need to see Miss Davies next ourselves.'

'Right, boss. That'll be at the library, I expect.' Lloyd

made a tick in his notebook. 'Well at least we've got the weapon, both weapons,' he added encouragingly, since there wasn't that much else to be pleased about.

'With no prints on either, and not much chance of DNA matchings,' Parry provided gloomily.

The early pathology and forensic reports had confirmed that the miner's lamp had caused the crushing head wound that had killed Delia Bewen. It was equally certain that the two-inch blade scalpel left deep inside the body – proving Dr Maltravers right in his dire foreboding – had been the implement used in the stabbings. It was almost certain that the instrument had come from the labelled carton of individually wrapped and assorted scalpels kept in clear view in Dr Bewen's consulting room. In addition, it had been confirmed that the stabbings had been made after death, but only a matter of minutes after – allowing time for the murderer to have collected the gloves from the kitchen, and the scalpel from the consulting room.

The lamp had been washed in the same brand of dishwashing liquid as the one found in the Kingfishers kitchen – but not washed in the course of her work by Mif Evans, who had claimed that she wiped the object over once a week with a cloth dampened only with plain water. Parry had told the collator that this point needed double-checking with the girl.

Although the lamp had appeared clean to the naked eye, its worn surfaces had provided many small crevices, and traces of blood and skin had been lodged in several of them, plus a particle of hair. It seemed certain that all this human detritus had come from the body of Dr Bewen – unfortunately so, since there had been hope that some might have belonged to her assailant.

The green plastic kitchen bowl, kept in the stainless steel sink at Kingfishers, was also being tested. It had been removed with other material the night before, at the insti-gation of DS Wilcox. There was a better than even chance that the bowl had been used for washing the lamp. One indicator to this lay partly in the disappearance of Mif's yellow rubber gloves which she kept in the cupboard under the sink. If they had been used by the murderer while he was washing the lamp, as well as during the stabbings, this increased the chances of DNA samples being found on them too. After Mif had revealed their absence to the police, a search for the gloves had been made in the house. The hunt had since been extended to the area around and well beyond Kingfishers – down Picton Grove, and along Valley Lane in both directions. This had meant examining the contents of every dustbin in the vicinity, to the embarrassment and irritation of some householders who didn't care to have their refuse turned over in public by strangers. That official refuse collectors were at liberty to do the same thing was not considered comparable to having policemen do it.

The pathologist had found no semen in or on the body, suggesting that there had been no carnal intimacy, whether consenting or otherwise, prior to the murder. This also offered the possibility that the killer could have been female – except that the angle and weight of the head blow had seemed to point to a right-handed male assailant, although this last was largely based on empirical deduction.

'Those rubber gloves have got to be somewhere,' said Lloyd reflectively, while still toying with his empty glass.

'Assuming young Mif is telling us the truth.'

'About just the gloves you mean, boss?'

'About a lot of things. You don't think she overdid her devotion to Dr Bewen?' Parry answered, in a speculating tone.

'Why should she?' Lloyd had been sorry for the girl.

'Possibly because Delia Bewen left her something, money or property, and she knows about it. Lewis said he doesn't believe she made a will. Treace and her bank manager said the same. But they weren't positive about it. If she did make a will, any number of people named in it could be standing to benefit from her death.'

138

'Who wouldn't do, not once she married Mr Treace, boss?'

Parry shrugged. 'That's impossible to say, but if she had made a will, it's pretty certain she'd have made another when she got married again.'

'Leaving everything to Mr Treace, like? But couldn't she have done that already? Kind of in advance of the marriage? Making him the only one to benefit?'

'Not the only one, probably. She has a mother living, remember? But her having left anything substantial to Treace offers fresh possibilities, of course.'

'You mean like Mr Treace could have murdered her himself, boss, for the money, without having to marry her, or lose his job, or his present wife?'

'I never said that, and it's hardly a probability, is it? Anyway, her lawyer is the most likely person to know if she made a will.'

'There was no lawyer listed in her organizer, boss.'

'I know. But it doesn't mean she didn't have one, or that she didn't make a will.'

'A lot of people don't make wills, of course.' Which, as it happened, included the speaker. 'But we can check again with her secretary. About her having a lawyer at least.'

'And with her mother, Mrs Elliott. By the way, she's coming down by train in the morning.' Parry paused, shifting his empty glass on the table. 'If Dr Bewen hadn't made a will before her husband died, it's possible she did afterwards. Widows often do. You're right though. There was no copy of any will in the house, and she didn't have a deed box or anything to keep it in at the bank.'

Their short interview with the dead woman's bank manager had been formal but enlightening – so far as a modern bank manager is allowed to enlighten anyone about anything which doesn't promise to produce immediate profit for the corporation. This one had accepted that a police murder investigation justified his answering the questions put to him about the balances in his dead customer's current and deposit accounts. The policemen had also been given a sight of the doctor's March bank statements, although they had been refused copies of these to take away with them, pending authorization by whoever was appointed as the customer's executor. They already had Dr Bewen's own copies of previous bank statements going back several years. These had been stored in the filing cabinet in the consulting room. The March statements, viewed at the bank, had showed nothing unusual, in terms of payments in or out, compared to the pattern of previous months.

'Are you thinking that what with the house and everything, Dr Bewen's going to carve up to –' Lloyd stopped, and shook his head. 'Well, there's an unfeeling thing to say, if you like. What I meant was, she's left quite a bit, what with the house, and the investments, and money we know about. It's got to go to someone.'

There had been six hundred pounds in the current account, and over three thousand on deposit. In addition, Parry had estimated that the house, without the contents, was worth better than a quarter of a million pounds. The doctor's building society passbook had revealed that there had been an original mortgage on the property of a hundred and eighty thousand. This had now been reduced to just under thirty thousand. Most of the dramatic reduction had occurred fifteen months before, thanks to one large deposit made then of a hundred and twenty thousand pounds. Olaf Lewis had volunteered that this had come from the benefit the doctor had been paid through an accident insurance policy on her husband's life, with a further thirty thousand pounds of it invested in unit trusts and savings bonds.

In short, Dr Bewen had been a woman of substance.

'Going back to Mif,' said Parry, 'if she knew she'd been left a bundle in the doctor's will, was she bright enough or . . . or knowledgeable enough to twig she'd probably lose it come the marriage to Treace? And if she did twig that, was she likely to commit murder to protect her expectations?'

'She mightn't have been, boss, but what about her boyfriend? The one that made her pregnant?' His sympathies didn't extend to Mif's irresponsible lovers.

'Who she says she'd dropped,' Parry put in. 'But we've only her word for that, of course. He could still be around, and he could be a lot brighter than she is. He might have been her pimp, of course.'

'You don't think she's still on the game, boss?'

'No. But I think we need to pay a visit to 8 Isabella Street. To find out what the setup is there.'

14

'I'm back then. I'll make you some tea, shall I?'

Sybil Treace was standing in the doorway of the vicarage study. She was dressed in her green woollen outdoor coat, a small and battered suitcase in one hand. Her husband had been sitting behind his desk, trying to work at his computer. The smile on his face had frozen as soon as he raised his eyes and saw her. 'Sybil, I . . . I thought you were Janet. Your voices are . . . they're so alike.' Confused, he pushed back the chair and got to his feet. The two women's voices weren't that much alike. It was just that he hadn't been expecting Sybil, hadn't wanted her here.

'Well, I'm not Janet. I'm me, and I've come to look after you.' She put down the case and moved into the room towards him. Her movements, as yet, were bolder than the expression in her eyes, which was a lot short of confident. 'I was sorry to hear about Dr Bewen. What a terrible thing. You must be ever so upset. We all are, of course. She was very well thought of, you know. By people who'd met her.' She'd practised saying that, but it had sounded wrong, and she knew it. It was as if she'd meant that not many people had met Delia Bewen – that there hadn't been enough of them to form a proper opinion, a consensus.

'Indeed.' He swallowed, clearly at a loss over what to say next. On top of a bad and sleepless night, to this point he'd had a worse day, after steeling himself to carry on as usual, saying matins in the church mid morning, doing

142

his sick visiting, and the rest. Now the prospect of the day getting any better had disappeared entirely.

'So it's all over for you with Delia, before it began really,' she said, standing close in front of him now. She began picking loose hairs off the front of the dark blue, high-necked sweater he had on, below his clerical collar. 'Chance for us though,' she went on. 'Specially for me. You see, you've brought me to my senses at last. I . . . I shan't be drinking any more. Not ever. Shock therapy, they call it. That's what you gave me, love, with a ven-geance. No, hear me out.' She had put her fingers over his lips, to stop him speaking. 'You were right on Tuesday. I'm ashamed of myself. But I'll make it up to you. Starting from now. That way, Delia's death won't go for nothing, will it? There's something really positive to look forward to now, thanks to her.'

'Sybil, Delia's death can't make any difference to our relationship.' He had spoken slowly, still unsure of his words – and even why he was saying them. What his wife had uttered had taken him more by surprise than even her appearance had done.

'Oh, you wait and see, love. It'll make all the difference in the world. I'm only sorry it's a blessing she's bought for us at such a high price to herself. The highest price, of course. We must try to be worthy of her sacrifice.'

'Sacrifice? You don't know what you're talking about.' Her last sentence had at last galvanized his thoughts. And then he wondered suddenly, did she know exactly what she was talking about? Did she know a lot more than she should have done? He moved back a step from her in a reflex gesture, spawned as much by doubt as by sickening apprehension.

'Oh, but I do know, Peter. She's dead, poor dear thing, and without me you'll have no one to look after you. No one to be with you, to help finish your work here, and then move on to higher things.' She took a deep breath through her mouth. 'I've seen the archdeacon.'

143

'You've what?' She had shocked his mind back to where he had been when she had first appeared.

'I said, I've seen the archdeacon. Today it was. Just after lunch. Thought I'd just catch him then. At his house. I got a taxi over. We had a lovely talk. I –'

'How . . . how dare you go to see the archdeacon without telling me.' It was an admonition, but the tone had been feeble by Treace's normal standards. Both his open hands had moved to grasp at his brow, while his eyes stared at her in total incredulity.

'I didn't want to bother you, not with everything so topsy-turvy. Now, why don't you sit down while I tell you? Go on. Sit down, comfy.' To her surprise, he did as he was told, still in a kind of daze. He dropped into one of the two upright chairs with wooden arms arranged close to each other in front of the desk. The chairs were there chiefly for young couples who came to arrange their banns and listen to pastoral advice on marriage. 'The archdeacon was very worried about you.' Sybil had now sat in the other chair, pulling it closer to his. 'He said he didn't know whether he should have been in touch already today. I said it was better to have left you alone for a bit, at least.' She moved her glasses up the bridge of her nose. It was one of her more confident gestures. 'Anyway, we agreed that what's happened to Delia, terrible though it is, makes a marvellous chance for you and me to patch things up. Face the future together. The archdeacon and I even said a prayer about that. After I asked him if we could.'

'You and the archdeacon prayed together.' It was a statement, not a question, as though he needed to marshal all the facts before he could make his mind up about something important.

'That's right. He's a lovely man, that's when you get to talk to him properly. Very saintly. I've never spoken to him like that before. Well, we'd only met properly twice, up to today, that is. He wanted to know how the parishioners were taking the news of Delia's death. I told him

144

that so far as I could tell at the moment, there's very great sadness all round. Especially for Delia herself. And hope that good will come out of what's happened, after all. I mean, no one's saying it's divine retribution because of what she was doing.'

'You told him that?' He had begun to breath noisily, his eyes now fixed on hers.

'Yes, because he asked about it. Like I said.' Her voice faltered slightly, the tone defensive. She was wanting to drop her gaze, but was willing herself not to. 'I said the . . . the good people of this parish . . . they don't have minds of that kind. Well, some might, but –'

Treace had suddenly got up from the chair, knocking it over behind him, towering over his wife, his face suffused with anger. She cringed, letting out a frightened little whimper as he grasped at her coat lapels, and hissed at her. 'Where were you last night, when she was murdered? Tell me that? Where were you at nine last night? Were you there? At the house?' Now he began to shout, pulling her face closer to his, shaking her violently. 'Tell me, you bloody hypocrite. You think I can be morally blackmailed, do you? Is that it?' He was roaring more abuse at her, shaking her still, after pulling her halfway out of the chair, when his daughter dashed in. Aghast at what she had heard already, she rushed over to the struggling couple.

'Sorry to break into your work, Miss Davies. Case of needs must, I'm afraid. The sergeant and I are inquiring into the death of Dr Delia Bewen.'

'I thought it might be that. I expect my assistant can cope provided we're not too long. But I did speak to one of your colleagues about the . . . the murder this morning.' Maud Davies dabbed at the end of her nose with a tissue, straightened her knitted jumper – this one had marigolds on it – and looked across at Parry questioningly. She had shown the two policemen into what was termed the staff room of the modern but small Bryntaf Library. The room was on the upper floor, and was little more than a glorified locker room, with a wooden table and chairs in the middle, some metal shelving holding books to be catalogued or repaired, and a washroom beyond the small bank of lockers. The three were already seated at the table.

'Yes, that was Detective Constable Vaughan you saw, Miss Davies,' said Parry. 'We've got more information on the case since you talked to him. We're hoping you may be able to help us further.'

'If I can. I really don't know how, though. I mean, as I explained to Mr Vaughan, I'd never even met Dr Bewen. She wasn't a member of the library.' The speaker's tone was dismissive on the subject of the murdered woman – but nervous with it.

'But the doctor attended your church, didn't she? St Samson's?'

The librarian touched the heavy silver crucifix – of almost episcopal proportions – that was hanging on a substantial chain around her neck, while a sober, indulgent smile crept over her face. 'Did she? Not to the eight o'clock, I'm sure. Perhaps to the ten thirty parish communion. That's very popular. Very crowded too. I'm always at both. Yes, she may have come to the ten thirty once or twice, without troubling to make herself known. That would be quite recently, I expect. But she never came for coffee in the church hall afterwards. If she had, I'd certainly have met her. Of course, it was just the vicar she was interested in, wasn't it?' The last putatively barbed sentence was delivered in a tone of disarming, quiet innocence. Miss Davies had leaned forward at the end of it wearing an expression of earnest enquiry, as though she was really seeking an answer to her question.

'Was it? Perhaps that's right,' the chief inspector replied neutrally. 'Anyway, we understand you told DC Vaughan that you know the Reverend Peter Treace very well.'

'Yes, I do, but that's not the same as knowing Dr Bewen, is it? I mean, they've never been thought of as a . . . as a couple. Not until this week. Well, there's no reason why they should have been. Quite the opposite, really,' she

146

added with sober propriety. 'I try to be a useful member of the congregation, of course. That's why I'm . . . I'm involved in a lot of activities with the vicar, yes.' She pulled down the bottom of her jumper, then smoothed the top of her skirt under the table, using both hands for the neat, precise movements. Then she looked to Parry again expectantly.

'And I believe you were at the meeting in the parish hall on Tuesday evening?'

'The one about the planned supermarket? Yes, I was there.'

'So you heard the vicar announce that he was divorcing his wife, and then the protests of Mrs Treace before she was helped away?'

'Yes, poor lady. I felt so sorry for her.'

'Was that the first you knew of the vicar's . . . surprising plans?'

'Certainly it was. Although he's a wonderful pastor, very wonderful, he's quite a private person as well. He's looked after a problem wife for many years, really without complaint. Not to outsiders. Not even to friends, really. We wouldn't have expected him to tell us he was leaving Sybil for someone else, not until he was quite ready.'

'He wouldn't even have told you, Miss Davies? I imagine you're a lot closer to him than most other people?'

Her cheeks flushed immediately, and in a token effort to disguise this embarrassment, the flattened fingers of both open hands moved up to adjust the frames of her spectacles at the outer edges. 'I don't think that's true. Not really,' she said, deliberately. 'There are many members of the congregation who are . . . close to him. Closer than me, I expect.'

Gomer Lloyd cleared his throat. 'But we've been told you're as good as an unpaid curate to the parish, Miss Davies,' he said.

'Oh, I wish that were true. In any case, I couldn't be that.' She had removed her hands from her spectacles,

147

before she added, a touch primly, 'You see, I don't approve of women priests.'

'Ah, yes.' The sergeant nodded sagely, heavy eyebrows knitting, his whole expression implying a total understanding of the intricacies, complications and conflicts affecting the ordination of women. 'Anyway, you're saying you didn't have an inkling of his . . . his new marriage plans?'

'That's right.'

'Did you even know he was seeing Dr Bewen?'

'I knew she was one of the people who'd been to him for private counselling. That was some months back.'

Parry looked interested. 'How did you know that, Miss Davies?' he asked.

'He mentioned it to me one day. In passing, it was, in the vestry. Nothing confidential, of course. We were looking out some vestments for cleaning and repair. That's one of my little jobs. Caring for the vestments,' she put in, before continuing. 'I remember him asking if I knew Dr Bewen. He said it was very sad her husband had died so tragically, and that he was trying to help her in her grief. That was all. Oh, not quite.' One hand had quickly gone to her mouth in a nervous, forgetful gesture. 'I remember now he said Dr Bewen might be useful to the parish some day. To be on the list of volunteer counsellors we keep. People ready to advise young members of the congregation. To help young women, he must have meant, in Dr Bewen's case. She being a . . . a gynaecologist.' She had dropped her voice before the last word, as though she was uncomfortable about saying it. 'Nothing came of that, though. I know, because I'm in charge of keeping the list up to date,' she completed.

'Another of your . . . little jobs,' commented the chief inspector with a smile. 'But, as you say, you'd know, of course, if anything had been done about it. Thank you, Miss Davies, that's very helpful. Can you tell us now what your first reaction was when Mr Treace made his personal announcement on Tuesday evening?'

'Is that important? My reaction?' The surprise in her tone sounded both genuine and concerned.

'It might be, yes. You see, we're trying to build a picture of the general response to the news in the parish. Whether people approved or disapproved.'

She frowned as though she found Parry's explanation still wanting, which he was perfectly aware it was. 'I suppose I was shocked at first, like most people were,' she answered slowly. 'Then I tried to bring myself to understand that he'd been driven to it all. That it wasn't his fault.'

'So whose fault would you say it was?'

She paused, fingering the crucifix again, restively. 'I really couldn't say.'

'Despite your effort to understand, would you have preferred it if he'd announced later, say, that he wasn't going through with his plan after all?'

Again she was silent for a moment. 'Perhaps so. Yes, I think so. For the good of the church, anyway.' She looked up. 'There's enough scandal nowadays, isn't there? I mean, in the Royal Family, for instance. Not with the Queen, of course, just the younger generation. And in politics. And in the church as well. You don't want it adding to, do you? Not if you can help it. The newspapers are so unkind in the way they report things. Build them up. Make them much worse than they are.' Her unexpected, voluble outburst had been more nervous than convincingly relevant.

'So you thought what he announced was scandalous, Miss Davies?'

'No, I didn't say that. Not exactly that.' Her more managed tone was now thoughtfully interpretive, not defensive, and suggested that she was trying to control her words better. 'At least, I didn't mean it that way. I said I thought the media could have turned it into a scandal.'

'Sorry, I understand now. And when you told us you couldn't say whose fault it was that Mr Treace was going to leave his wife for the doctor, did you really mean you couldn't say, or that you . . . that you wouldn't say?'

'I meant I don't believe it'd be a very charitable thing to say. To talk about.'

Parry brought his chair back on to its rear legs. 'Putting it in another way, if you'd thought of seeing either Mrs Treace or Dr Bewen, to plead with one of them – his wife to try harder to keep him, perhaps, or the doctor to give him up – which one of them would you have chosen to see?'

She half lifted her head, then lowered it again as if, after all, she was avoiding having to look Parry in the eye. 'Why should I have wanted to do that? To see either of them? It wouldn't have been my place.'

'As the much respected, unpaid curate of the parish, it might have been your place, miss, easy.' This was Lloyd, adopting his best avuncular manner. 'Are you sure you didn't do just that? Go to see Dr Bewen? For the good of all, like?'

'When?' This time she had looked up – but apprehensively.

Parry brought his chair back to the upright, letting the front legs bang hard on the tiled floor. 'I'm afraid we have a witness who saw you go into Picton Grove, on foot, at ten past nine last night, Miss Davies. Were you on your way to call on the doctor, perhaps?'

'I . . . I don't quite remember.' Her jawbone had tightened, and she had begun to blink compulsively behind the spectacles, all semblance of calmness evaporated.

'You see, you told DC Vaughan you spent the whole evening at home, miss,' said Lloyd, still much more curious than accusing.

'Did I? Oh, dear.' She looked across at him. 'Come to think, I . . . I may have gone out for a little time. For a . . . for a short walk. I've not been feeling too well lately. Not enough fresh air, I expect. It's close in this building, don't you find?' She looked about the room in a feeble attempt to illustrate her point, except to the policemen it seemed more that she was seeking a way of escape.

'And did you walk as far as Picton Grove at nine last night, perhaps?' Parry put in, ignoring her own question. He paused, waiting for her response, and when he got none, went on. 'There are six other houses in the road, and you could have been going to any one of them, of course, except we've now interviewed all the occupiers, and none of them remembers having a caller during the whole of last evening.'

'So there's only Dr Bewen left you could have been going to see, miss,' Lloyd explained, when Parry had stopped speaking and Miss Davies had failed to respond again. 'Unless you decided to take your walk up a little cul-de-sac like that, which doesn't seem very logical. Not to us, anyway. It's a bit dark up there, for a lady on her own at night.'

Maud Davies put the crumpled tissue to her nose again. She was staring at her lap, and although her lips seemed to be attempting to form words, she still made no audible response – only her whole demeanour had begun to signal distress.

Lloyd broke the silence once more. 'It seemed to us you'd probably forgotten you went out, and that's why you didn't tell DC Vaughan, miss. Easy enough thing to do, of course. Especially when you haven't been very well.' But more especially, both he and Parry were thinking, when they had only the word of an octogenarian with defective sight, as well as hearing, to back a vital, possibly incriminating premise – with no immediate hope of corroboration from any other source. 'It wouldn't matter that you made a mistake before. We can easily put the record right,' the sergeant completed with an encouraging smile, while inwardly willing her to admit, without penalty, that she'd lied.

The librarian brought her gaze up very slowly. 'I . . . I'm afraid I did go up Picton Grove, yes,' she said in a half whisper. 'I wanted to see Dr Bewen. It took all the courage I had to go there.' She paused. 'I'd . . . I'd thought about it all the night before, and yesterday.' She looked at Parry.

'It was what you said. I was going to ask her, beg her, on my knees if I had to, beg her to give him up. I'd thought it was my duty. My Christian duty. I didn't mind debasing myself.' She caught her breath and only half suppressed a sob. 'I'm sorry,' she continued, tearfully now, her voice beginning to break.

'And did you see Dr Bewen?' asked Parry, more gently than before.

She shook her head, then took off her spectacles, dabbing at her eyes with the tissue. 'I stopped in the road outside her house, getting up courage, practising what to say. Except . . .' She swallowed hard. 'Except it was then I . . . I suddenly knew why I was there. Why I was *really* there.' She stopped speaking for several seconds, her body heaving with very audible sobbing. 'You see, I knew then it wasn't for Sybil's sake. It wasn't for the church either.' She was breathing heavily through her mouth, but words appeared to have failed her again, and tears were running down her cheeks unchecked.

'Go on, miss. Better to tell us everything. Get it off your chest, like,' said Lloyd.

She nodded, blinking at him through the tears. 'I was there because I couldn't bear anyone else getting him . . . not if . . . not if I couldn't have him.' Unexpectedly her voice had become stronger. 'It was too much, do you understand? No, you don't. You can't,' she uttered, very distinctly. 'It's so shaming to say, but . . . but I . . . I love him so much.' She looked from Lloyd to Parry in evident relief and almost triumphant defiance as her confession ran on. 'It was all right when there was only poor Sybil. I could share him then. With her. Without her knowing. Not sharing him in the filthy way people would think. Only . . . only in a loving way. A clean, innocent way. But I couldn't bear him going off with . . . with her.' She was out of breath now, and trying to calm herself, pressing her clasped hands against her mouth.

'And that made you very angry, did it, miss?'

She nodded, biting at her knuckles.

'And more determined to see her? To hurt her, perhaps? Understandable too,' Lloyd continued to prompt.

She was blinking again. 'I don't know what I wanted. Oh yes, I hated her enough to hurt her, probably. That's what you want me to say, isn't it? Well, it's true.' She swallowed. 'But, you see, when I . . . when I went to go up the drive, I . . . I couldn't go on.'

'Was that because of the car, miss? Did a car come out of the drive just about then?'

There was growing apprehension in the eyes again as she replied. 'I . . . I heard a car start, yes. At the top of the drive. It must have been parked past the front door, because I hadn't seen it. Then the car lights came on, and . . . and I was so ashamed, in case . . . in case the person in it saw me. I could only think of hiding myself. You see, I was sure it . . .'

When her voice halted dramatically, Parry put in: 'You were sure it would be Mr Treace, I expect. And was it?'

She was shaking her head violently already. 'No, no. It wasn't him. I swear it wasn't him.'

'Then who was it, Miss Davies?'

She fell back in the chair, an exhausted, diminished figure, very much at bay, but with eyes that were darting – and fighting to be alert. 'I . . . I don't know who it was. I couldn't see. I swear I couldn't see.'

The nonsense her last two conflicting assertions would be making to the policemen had not occurred to the wretched, panicking Miss Davies. But if she hadn't seen who it was, how could she have known it wasn't Peter Treace?

15

'She swears she never went in the house, or even up the drive,' said Parry. 'She's just as firm she never saw who was in the car. And she didn't spot the make or colour.'

'Where was she when it passed her, then, sir?' asked a shirtsleeved, sandy-haired young detective called Dewi Morgan, standing at the back of the group that was gathered in the incident room.

'Making herself invisible behind a tree in the next door garden,' Parry replied. 'Where she'd gone to avoid being seen. It's why she insists she didn't get a look at the driver.'

'But she first swore it wasn't Mr Treace in the car, you said, sir?' pressed a female questioner.

Parry nodded. 'Yes. And she explained that by insisting she knows the sound of his car engine too well. That she'd have recognized it anywhere.' It had been Maud Davies's most telling insistence, if made a little late in the interview.

'That's possible, sir.'

'And no doubt it'd be more than possible to the Crown Prosecution Service, if it was the only evidence we offered for Treace not being the driver.' There was a good deal of acidity in the chief inspector's tone. 'Incidentally, Treace himself denies it was him. Personally I think Miss Davies may well have seen who it was. And it was either Treace, or someone else she knows, who she's just as keen to protect. Or nearly so. Like Simon Treace, for instance. Either way, she's not going to admit knowing who it was.'

'Since she swore this morning she was in all last

evening, her word on anything isn't worth much anyway, is it, sir?' asked DS Mary Norris.

'Normally I'd say it's worth more than most people's. She's a very committed Christian. Religion seems to be her life, or maybe it's just the vicar who's really that. In her case, I expect it amounts to much the same thing.' Parry's lips squeezed together, while his eyes confirmed he was applying tolerant comprehension before he went on. 'But in this instance, you're probably right, Mary. When we found she'd lied to Alf Vaughan this morning, we thought it was because she just could be the murderer, even though you'd have to admit appearances are against her. This afternoon, it seemed more likely she was shielding Treace. And that's more credible, too. Except we can't prove it. And I'm not yet ready to accept she wasn't in the house either. But once she'd been surprised by the car, I think she could have lost her nerve about going on. For her that wouldn't have taken much doing. She's really a church mouse, by character and instinct.'

It was six twenty. Parry was in the Delia Bewen incident room, standing before an easel with a mammoth flip-over pad mounted on it. The exposed page of the pad showed the headlines of the latest developments on the case, lettered in large capitals.

A few minutes earlier, the chief inspector had been conducting a news conference downstairs. What information the police had been ready to pass to the reporters present, including two from television news teams with cameramen in tow, had been limited and fairly unrevealing. In contrast, the questioning from the audience had been the opposite by intent – but with the cautious answers exactly what had been anticipated by the questioners. In short, the standard ritual had been observed.

Several lines of inquiry were being pursued – developments were expected soon – it was too early for an arrest to be regarded as imminent. These had been the official, cryptic and ambiguous kind of phrases used to indicate that so far the police were baffled, and looking in all directions (with no immediate signs of finding a promising one), in their search for the killer of Dr Bewen.

In truth, the representatives of the media were hardly disquieted about what the police were achieving, or not achieving. This was because those same representatives were inured to the slow plod usually attendant on the solving of murder cases. On top of which, it had to be accepted, murders were fairly commonplace these days. It was fortunate, in the journalistic sense, that this particular murder was more promising than most in terms of extra human interest.

The bloody slaying of a medical consultant, employed at a famous hospital, could be relied upon to shock and horrify the reading and viewing public more than the murder of someone a lot further down the social scale or, as was so often the case, someone so low down on that scale as to have dropped off it altogether. Since the medical consultant was youngish, female and pretty, then the matter was more newsworthy, but not, on the face of it, that much more. It might have been a two-day startling event, as opposed to a one-day wonder, except for the embellishments, scandalous ones – and scandal is a lot more enduring and involving than crime, even the crime of murder.

The amatory activities of the vicar of St Samson's and his dead lover meant that reporters and cameramen were more usefully engaged outside the Bryntaf vicarage, pestering its inhabitants and the people closest to those inhabitants, than when they were attending briefings at the Fairwater police station that disclosed little that was new. And this was something that suited the police well enough. Allowing that they called in representatives of the media at reasonable intervals, they could otherwise get on with their proper work and leave those others to do the same.

In short, it had been an adequate news conference.

Gathered in front of Parry now, in a variety of postures, were nine members of the murder investigation team – five were CID officers, the rest civilian police employees.

Gomer Lloyd was not present. He was on his way to Bristol to keep an appointment, made that afternoon, with a member of the Somerset and Avon CID.

'She's no murderer, sir,' offered DC Vaughan, seated back to front on a typist's chair. At forty-eight, he was the oldest person in the room. 'Suicide type, perhaps, but taking someone else's life wouldn't be on. She's too holy, by a long shot. And she's about the only one I interviewed all day I could say that about.' He lit a cigarette, and was thinking uncharitable things about Mrs Agnes Craig-Owen as he went on. 'Miss Davies lied to me this morning, like you said. I sensed it at the time, as well. She's a bad liar. No practice at it, I should think. But she'd have been too ashamed to do anything else but lie about being up there last night, even without the murder, and even if she hadn't seen the car. She couldn't admit she'd been intending to plead with her rival, like.' He scratched the back of his head. 'Well, rival in a sense, even though the man she's crazy about is a married clergyman and, in her language, beyond her reach. Seeing the car would have put the kibosh on things, especially if she knew the driver. And I think you're right about that. She did know who-ever it was.'

'So she hated Dr Bewen enough not to help us find her killer, even though she says she'd never even met her, sir.' This was Sergeant Mary Norris again, perched on a desk beside the lanky, angular DC Alison Pope.

'Is that so surprising? Wouldn't she have hated anyone who was making off with her idol?' responded Parry, who, though pressed for time, was anxious to hear all available inputs.

'Not necessarily surprising, sir. Not if she's such a good Christian, either,' said DC Pope, only a touch nervously. She was usually too uneasy in the presence of senior officers to speak out on such occasions, but her courage had been boosted by her Ianto Price interview earlier – so far the most productive encounter of the day made by anyone.

'That's right,' put in one of the civilian workers, a mature woman, a fingerprint expert, and, as it happened, a Samaritan counsellor. 'It's complicated, but for her it sounds like it'd be the sin involved she'd most despise, not Dr Bewen as such. If she's angry with anyone, deep down it has to be Mr Treace. Only she has to transfer his guilt on to someone else, because consciously she can't accept he can do wrong. Any wrong. Maud Davies didn't have to know the doctor to blame her for everything. I'd guess if it was Mr Treace in the car, she knew it, but will never admit it.'

Parry half agreed with the last contention, but he still couldn't hit on a motive that would have made Treace want to murder Delia Bewen. And if he had murdered her, why should he have assisted the police by directing them to the weapon used? This last was a small point, but still an irritatingly inexplicable one if the man was guilty. 'We don't know when the car arrived at Kingfishers,' he said, 'but it left with time enough to get Treace to the vicarage by the approximate time he gave us. And that was confirmed close enough by his daughter Janet.'

'But he's supposed to have come home on foot from the church, sir,' someone else offered.

'That's what he says. His daughter never mentioned how he came back.' Parry looked at DS Norris. 'Let's dig around on that, Mary, can we? For a start, see if we can find out where his car was parked while he was giving his Lent lecture.'

'Right, sir.' The sergeant made a note while asking: 'And you think Mr Treace was going to confess to something when he first asked to speak to you this afternoon, sir? It didn't sound that urgent when he phoned here at four.'

'Possibly it was urgent then, but not when I talked to him half an hour later,' Parry replied. Treace had refused to speak to anyone else, but when Parry had got the message, he hadn't been able to deal with it immediately. 'I think he had cooled off by the time I reached him. But I

158

don't believe he was going to confess to murdering the doctor.'

'Or to accuse someone else, sir?' This was DC Vaughan.

Parry hesitated. 'We'll never know that, but his attitude was apologetic. He was sorry he'd troubled me. Thought he might have misled me in something he said last night. Something pretty trivial. I think the original purpose may have been to tell me something about his wife, and he'd thought better of it.'

'Why do you think that, sir?' someone asked.

'No supportable reason. She's gone back to the vicarage though, and I imagine their present relationship will generate any number of illogical events.'

'But he denied driving up to Kingfishers, sir?' said DC Pope.

'Categorically, yes.'

'You know the vicar's car's got a B in the number, sir?' asked Alf Vaughan.

A ripple of amusement went around the group. It seemed that almost every car that could remotely be involved in the case had either a B or a P or a D on its numberplate – and this included the Rover 800 belonging to the Craig-Owens, which had D and B in its registration. Not that all the venerable Ianto Price's evidence had gone for nothing. If it hadn't been for him, Maud Davies's original story about being at home all evening would not have been challenged and disproved, and neither she nor Peter Treace would now have been under suspicion. Even so, it was Mr Price's indecisive contribution on the numberplate issue that had prompted Parry to have the letter D added to the other two the old man had offered, since each could be mistaken for either of the others at a distance – and in witnesses' testimony too often was.

'If Mr Treace did the murder, he'd have needed all the time between the end of the lecture and when he got home, sir. To do everything, like,' offered DC Dewi Morgan, pulling at his trouser tops.

'And if he went straight to see his daughter when he

got to the vicarage, where did he change?' put in Alf Vaughan. 'The murderer may not have been covered in blood, but the chances are he must have had some blood on him. Must have had,' he repeated. 'On his cuffs most likely, or the sleeves of what he was wearing. If it was Mr Treace, his daughter would have noticed. And he did say he went straight in to see her.'

'But would she have let on if he'd had blood on him?' questioned someone.

'Possibly not, but it wouldn't have arisen,' answered the woman fingerprint technician. 'He'd have made quite sure there was no blood on him when he joined her. He wouldn't have risked her needing to choose between loyalty to him and her public duty. Even if he was certain she'd support him.'

'I think you're right again,' Parry agreed.

'He could have changed in the church vestry, couldn't he?' put in Alison Pope. 'With no one to know. He'd have had other clothes and everything in there. Including a spare cassock, at least. More than one probably.'

'And all jet black to disguise bloodstains. Good thinking Alison,' Vaughan complimented the young woman, then inhaled heavily on his cigarette before adding: 'And he could have left anything incriminating there, too, till he was ready to fetch it. Anybody know what he was wearing for that lecture?'

The two seconds silence made it clear nobody did. 'Well, that's easy enough to check now,' said Mary Norris, scribbling in her book. 'May be harder to find out if he was dressed the same way when he got home. Anyway, we've established a vicar has more than one place where he keeps clothing legitimately, not like most murderers. They only have their homes for that, usually.'

'There's still the problem of the time he had available,' insisted Dewi Morgan.

And still the question of his motive, Parry was thinking again, except the exchange had already moved his mind on to another member of the Treace family.

Mary Norris crossed her legs under the notebook. 'We could be wrong about the time, couldn't we, sir?'

'Only if Treace *and* his daughter have misled us. That's about when he got back after the lecture,' said the chief inspector, looking in the direction of the fingerprint technician cum Samaritan. 'And if we're going to search the vestry, it needs to be done now. Clothing that he or anyone else left there, incriminating or otherwise, won't go unnoticed by Miss Davies. Or not for very long. One of her jobs is what others refer to as being vestment virgin.'

'That's supposing she hasn't been using the place for hiding incriminating stuff of her own, sir,' said one of the male civilian employees.

'That's true, yes.'

Mary Norris got down from the desk. 'DC Pope and I were on our way out for more interviewing, sir. We'll go to the church first.'

'You'll need to get keys from the vicarage. Just say I've told you to check the church for evidence. The church and the vestry. Vestries are usually locked.'

'Can the vicar refuse to give us the keys, sir?' asked Alison Pope.

'To the church? No, he can't. Or if he does, we can regard it as grounds for obstruction and demand the keys.' Parry checked the time. 'Anyway, he won't be there. He told me on the phone he had to be at the archdeacon's house at six, and that's a ten-minute drive away for a start. If Mrs Treace or either of her children are in, ask for all the church keys they have, and check where they're kept and how many sets there are. We also need to know how many people have their own church keys, and how many others have at least access to keys. I think it follows that both the vicar's children come in the last category.'

'If there's a safe in the vestry, can we demand to have it opened, sir?'

'Yes. Only ask nicely first. Of course, the chances are the vicar will have his own safe key with him.'

'Probably one or both the churchwardens will have keys

to it as well,' volunteered the Samaritan knowingly. 'You could try one of them.'

Parry agreed, adding: 'And get whoever it is to come round and open the safe in your presence. If there's a bloodstained cassock inside you won't have to apologize for the inconvenience, will you? Or risk being accused of planting evidence.' He grinned. 'And now I've got to leave. I'd planned to be in Isabella Street five minutes ago.'

He was also due at a concert in St David's Hall at seven thirty.

16

The facade of 8 Isabella Street had seen better days – far better. So had the facades of all the other identical houses in the matching terraces that lined both sides of the road, which ran southwards, toward the bay, a mile away.

In mid Victorian times, these narrow, three-storey plus basement, town residences had represented the essence of respectability, with their space extending, wide bay windows, their railed steps up to dark porches under pointed arches, and front doors beyond, with heavy iron-work embellishments. They had been the homes of lesser managers and chief clerks in the shipping, insurance, rail-way and dockyard companies that once served the largest coal and steel port in the world.

Today, peeling paint and crumbling brickwork showed neglect bordering on abandonment. Even the Doric-columned, long-disused Baptist Chapel, that had grandly closed the vista in the crossing road at the lower end, had recently been converted into a warehouse for a Jacuzzi manufacturer – making a comical turn in commercial evolution.

Being a quarter mile to the west of the new, three thou-sand acre Cardiff Bay Development, the area around Isa-bella Street was in a kind of no man's land. To the east and south, old, heavily urbanized districts had been flat-tened for rebuilding. The expectancy was that a prosper-ous overspill would eventually be generated. Meantime, property in Isabella Street had been changing hands with increasing frequency, as successive impatient freeholders let their properties go (along with their unrealized ambitions) for disappointing sums to fresh hopefuls, the new owners fired, in their turn, by the prospect of pending capital gain.

As he stood on the doorstep of number eight, Merlin Parry passed the time since ringing the bell by contemplating the multitude of estate agents' boards that, at various heights and drunken angles, were further disfiguring the rundown thoroughfare – like the dishonoured banners of some straggling, defeated army.

When there was evidently going to be no answer to the bell, an indication either that there was no one at home, or, more likely, that the device wasn't working, the policeman applied himself to hammering on the knocker, an impressive implement lacking in modernity, but proving rich in sonorous capacity. In immediate response, a large black cat shot out from behind a dustbin in the basement area, tore up the steps and out into the street. A few seconds after this, the door was pulled open with a good deal of effort and muttered complaint from the other side.

'Yes?' The young woman looked a year or so older than Myfanwy Evans, and a great deal better nourished. She had a well-developed body, bordering on the plump, and was dressed in a loose, cream blouse hanging over a calf-length black skirt. Her straight dark hair was pulled up and back into a high ponytail, away from a dimpled, and carefully – if heavily – made-up face. The eyes were unsmiling and busy. The nose was a blob with pulsing sides like alerted antennae. The mouth was wide and full-lipped. She was wearing eastern-style, long filigree earrings, and a gold ring set with zircons on the third finger of her left hand. There were three long strings of coloured beads around her neck that hung down along the deep valley of her cleavage and the line of the loosely buttoned blouse. She was a touch below average height, though the ponytail drew attention away from this. Parry thought how little she resembled her mother, except for the almost somnolent eyes.

164

'Miss Dilys Hughes, is it?' he asked.

'Y-es.' With her reluctant admission, Miss Hughes had still managed to convey an answer that was more neutral than it was positive – or one that could have been rescinded without too much adverse reflection on the speaker.

'I'm Detective Chief Inspector Parry. I'm investigating the death of –'

'Delia Bewen,' she interrupted, her chin lifting sharply. She opened the door wider. 'Better come in, I suppose. This way.'

He followed her through the freshly painted white hall, past the oak staircase – both newly carpeted – and through the second door on the right, into a sitting room that was comfortably arranged with well-designed modern furnishings. There were French windows at the far end looking out on to a derelict strip of garden. Lights were burning inside the room, although the curtains had not yet been drawn.

A strikingly handsome black man, aged around twenty-five, looked up from the heavy tome he had been reading as Parry entered, his face more welcoming than Miss Hughes's had been. He was heavily built, with short crinkled hair above a broad forehead, intelligent eyes, a patrician nose, and a square chin, the last bordered by an even, well-trimmed beard. He was dressed in an open pink shirt, good quality, dark blue slacks, pink socks and black leather moccasins. There was a large spiral-bound notebook under his right hand, resting, like the book, on the wide piece of polished wood that was balanced across the arms of the low-slung armchair. There were more fat, serious-looking books on this improvised book rest and on the small table to the man's right, with several more on the floor around his feet. A simulated log fire, powered by a gas jet, was burning in the hearth to his left, but the source of the real warmth in the room was a long, slim radiator on one wall. There had been a similar, smaller radiator in the hall.

'Hi. So what you selling, man?' In repose, the face of the man in the chair had seemed grave and almost fearsome, but not so when he grinned, which he was doing now.

Parry reached for his warrant card again. 'I'm –'

'Chief Inspector Parry,' the other interrupted, with a deep-throated chuckle. 'Sorry, I was joking. I heard you tell Dilys. My name's Alex Vespucci. Yes, the same surname as the man who didn't find America.' His accent had changed now, from the broad West Indian of his first pronouncement, to a soft and cultured, English Home Counties one.

'Amerigo Vespucci? He had a continent named after him, all the same,' Parry answered lightly.

'With no enduring benefit for the family, even legitimate family,' said the young man, before hunching his shoulders, glowering, then quoting in the instantly recognizable voice of Winston Churchill: 'Shum men are born great, shum achieve greatness, er-and shum have greatness sh-rust upon them.'

'Which wasn't by Churchill. Shakespeare in ... *Midsummer Night's Dream*, wasn't it?' Parry put in agreeably, 'but it nicely describes your ancestor's situation. Convincing imitation, too.'

'Ah, recognition at la-shed,' Vespucci guffawed. 'Well, thank you, sir. Not just an historically informed and literate policeman, but an appreciative one as well. I'd get up to shake your hand, except I'm hemmed in here by my portable study.' He waved a hand over the scatter of books and the board that encased him. 'But why don't you sit down, Chief Inspector? It would even things up a little. Can we get you a drink?'

'No, thanks all the same. I'm not stopping long,' said Parry, as he settled himself at the far end of the sofa, opposite the fire. Like the carpets, here and outside, the sofa looked new, as did everything else in the room which had evidently just been decorated. 'Thank you for seeing me, sir, and you, Miss Hughes.'

166

'Alex and Dilys, please. We're very informal,' Vespucci broke in. 'In fact, you could call us downright casual. Isn't that right, my sweet?' He looked across at Dilys Hughes, who was now seated on the arm of the sofa closest to him, and who had so far not only failed – and pointedly failed – to join in the light-hearted exchanges, but had looked daggers during her boyfriend's Churchillian portrayal. She only half responded now with a nod at the visitor.

'Obviously you know about the murder in Bryntaf last night,' said Parry next. 'One of your tenants –'

'Mif, downstairs? She worked for Dr Bewen. She'll be at home now. Do you want her up here?' It seemed that the plummy-toned Vespucci enjoyed anticipating the ends of other people's sentences – even if he didn't always accurately prejudge their intentions.

'No. Well, not for the moment, at least. I might look in on her when I leave. It's you two I've come to see,' Parry responded. 'I take it you both live here?'

'We cohabit, yes, Chief Inspector,' admitted Vespucci, grinning again, after elongating the operative verb.

'And, just for the record, would you mind telling me what you both do?' Parry had produced a notebook.

'Of course. For a start, I'm Jamaican. Well, you can tell that from the accent.'

'Hardly,' said Parry. 'Or only when you were sending it up.'

'And thus denying my roots,' the other responded. 'Been here too long, I expect. I graduated two years ago, in London, at the LSE. I've stayed on in glorious Britain because I got a research bursary. I'm doing a doctorate now, at Cardiff University. On economic and political relations between Wales and the West Indies in the eighteenth and nineteenth centuries. Well, that's my excuse. Dilys is the real reason for staying, but don't tell her. It'll go to her head.' The speaker reached a hand out far enough to squeeze her exposed knee – the long skirt was split at calf level. Dilys didn't seem to be particularly amused either by the badinage or the knee-squeezing. 'I also dabble a little in property,' Vespucci continued. 'Like this house, and one or two others in the street. Going to make us a pile of money one day. But they all say that, don't they?'

'I don't know. Anyway, I wish you luck,' said Parry. He turned his eyes to the woman. 'And I believe you're a teacher, Dilys?'

'She's a dropout, with four good A-levels, who ought to be at university, and probably will be one day. Meantime –'

'I teach at a kindergarten. In Greychapel. Not very well. And hardly at all today. I came home with a bad migraine at lunchtime.' It had been Dilys's turn to interrupt, which she had done without the humour of her companion. She had seemed anxious to give Parry all the information she had offered, speaking quickly, as though it had been a prepared statement. Greychapel is a western Cardiff suburb, halfway between Isabella Street and Bryntaf.

'Thank you,' Parry replied. 'I'm sorry about the migraine. I understand from Mif that you were here last evening between eight and ten, Alex. Were you here as well, Dilys?'

'She was here, yes. On the next floor, actually, painting the bathroom window. I was in the basement flat with the delectable Mif. No shocking intimacies took place, worse luck.' There was another complaining look from Dilys at this aside as Vespucci went on: 'We're decorating down there, too. I'm better at reaching the ceilings than the ladies.'

'Up here looks very spick and span,' Parry observed approvingly.

'Good. Structurally the houses in this street are sound, even if they don't look it. No point tarting them up outside. Only attracts burglars. We move in, do a job on the inside, renew the plumbing, heating and electrics, put in carpets and curtains, sell the place after a year, then move on to another one. Well, we've done it once so far. But it pays all right.'

Parry wondered how this young man got the seed money to buy houses, even nearly derelict ones. Maybe a degree in economics was the key, or maybe he was just a very rich Jamaican. 'And Mif was with you the whole time last evening, Alex?' he asked.

'Yes, she was. Oh, except when I came up to check Dilys didn't need help, which I did a couple of times, probably.' The speaker frowned and stroked his beard. 'You're not supposing she had anything to do with the doctor's death, are you? She idolized the woman.'

'We just need to know for sure where everyone closely connected with the doctor was last night, that's all. I believe you knew her as well, Dilys?'

'That's right. She was special. Really special.' The girl was showing some animation for the first time.

'Did you know her as a fellow Bryntaf resident? I believe you grew up there, living with your mother till recently.'

'I . . . I met Delia in Bryntaf, yes. But at the cottage hospital. I still count as a resident there if I . . .' She took a quick breath. 'If I need medical treatment. It's been easier to get an appointment there than in the city.'

'Dilys and I've been together for well over a year now,' said the big Jamaican. 'Sad to say, I'm afraid I don't really hit it off with her mother, Mrs Hughes. Not any more. And Dilys doesn't socialize much in Bryntaf nowadays.'

'I understand,' said Parry, believing he might have guessed the reason for the rift without asking for it, as he added: 'Your mother has been very good to Mrs Treace, don't you think, Dilys?'

'Yes. I heard she was staying with Mum last night. Mum's a very kind, good person. She's got blind spots, like everyone has. It's my fault we're not –'

'It was in the paper about the vicar leaving his wife,' Vespucci broke in quite loudly. 'Sad business altogether. Do you know yet who killed the doctor, Chief Inspector? Burglar was it? Young tearaway?'

Parry closed his notebook. 'Too early to tell, I'm afraid.' He glanced at the time, then stood up. 'Well, I think that's all I need. Thank you both, very much. And I won't trouble Mif again, after all. Not this evening.'

It's claimed that the Cape Cod, in Bristol, first opened its doors in 1772. Recently it had been refurbished to look the way it might have done before it was bombed in the Second World War. There was nearly enough antique nautical gear attached to the bar, the walls and the ceiling to have stocked a middling-sized ships' chandlers. In truth, before it was bombed, the place had been called the Maltsters, and had consisted of a four-ale public bar with benches, a saloon bar with chairs, and a ladies' bar where mature members of that gender had gathered – mostly to consume Guinness, then a popular ladies' tipple.

Gomer Lloyd was only surprised that the pub was as full as it was at eight o'clock. One of the attractions was a three-piece jazz combo – synthesizer, clarinet and drums – which had already been playing hit tunes from the thirties when the sergeant had arrived half an hour before. His local police contact had confirmed that the Cape Cod was recognized as a heterosexual singles bar and grill, and that the clientele tended to be middle-aged and respectable. The fifty-three-year-old sergeant had figured he fitted the profile pretty well.

It was 8.15 when the diminutive, but otherwise over-developed, bubbly, long-haired blonde had come in. She was balancing on red, very high-heeled shoes, the chunky jewellery at her wrists glinting like her shining white shoulder bag. At a distance, her age could have been anything between sixteen and thirty, and her appearance was, metaphorically, noisier than the music. Her progress from the door was almost triumphal, as she acknowledged the greetings of acquaintances, waving at some, briefly embracing others, and making kissing movements with her heavily made-up lips at yet more.

When she reached the long bar, she was quickly engaged with the head barman, who had leaned two-thirds of the way across the counter to speak to her, a deeply confidential expression on his face. He then nodded in the direction of Lloyd, who was seated at a table for two at the rear of what was designated, in gold script, as the Poop Deck – this being a raised half-floor with a brass-railed edge, built out over a candlelit restaurant area, in turn called the Captain's Galley. The Poop Deck was reached via a short metal spiral staircase, also with brass fittings. As yet, only one other table there was occupied.

'Thenks tewibly for the dwink, Goma. That's a Welsh name, isn't it? It's quaint, quate quaint. Well, here's knowing you.' The blonde's cut-glass accent was so phoney as to be comical. She took a modest sip from the champagne cocktail she had brought up the staircase with her – straightbacked, with no spillage from the glass – before crossing her legs under the tight, red cotton miniskirt. Once she was seated, her white double-breasted jacket, with gold braiding along the edges, was long enough to give the impression that she had nothing on under it except the black Lurex tights and the fancy shoes.

The woman's legs were not particularly well shaped, too much bulge and not enough tapering, Lloyd had divined already, but he was still taken by the way she tautened then relaxed her calf muscles, dancer fashion. 'Cheers, Fiona. Nice to meet you.' He lifted his own glass, without drinking from it. He didn't much care for ginger ale, but it passed for whisky when such appearances were needful.

'So what can I do for you?' asked Fiona. 'George, behind the bar, says it's off the record. Can I rely on you, but abso-lootely, on that, Goma?' She fluttered the long eyelashes that were as bogus as the accent.

'You've got my word on it, love.'

'I mean, I won't have to go to court? To be a witness, or anything bor-wing, like that? I don't care to call attention to myself.'

'Nothing like that,' he answered, suppressing his amusement at her last comment. He couldn't be certain that the promises he had just made would be honoured, but, in any case, he had it on good authority from the local CID that Fiona 'owed us one', and would be co-operating in her own interests, whatever the outcome.

'Is it hot in he-ar tonight, or is it just little me?' Fiona first undid her jacket button, then shed the garment entirely, in a stagy movement that allowed it to fall from her, to the not inappropriate accompaniment from the combo downstairs of 'I've Got My Love to Keep Me Warm.'

'Oh, thanks or-fully, Goma.' She gave Lloyd a languid, penetrating smile as he half rose, and draped the jacket over the back of her chair. Her neck, shoulders and arms were now quite bare. All she was wearing above the skirt – visible again – was a white sarong top, with uplift for her pronounced and redoubtable breastwork somehow provided under it.

The sergeant had concluded before this that beneath the make-up and the mass of wavy hair, his companion was nearer forty than thirty. 'It's about last night, Fiona,' he said. 'Bloke called Olaf? Says he met you here?'

The eyes widened. 'That would be his right name, would it, Goma? People can be funny about names sometimes, don't you find?'

Including quite a few with names like Fiona, the sergeant thought to himself. 'You didn't meet any Olaf?' he asked.

'One meets so many people. No, the name doesn't come to mind, Goma, not st-wate away.' Her hand went decorously to adjust the edge of the skirt, though since the garment was skin-tight, the gesture was only token. 'Would he have been anuv-a Welshman, perhaps?'

'Yes, he would. This photo might help.' It was one that Olaf Lewis had supplied himself.

The long eyelashes fluttered. 'Oh, yes. I remember him, all right. I don't think he was an Olaf, though. More a Reggie, as I recall.' The invented accent and lisp had been momentarily replaced by a much warmer, native Bristolian.

Lloyd noted the last fact, which he supposed was somehow a credit to the mesmerizing effect of Olaf Lewis's photograph. 'You mean, he told you his name was Reggie?'

Fiona looked up slowly. 'He told me a lot of things, Goma.' The fruity inflection had returned. 'Anyway, he was in he-ar, all right. As a matter of fact, we'd met before. He-ar, at the Cape Cod. Only b-weefly though. Weeks ago, that was. It wasn't till last evening that we-lations were cemented, as you might say. And I hope you're not intending to press me more on that.' The eyes lowered, and the false lashes fluttered quite prettily.

'No, love. But I hope you can tell me what time he came in.'

'Oh, yes. That's easy.'

The policeman was grudgingly expecting to be given some further manifestation of Olaf Lewis's personal magnetism – a claim, perhaps, that he stopped clocks, or set off alarms when he entered rooms. 'So what time was it, Fiona?'

'Anyone who was he-ah could tell you that. The band had just started to play "Anything Goes", you see?' – which was exactly what the band had started to do as she finished the sentence.

She picked up her glass again with the look on her face of someone who normally aimed to please, and who was satisfied that she had just done so with honours.

17

'But I told you before, it was the Vaughan Williams I really wanted to hear, honestly,' Perdita Jones insisted, pulling more of the sheet up over her body. 'Anyway, it wasn't your fault I missed the rest.'

'But if I'd met you at the station –'

'The train would still have been late, and we'd both have missed the Mozart. So stop blaming yourself.' She snuggled closer to him. 'Why are your feet always so cold?'

'Legacy of years as a bachelor on the beat, with holes in my socks. Terrible chilblains I used to get. Lonely widowers have the same problem, of course,' Parry observed in a stoic voice, then kissed the top of her forehead.

'Except beat constables had Panda cars in your time, and chief inspectors can easily afford new socks. In any case, I'm a lousy darner. Good at other things, though,' she replied archly.

'Things I'd gladly go barefoot to enjoy,' he rejoined with feeling.

'Because we'd look pretty silly making love if you kept your shoes on,' she giggled.

Parry had reached St David's Hall in time for the start of the concert after all. It was Perdita who had arrived only just before the interval, after he'd assumed she wasn't coming at all. A bomb alert at London's Paddington Station had delayed her train. They had eaten at Quayles following the performance, and were now bedded at his Westgate Street flat – with a half-empty bottle of chilled Chablis which they hadn't had time to finish at the restaurant, but had brought away with them at the management's suggestion.

'Anyway, I don't have to be back at the hospital till early afternoon,' she said, but half-apologetically.

'Big deal.' He took a sip from his glass, then put it back on the bedside table.

'I thought you'd be pleased.'

'I am. Means you can catch the 11.25, or even the one after that. I thought you might have to go earlier.' He'd arranged to take the morning off to be with her. 'A weekend would still be better. A lot better,' he added.

She sighed, rearranged the pillow against the bedhead and reached for her own glass. 'Sorry, darling. The odd weekday night's the best I can manage at the moment.'

'Well, all in a good cause.' He kissed her again. 'Would you be an angel and do my neck?'

'Sure. Turn over.' She ran a hand over the top of his spine. 'God, this is really knotted again, isn't it?'

Massage was one of the 'other' things Perdita did well – and professionally, a relic from her days as a physiotherapist, before she had returned to studying medicine.

'That's bliss,' he uttered in a muffled voice, moments later, with his face buried in bedclothes.

The naked Perdita was sitting astride him, strong fingers manipulating his shoulders. 'If you relax completely, it'll work better,' she said, pushing her loose, corn-coloured hair away from her face as she bent to the task. 'I meant to tell you, I can probably take a week off in early June, if that suits. After I've stopped working for the firm I'm with now.'

'The consultant, you mean?' Hospital jargon still occasionally confused him. 'And of course it suits. Is that the gynaecologist you're so crazy about?'

'Yes. Dr Reynald-Kane. She's brilliant. I'm learning so much from her.'

'Weren't you working with her before? Last year?'

'That's right. It was her idea I came back for an extra month.' Perdita paused in the massaging for a moment,

175

and looked thoughtful. 'She says I should seriously think of becoming a gynae. That I've got a flair for it.'

'That's encouraging. But won't specializing take years longer than just being a GP?' he asked, half turning his head.

'Yes,' she replied, firmly turning it back the way it was, before she went on. 'And it probably won't happen, because I won't be good enough. But if it does happen, I promise it won't make any difference to us. That's if you still want to marry me when I'm qualified.'

'Well, that's all right then. Do gynaes make a lot of money? If they don't, I may jilt you.'

She grinned. 'I don't think they make more than other consultants. Less than some. Dr Reynald-Kane has a pretty house in Swiss Cottage. Her husband's an orthopaedic surgeon.'

'So between them they must be coining it?'

'Hm. They've got two kids at private schools, and a German au pair. That must set them back a bit. I know they work very long hours, both of them. Hardly any time off. Not even for shopping. Things are ordered by phone and delivered. I'd miss never shopping. Choosing my own fruit and veg.'

'But they probably have long holidays,' Parry put in.

'A week's skiing in Austria, and they rent a house in Corsica for a month in the summer, she told me. There, you'll do.' She smoothed her hands down his back.

'Marvellous, thank you, darling. That's so relaxing. You've no idea.'

'Yes, I have. It's why I'll teach you to do it to me some day. Not now.' They were lying side by side again.

'D'you want your glass?' he asked, reaching for his.

'No thanks.'

'Pity you never knew Dr Delia Bewen.'

'I'm sorry too. Like I said, I knew the name, that's all. We never met. From what you've found out, she seems to have been the dedicated type.'

He had briefly mentioned his current case during supper, but only because of the medical connection. 'Are all gynaes dedicated?' he asked.

'Not necessarily. There's a case for thinking the female ones are more involved than the males. Simple matter of gender sympathy. From what you said about Dr Bewen and those young women patients, she was strong on sympathy.'

'Yes. Beyond the line of medical duty, too.' He had Mif in mind.

Perdita looked unsure. 'Maybe she'd wanted daughters of her own to guide.'

There was silence for a second before he said, 'Well, on the whole, I think I'd like you to specialize in gynaecology. I mean, on the positive side, there can't be anything much better, more worthwhile, than helping women to conceive. I mean, it's like giving God a hand with the . . . with the really basic good work, isn't it?' Open-mouthed, he ran his upper teeth along the lower ones and back again – a habit that helped his thinking.

She smiled. 'There's a bit more to it than that.'

'But on the whole it's all pretty positive stuff.'

'Depends what you count as positive. I helped Dr Reynald-Kane do eleven abortions before lunch today. By the suction method. Very simple, quick and safe. No waiting either.' She paused, looking sideways at him, her eyebrows arched. 'But, positive? Depends who you are. Very positive if you're a woman who doesn't want the baby she's conceived. I don't know whether God approves of that.'

'Do you?'

'Sure.' She paused. 'A lot of people don't, of course.'

'Doctors?' he asked.

'A few I know. But a bigger percentage of lay people, I'd think. Probably your vicar's wife for one. And that . . . vestment virgin you mentioned.'

'Miss Davies? I don't know. What about Dr Reynald-Kane?'

'She doesn't have hang-ups about what we were doing

177

this morning. Or any of that side of the work, for that matter.'

'Well if the . . .' his nose wrinkled, 'the suction method is all it sounds – '

'It is. But not all abortions can be done that way. I mean, a good many would be too far advanced.'

'I understand. Except, I'm not sure I want to,' he added grimly.

Perdita nodded. 'Dr Reynald-Kane told me once she used to have qualms after delivering deformed or brain-damaged babies. And that was common in her early days still. Hardly happens now because it doesn't have to.'

'Because of . . . ?'

'Oh, prenatal clinics,' Perdita interrupted, adding. 'So which qualifies as what you'd call God's work? The creation of a badly impaired human being, or its . . . its timely elimination? I'd give a prejudiced answer to that, of course.'

Parry was exercising his teeth again. He was quite sure Delia Bewen would have given the same biased reply as Perdita. But there were many more than the two people mentioned already, and involved with the doctor, who might give a diametrically opposite answer on principle. Worse, there were plenty who might have regarded Delia Bewen's attitude to abortion as wrong, and deserving of some kind of divine retribution, because they regarded that part of her work as amounting to murder. Whether they would be the same people who would take it out on her for breaking two of the other Ten Commandments – the one about not committing adultery, and the one on not coveting your neighbour's wife – he wasn't yet sure. For his own part, he was still far from certain that Treace and Dr Bewen ever had committed adultery.

Also, to be strictly accurate, it was Sybil Treace's *husband* the doctor had coveted. And come to think of it – as Parry just had, and was doing again now – according to the Bible, the sin really was in coveting wives: husbands weren't mentioned. Except that in Old Testament times, wives generally weren't considered relevant contenders when it came to their coveting anything. But if there were religious people nowadays who still took the scriptural wording literally, wouldn't Treace still have been the more suitable victim?

Perdita cleared her throat. 'Keeping you from your work, am I?' she questioned pointedly.

He smiled, and turned to her. 'Is it psychoanalysts who can read patients' minds?'

'Yes. Or think they can.'

'Well, please don't become one of those. You're too good at it, and it's unnerving. Now I promise to think about something else.'

'Which makes two of us,' she purred, moving closer to him.

'Come this way, will you, Mr Davies? I'm sorry you were kept waiting,' said Sergeant Mary Norris, holding the door open for the elderly visitor to come through from the reception area of the Fairwater police station.

'That's all right, miss. I know it's very late. You're in charge of the whole place then, are you? Big establishment like this, as well.'

He had sounded unduly surprised, because she was female, probably, she thought. 'No, sir. I'm not in sole charge of the station. It only looks that way.' She smiled apologetically despite herself. After all, she and Mr Davies came from widely different generations with wildly different expectations. She was in charge of what he'd come about, all right, more so than the station's duty inspector could be. But she was tired, had been caught off guard, and wasn't even on duty. 'You had to wait while the desk sergeant found out if there was anyone still here. Anyone working on the Dr Bewen case, I mean. Actually the incident room upstairs is closed now, till six in the morning. But it's all right,' she added hastily, seeing the beginnings of despair developing on the old man's already hangdog countenance. 'I'm one of the detective sergeants on the

179

investigation. As it happens, I'd come back to pick up something I'd left behind earlier. Just dropped in on my way home. I only live round the corner.'

'Been out for the evening, have you, miss ... er, Sergeant?'

'To the pictures, yes, sir.'

'Good was it?' He seemed glad to be staying off the subject he said he'd come about.

'It wasn't bad. We can go in here, sir,' she added, opening the door to one of the interview rooms, and waiting while he sidled ahead, which he did, awkwardly, and obviously uncomfortable that he was going in front of a lady. 'Please take a seat.' She pulled out a chair for him on one side of the small table, then seated herself opposite. 'And you are Mr Gareth Davies of Flat 11, Old Vicarage Mansions, Bryntaf?' She was reading from the slip the desk sergeant had given her.

'That's right.'

'And you have something to tell the police about the case?'

'Yes.' He sighed. 'Except I've probably done the wrong thing coming. Maud will think I've let her down. That's if she finds out.'

'Would that be your daughter, Miss Maud Davies, the librarian, sir?'

'That's right. Know her, do you?'

'I know who she is, sir. She's been helping us with the investigation today.'

'Right. Well, she went to bed quite early, but I had to wait till I was sure she was asleep before I came out. If she wakes up, she'll think I've gone for a late walk. I sometimes do that.' He ran his fingers along the wooden edge of the table as though he was checking the finish – which, subconsciously, out of habit, he was – before he asked, 'So you're not one of the police she's talked to?'

'No, sir. But she was seen by three of my colleagues today.'

180

'She told me that. Interviewed twice. And not telling what she could have told.'

'Not the first time, you mean, sir? When there was a slight error over what she remembered. She's put that right, of course.'

'That was about her going out last night, wasn't it? She told me. But it didn't count, did it? Not really. At the time she didn't see the reason to tell anybody else about her movements. That's including the police.' He rubbed the side of his face with his weathered hand. 'Well, that was wrong, I expect, but excusable in the circumstances, like. Been depressed over the whole thing, she has. Deeply depressed, since Tuesday night.'

'You mean Tuesday night, sir? Not Wednesday?'

'No, I mean Tuesday, all right. Ever since Treace made his announcement about deserting his wife. Maud came home from that meeting in a terrible state. She tried to hide it, but I could see it, right enough.'

'And did you mean just now that she hadn't told everything she knew at the second police interview today, sir?'

'No, no, I didn't mean that at all. But somebody else is sure she was holding back, though. And that's something she should have told you by now, but she hasn't. I know she hasn't, and I know she won't. There, I've said it now. Will you need to tell her I've been to see you?'

'Well, that's difficult for me to say, sir. Not knowing exactly what it is you say she should have told us.' She smiled encouragingly, not indulgently.

Davies looked bewildered. 'Oh, that's right. I'm sorry. Getting old, I am. Old and stupid.'

'So was it something to do with your daughter being in Picton Grove last night, sir?' the sergeant pressed, when the interviewee's eyes suggested he might have lapsed into an introspective silence.

Davies rested his hands, fingers clasped, on the table in front of him. As he started to speak again, his left thumb began kneading the upper knuckle of his right forefinger. 'I didn't know she'd been out last night. She didn't say, see? Not when I got home. Playing in a darts match, I'd been, down the pub. It was that old fool Ianto Price blabbing his mouth off. That's how I found out. Like everybody else.'

'Mr Price only told us about what he saw, sir, he –'

'No, no. I don't mean what he said to the police. I mean him telling the whole bloody village, excuse my French, about Maud being up there. Told Agnes Craig-Owen in the shop, he did, before midday today. Might as well have put it out on the BBC one o'clock news.'

'Do you have reason to think that Mr Price got anything wrong, sir? In what he's said?'

Davies looked up. 'Not him, no. It's Maud who hasn't come clean, for reasons of loyalty. Dangerously misplaced loyalty, if you ask me. And meantime, she's left everyone thinking it's she who's done the murder herself.'

'Oh, I don't think so, sir. Miss Davies told us exactly what happened when she was in Picton Grove. That was during the second interview today.'

'She said she didn't see who was in the car up there, didn't she?'

'I'm afraid I'm not allowed to divulge the testimony of a witness, sir, even though it's your own daughter.'

'Well, it doesn't matter, because she's told me what she said. And it was the truth, d'you understand? Only some people don't believe her. One in particular. And that could put her life in danger, grave danger.' Davies was now earnestly leaning over the table, his forehead sparkling with beads of perspiration.

'You said one person won't believe her, sir. Who exactly is that?'

'Like I'm telling you, the vicar, of course. Treace.' He hadn't told her, but she let it pass as he continued. 'He rang when she got home early this evening. Told her she must never, ever say who she might have seen in the car in Picton Grove. She said she never would.'

Mary Norris looked up sharply. 'Did she really say she never would, sir, or was it never could?'

'Would, I think, but I couldn't swear on it. It matters, though, doesn't it? I can see that.'

'Well, if you're not certain, never mind for now, sir. What else did he say?'

'He told her she should never admit she saw who was in the car, that it was right for her to protect whoever it was, because that person was innocent.'

'Mr Treace didn't say she was protecting him, sir?' The sergeant was scribbling hard in her notebook.

Davies looked confused. 'Well, not in those words, no. But it was obvious. He was speaking in code, I expect. Being it was on an open line. And here's the last bit. He said they must never speak on the subject again. And I'm sure those were his very words: "We shall never speak of the subject again, in private or in public, because it'll be too dangerous. We must wash it from our minds." That's what he said, at the finish. Then he rang off. So what do you think of that then?'

The sergeant was still writing. 'So how did you come to overhear both sides of this conversation, sir?'

'I didn't hear all of it. See, there are two phones in the flat. I'd heard the bell go when I was . . . when I was in the bathroom. Maud answered it in the kitchen. When I came out, I picked up the phone in my bedroom to see who it was. In case it was for me. All I heard was Maud protesting, in her way, her weak way, while he was saying she must have seen who was in the car. That everyone was saying so.'

'You're sure it was Mr Treace speaking, sir?'

'Positive. I've heard that voice often enough on the phone. Calls her all the time, he does. "Do this, Maud. Do that, Maud." Vicarage skivvy she is.'

'And does your daughter know you overheard them talking, sir?'

'Oh, no. Certainly not. She'd never forgive me if she did. Or for telling you about it, for that matter. That's why I've been between the devil and the deep blue sea ever since. I did ask her later who'd been on the phone. She said someone from work. From the library. Her eyes were all red, though.'

'You didn't think to confront Mr Treace, sir?'

'Yes. Then I thought, for starters, he's going to deny making the call, and then get Maud to deny it too, as like as not. He's got such a hold on her, you'd never believe. Then he'll say he wasn't in the car. Well, that's for sure. So seeing him wouldn't get me anywhere, would it? Only put Maud's life in danger. Mine too, if he knew I'd heard them talking.'

'I don't think that follows, sir, so you shouldn't distress yourself.'

'Distress myself? I'm round the bloody bend with worry already. Sorry, miss.' He gave a deep sigh. 'She's so barmy about him. It wouldn't surprise me if she confessed to the murder herself, just to save his skin.'

'Could you tell me the time of the phone call, sir?'

'Yes. Five past six.'

'You realize we can easily check if it came from the vicarage?'

'You may be able to. I couldn't. To be sure, like, I tried checking it by ringing that number . . . what's it? . . . 1471, from my bedroom, just after. In any case, I wanted his number without going in the kitchen to look it up in our directory. You see, I'd had half a mind to ring him back right off, without telling Maud. But that awful automatic voice just said there was a call at 18.05, but they didn't have the caller's number. Something like that.'

'That meant the call was from a cellphone or some other non-BT network, sir. Or from a payphone. It only tells us he wasn't using the vicarage phone. And there could have been any number of reasons for that, of course,' she explained indulgently.

'Ah, that's it, is it? I'm never sure about these new things.'

'You didn't think to get the vicarage number from directory enquiries, sir, and then try to ring the vicar back?'

'No, I didn't. Well, I did, but by then I'd thought better of it. For the reasons I've said.'

'I understand, sir. You're right, though. Whatever happens, we have ways of finding out where that call came from.'

'Good. And you'll see Treace?'

'When we've established that he made the call, sir.'

'What if you can't?'

'If we can't, we'll probably see him anyway, sir.'

'Probably?'

'In the circumstances, almost certainly, sir.'

'And you won't need to tell him you found out anything through me or Maud?'

Sergeant Norris hesitated. 'On the face of it, sir, we shan't want to disclose the source of our information. And if it's any comfort, I don't think we'll want to tell your daughter either, at least for the moment.' In practice, she thought later, all that was pretty small comfort when you analysed it, but it seemed to placate Gareth Davies.

18

'Looked like a sensational development, boss. Sensational,' Gomer Lloyd repeated. He was referring to the report of DS Norris's interview with Mr Davies late the night before. 'And it still is, in a way, like,' he went on. 'But not so far as it involved Mr Treace. Or at least, it doesn't look like it, not any more. When Mary Norris checked the story out this morning, she found he was in church from 5.58 to 6.42 yesterday evening, conducting a communion service. He had plenty of witnesses, too. Well, five, anyway.' The attendance at evening services wasn't overly heavy at St Samson's, even in Lent.

'And Maud Davies wasn't one of the five,' observed Parry.

'Definitely not, boss.'

'Hm. Well could Gareth Davies have got the time of the phone call wrong? Was it a bit earlier than he said?'

'No. Not possible,' Lloyd answered firmly. 'There was only one phone call made to the Davies flat at around that time. It was at 6.04. Within a minute of when Mr Davies said. So it couldn't have been made by the vicar. And it wasn't from the vicarage, either. Came from a call box. In Cardiff Central bus station.'

It was shortly after noon. The two men were in the otherwise fairly empty incident room at Fairwater. Parry had just arrived there after seeing Perdita off on the London train. Most members of the inside team on the Dr Bewen case had already gone for lunch in the canteen, so were available on the premises. DC Alf Vaughan was

186

still bent over a keyboard on the far side of the room, transferring longhand notes from his book on to a computer, and, judging from his expression, wishing he wasn't.

'So has anyone gone back to Gareth Davies?' Parry asked.

'We can't find him, boss. He's not in his flat. A neighbour saw him leave by car around half-nine. Gone into Cardiff probably.'

'What about his daughter?'

'She's at the library. Mary thought we should leave the decision to you, whether we ask her about the phone call. Because of what was promised to her father.'

Parry pouted while looking at his watch. 'If he doesn't show up at the flat by one, we'll ask her. We'll probably have to anyway, even when we do find him. If he's still so certain it was Treace on the phone, there's no alternative. She has to know who she was talking to, for heaven's sake. And so do we.'

'Right, boss.' Lloyd flipped over the pages of his notebook. 'And I'm afraid that's not the only phone call giving us trouble. Now we've got the complete log of calls we asked for from BT, there was one made to Dr Bewen's house at 8.17 on Wednesday evening. Also made from a public phone box.'

'Sophisticated people, Bryntaf criminals. Know all the tricks,' muttered Parry.

'Great users of public transport as well,' the sergeant responded. 'Because this time the box was outside Bryntaf railway station. One of two they've got there. The call only lasted fifteen seconds.'

'Coin box, was it?'

'That one is, boss. The other one's for cards.'

'Hm. Easy to assume the caller wanted to avoid being traced. On the other hand, it could have been someone who doesn't like using cards.'

'Afraid the box was emptied first thing yesterday, too, boss.'

'So no chance we can check all the coins in it for prints.'
The chief inspector sniffed while thinking how laborious
and probably futile that exercise would have been. 'Anyway, at fifteen seconds it sounds as if whoever it was might
just have been making an appointment. No, confirming or
cancelling one, more likely,' he speculated. 'So, have the
station staff been questioned about people seen using the
box?'

'There's no station staff, boss. Not at that time of night.
They close the booking office at seven. After that you have
to get tickets from the machine. The phone boxes are on
the other side of the forecourt from the station, nearly in
the car park. We'll have a team there this evening to
question people catching or leaving trains from eight
onwards. There won't be many, though. Commuter
traffic's well over by then. Same with the cinema trade
to the city.'

Parry nodded. He had seated himself at an empty desk
and was scanning the top sheet of a handful of typed and
written reports he had just been given. He looked up.
'Anything else frustrating happened?'

'I saw Olaf Lewis's girlfriend, Fiona, in Bristol,' said
Lloyd. 'She's ready to swear on oath he arrived at the
Cape Cod at exactly 9.15 Wednesday. It's when the jazz
group they've got there takes a break every night. Seems
they always play the same tune before the break. That's
why she remembered.'

'Prostitute is she?'

'Not at all, boss. Describes herself as a party-giver. Careful to stay on the right side of the law, as well. She gives
what she calls bottle parties, at her house, most nights,
after the pubs close, or just before sometimes, like on
Wednesday. Well-conducted little orgies, they are, I
should think. Yes, harmless little orgies,' he completed,
reflectively.

'Did she say that?'

The sergeant stroked his moustache. 'Not in so many
words. But that's the feeling I got. Nobody actually brings

a bottle, they just pay her for what it would cost if they did. Could be a profitable line that. Fiona only drinks champagne.' There was a pause for more reflection. 'The women guests are regulars, lively unattached friends of hers, or that's what she calls them. Men get in by invitation only. Mature businessmen preferred. And how unattached they are's a debatable point, I'd guess.'

'You mean if Olaf Lewis is any example, Gomer?'

'Exactly. Anyway, the local force know all about Fiona. They let her alone because she doesn't cause problems. Helps avoid a few, more likely,' the speaker completed, a touch philosophically.

Parry grinned. 'So did you get an invitation, Gomer?'

'Yes. And if I'd accepted, which I didn't, I wouldn't have had to pay any bottle entrance fee either. And that would have been just as well. I'd guess what she charges would cover my drinks bill for a month. She first invited Mr Lewis when he was last in the Cape Cod. That was back in January sometime. He couldn't accept then. She offered him a rain check. That's why he was back Wednesday. Very popular, he was, at the party, or so she said.'

'Wouldn't it all have been a bit down-market for him?'

'Difficult to say, boss. Lot of middle-aged married men have a taste for those sort of parties. A night off appeals to their sense of adventure, I expect. And Fiona isn't a bit of the rough, either. Got a lot of style. Well, in her own way,' he added, ruminatively.

'Hm. Did you ask how long he stayed?'

'Yes. He was there from just after half-ten till about quarter past one, she said. That fits with the time he told us he got home, boss.'

'But that 9.15 arrival doesn't put him in the clear, does it?'

'No, it doesn't,' Lloyd pushed a peppermint into his mouth. 'And there's something else he told Fiona. He said he'd been disappointed in love earlier in the evening. That he'd come all the way from Cardiff to be cheered up.'

'That was careless, Gomer.'

'Ah, he thought he was well away from home territory, and safe, didn't he, boss?'

'Not if he'd had reason to think he might be involved in a murder investigation. That his movements might need to be traced. Along with the people he'd been with.'

'That's true enough. And he's not stupid, of course.'

'Only slightly less likely to be a murderer than we first thought.' Except there was no resignation in Parry's tone as he went on: 'Even so, if we take Fiona's word for it, Lewis and Dr Bewen had more than an accountant–client relationship.'

'Or he wanted it to be more, and wasn't getting it, boss?'

'Not after she'd hooked the vicar, perhaps,' Parry extended the point. 'Anyway, no point in spending more time on him now. Anything come out of the visit to the church yesterday?'

'No bloodstained cassock, boss.'

'But we got the safe opened, did we?'

'Yes, that was easy. The church itself was open when DS Norris and DC Pope arrived, so they didn't have to get keys from the vicarage. One of the churchwardens was at the church for some reason. A lady, it was. She had a key to the safe, like we expected. Opened it straight off. Nothing of interest there to us though. And Mary Norris didn't follow up on what keys were kept in the vicarage. Didn't seem any point.'

'But did she find out where the vicar's car was on Wednesday, after he finished that lecture?'

'Yes, boss. His daughter says it was parked in their drive from teatime onwards, and stayed there all evening. We've taken her word for it. We haven't checked with him, because he's going to say the same, isn't he? Specially since it's most likely true.' The sergeant sucked on his peppermint in a contemplative way before he added, 'Of course, he'd still have had time to walk to the doctor's house and back before he went home.'

'And murder her as well? Hardly, Gomer,' Parry replied.

'I suppose that's right. And we're pretty sure now he

didn't have a money motive for killing her. Dr Bewen did make a will. It was after her husband died, like you said, boss. She's left everything to her mother, Mrs Ann Elliott.'

'We got that from Mrs Elliott, did we?'

'This morning, yes. It was Mary Norris again who went to see her at Kingfishers. Sensible lady. Being very brave about the tragedy, but businesslike as well. She brought a copy of the will with her. Thought it might be wanted. Showed it to Mary. It was done through Mrs Elliott's solicitors in Chester. They handled all the legal work after the death of Dr Bewen's husband.'

'I see. So unless Delia Bewen made another will that Mrs Elliott doesn't know about –'

'Not very likely, boss,' Lloyd put in. 'From what she told Mary, the two of them were very close.'

'But not close enough for her to have ideas about who killed her daughter?'

'Afraid not, boss. She knew about Mr Treace. Never met him though.'

'And did she approve of their wedding plans?'

'She didn't disapprove, boss, or that's according to Mary. Ah, here she is. You can ask her yourself.'

Sergeant Norris had just come through the door with DC Alison Pope.

'Afternoon, Mary,' said Parry. 'I've been hearing about your interview with Mrs Elliott. I gather she couldn't help with the names of suspects?'

'Afternoon, sir.' The sergeant dropped her shoulder-bag on a chair next to the desk Parry was using. 'That's right. She says Dr Bewen didn't have an enemy in the world, or not so far as she knew. She thinks the murderer must have been some kind of demented burglar. Or a stalker who followed the doctor home.'

Parry sighed. 'Which puts her as close to solving the crime as we are.'

'Incidentally, Simon Treace rang us this morning,' said Lloyd. 'It was regarding two things to do with his movements Wednesday evening. First he says he now remembers seeing a mate of his at 9.20.'

'That's in the period he says he was just cruising around in his car, sir,' Mary Norris put in.

'Yes, well this mate was in a car as well,' Lloyd continued. 'Both vehicles were heading north. They'd pulled up abreast at a traffic light on the A4231, just south of Wenvoe. Young Simon was coming back that way from Penarth. The two lads waved at each other.'

'So that was the first thing,' said Parry, so far evidently unimpressed.

'Not quite, boss. The mate had a girl with him. She didn't know Simon, but she remembers the incident.'

'Ah, so Simon now has two witnesses who'll swear he was seven or eight miles from the scene of the crime at 9.20.' Parry simulated an arpeggio with his fingers on the desktop, then looked at Lloyd expectantly.

'The other thing was, he now believes it was nearer 8.10 than 8.20 when he left Helgarth Road, boss. It was a programme playing on his car radio that's jogged his memory, like,' provided the sergeant.

'Hm. Such a rush of honesty and accuracy all of a sudden,' Parry responded. 'None of which stops him from being a suspect. Only makes it a bit harder to prove he qualifies. Harder, but far from impossible. So he stays on the list of favourites, Gomer. Interesting that he came forward. Makes you wonder how many other people we'll have scared into improving on their stories, now they've had time to consider the consequences if they don't.'

'None of them knows the exact time of the crime, of course, sir,' said Sergeant Norris.

'Which means they have something in common with the police, at least,' the chief inspector responded grimly.

'We've just had sandwiches and Coke at the Waggoner, sir,' Sergeant Norris went on in a promisingly positive tone. 'We got chatting to Sally, one of the barmaids. She's been working there every night this week. Says the darts match on Wednesday didn't start till 9.15. Two of the visiting team players were late. They'd phoned through at opening time to say they would be. Sally took the message. When I asked had she noticed if Mr Davies was there before the match started, she said she'd served him with a pint at 7.30, but she hadn't seen him again till the match started. She thought he might have gone home, or something, in between.'

Parry looked at Lloyd, then back at the woman sergeant. 'Except he told you he was there from 7.30 to 10.30, didn't he?' he asked.

'That's what I understood he meant, sir.'

'The barmaid could have it wrong, of course,' offered Lloyd.

'But if she's got it right, why shouldn't he have mentioned he'd left for a bit and come back?'

'Perhaps because he didn't want his daughter to know he'd left at all, boss. That's if he didn't go home.'

Parry's eyes narrowed. 'Or because she knew where he was, all right, after she saw him drive their car out of Picton Grove at ten past nine. And . . . and now they've invented a phone call to suggest the vicar did the murder.' He paused, while shaking his head. 'No, that's too fanciful, isn't it? Still, since we want to see Davies anyway, we've now got some extra questions to put to him. Is someone phoning the flat to see if he's back?'

'I will, sir,' offered Alison Pope quickly.

'You rang in last night saying Mif Evans had witnesses for where she said she was Wednesday night, boss,' said Lloyd.

'Yes. Painting her flat with Dilys Hughes's Jamaican boyfriend, name of Alex Vespucci. But I'm still not happy with that trio in Isabella Street. Dilys Hughes was nervous as hell when I was there. Vespucci kept answering all the questions for her.'

'Didn't Amerigo Vespucci discover America? Or was it that he didn't discover America?' asked Alf Vaughan inconsequentially. He had now left his desk and joined the group.

'I knew I'd heard that surname name before,' said Lloyd, scratching his stomach. 'I thought last night I'd seen it on a list of wanted men.' He beamed at the others.

'Would have been if he'd actually discovered America, Sarge,' joked Vaughan.

'If he's her pimp, boss,' Lloyd went on, 'like you thought he might be, he'd have needed to answer all the questions himself, wouldn't he?'

Parry shook his head. 'He's no pimp. And she's no tom, and I'm pretty sure Mif isn't either. If Mif ever was, she's reformed – probably all thanks to Dr Bewen and her good works.' He thought for a moment. 'Have we got that list yet of the voluntary jobs people do in the parish? The one Maud Davies was supposed to be giving us, showing all the things she did herself?'

'I can tell you those, boss. She's vestment verger –'

'It's not her I'm interested in, Gomer,' Parry interrupted.

'Yes, we got it, sir. It's here,' said Mary Norris, pulling a paper from a folder. 'Except it's still in Miss Davies's longhand.'

Parry glanced at the tight, small handwriting. 'Hm. Mrs Bronwyn Hughes seems to be pretty devoted to good works as well,' he remarked, then squinted at the list more closely. 'Parish secretary for two, no, three Third World charities, two children's charities, one of those overseas, and another name I can't decipher. Anyway, she seems to be heavily involved fund-raising for good causes everywhere, with the emphasis on Africa and Asia. Can you make out what this other one is, Mary? . . . No, don't bother.' He kept the list himself as he continued: 'The names I can read make one thing clear.' He looked up. 'You wouldn't expect someone who gives as much time as Mrs Hughes to that kind of work to be a racist, would you? Except Alex Vespucci was making it pretty obvious to me that she doesn't want her daughter living with him because of the colour of his skin. In implying that to me, I'd guess he was not only wrong, but knew he was wrong.

And at the time, Dilys looked as if she knew he was wrong as well.'

'Could be it's nothing to do with him being black, sir. She just doesn't like him,' offered DC Vaughan, puffing on a cigarette. Like Gomer Lloyd, he favoured simple, straightforward solutions.

'If you'd met him, I don't think you'd believe that either,' Parry replied thoughtfully. 'He's a good-looking chap, well educated, well off, and plenty on the ball. I'd say any mother as unprejudiced as Mrs Hughes must be would find him more than just acceptable.'

'I still don't quite see the point, sir,' said Sergeant Norris.

Parry grinned at her. 'Neither do I, Mary. Not yet, anyway. But I'm sure there is a point.' And he was vaguely sure it would have a bearing on something quite trivial that Perdita had mentioned the night before, but which for some reason had lodged in his mind. He was about to enlarge on this when DC Pope called from the other side of the room that Gareth Davies was back at Old Vicarage Mansions and would stay there till the police arrived to see him.

'Right, let's get up there, Gomer,' said Parry, who was already on his feet. 'We can pick up a sandwich somewhere later.' Lloyd had delayed having lunch before the chief inspector arrived, and he had the feeling now that he had delayed too long. 'One other thing, Mary,' Parry added, when he was halfway to the door, 'can you find out what calls have been made to and from the Hughes house?'

'On Wednesday evening, you mean, sir?'

'No. From nine on Tuesday night, till, say . . . midnight yesterday.' He turned to DC Pope. 'Can you remember, did Ianto Price say what time his daughter gets home from her school dinner job every day?'

'Yes, sir,' she replied with a grin. 'In time to make him a cup of tea around three o'clock. That's when he wakes up from his afternoon nap.'

'Good. Their house is in Valley Lane, isn't it? We'll be going there later.'

'Will you want to see Mr Price alone, sir?' asked Sergeant Norris.

'No, it's his daughter we'll be after.' He joined Lloyd again at the door. 'We'll need to have a word with Mrs Elliott this afternoon, too. She'll be at Kingfishers, won't she?'

'Expect so, sir,' Lloyd answered, putting another peppermint in his mouth – certain there was no risk of it spoiling his appetite.

19

'Sorry if we've interrupted, Mr Davies,' said Parry, ten minutes later, as he and Sergeant Lloyd were being shown into the living room of the flat at Old Vicarage Mansions.

'You haven't. And your visit is very timely,' called the Reverend Peter Treace, who had caught the chief inspector's words. He was standing with his back to the television set when the two policemen entered with Gareth Davies.

'That's right. We'd just agreed we'd best ask to see you, Mr Parry. Right away. Both of us, hadn't we, Mr Treace?' Davies put in, sounding warm and even obsequious towards the vicar, in sharp contrast to his reported attitude at his late-night meeting with Mary Norris. 'You see, Mr Treace didn't make the phone call to Maud. The one I overheard last night.'

'Of course I didn't. To start with, I couldn't have done. I was in church at the time I'm told it took place,' Treace explained firmly, with a dismissive wave of his hand.

'We know that already, sir,' said Parry. 'One of the reasons we're here is to ask Mr Davies if he had any idea who it was –'

'Who was impersonating me? Criminally so, by the sound of it,' broke in Treace. 'Because that's what it amounts to, isn't it? Maud was threatened, you know.'

'What we don't understand is how you and your daughter were taken in, Mr Davies,' said Parry.

'Easy in my case, I'm afraid. To be honest, I hardly know the vicar. I'm not er . . . not much of a churchgoer, you see? Maud sort of makes up for the two of us in that department. Yes.' Davies gave a weak smile, then gave an almost furtive glance at Treace. 'Despite what I'm afraid I said last night to your young police lady, I suppose I didn't really know the voice well enough to tell the difference. I mean, between the real thing and a fake. So, like all eavesdroppers, I expect, I've only got myself to blame for going off at a tangent. Getting the wrong end of the stick, like.' He continued to look suitably chastened.

'But your daughter –'

'I'm also at a loss to understand how Maud was hoodwinked, Mr Parry,' Treace broke in. 'She not only knows my voice, if she'd thought for a moment, she'd have known exactly where I'd be at the time of the call. She's usually in church for the weekday services. Hasn't been for the last two days, for . . . for understandable reasons, poor girl. She's been very upset, of course, about one thing and another.' The speaker rocked on his heels. 'Probably wasn't thinking straight at the time. That's the most likely explanation.'

'Very likely, sir.' Parry turned to Davies. 'In fact, the other reason for the visit is to tell you we'll have to see your daughter about the call, Mr Davies,' said Parry. 'But in view of what you asked of Detective Sergeant Mary Norris, a senior and trustworthy officer, we wanted to warn you in advance. To offer to let you be present if you want.' He had also been concerned to leave the old man in no doubt about the rank and probity of the 'young police lady'.

'Thank you. But I don't mind any more about her knowing I listened in. Not now things are cleared up with the vicar,' Davies began to explain. 'I rang him when I came back half an hour ago. Decided to take the bull by the horns myself, d'you see? Said I wanted to talk urgently, didn't I, Mr Treace?' The vicar nodded as Davies continued. 'He asked what about, and when I told him, he denied straight off he'd made any call to Maud yesterday. Well, that set the cat among the pigeons and no mistake. I believed what he told me, of course. It'd been hard for me to accept what had happened in the first place. I was relieved, I can tell you. Better to have been hoaxed than . . . than –'

'Than to accept your parish priest has been guilty of criminal action,' Treace completed gravely for the other man. 'Naturally, I went to see Maud at the library straight away. Only left her a few minutes ago. She now accepts totally that I didn't make the call, but she says the voice was mine, or, as she now knows, incredibly close to sounding like mine. Mark you, I gather the whole conversation only lasted a minute or so.'

'Does she have any idea whose voice it could have been, sir?' asked Lloyd.

'Not the foggiest at the moment.'

Lloyd cleared his throat. 'This is a difficult thing to say, sir, but your son's voice is very like yours, isn't it?' In the last few minutes, Simon Treace had firmly been moved back to the metaphorical front burner in both the policemen's minds.

'Is it? I suppose it might be. They always say it's one of the things other people know better than you know yourself.' Treace gave an indulgent smile as he went on: 'But I have to tell you, Simon is a non-starter over the phone call. At six o'clock yesterday he was watching a new Woody Allen film at the MGM in Cardiff. His sister was with him. I booked the seats myself, by phone. The 5.10 performance. It was a treat. To get them both away from the . . . the pressures. You're welcome to ask Janet if Simon went out for a bit, around six, but I'll give you any odds you like he didn't. He's a very serious film buff. Woody Allen is his favourite actor and director. It would have been . . . sacrilege for Simon to miss seeing a chunk of the production.'

'Thank you, sir,' said Parry, busy estimating that the half mile between the cinema and the bus station would have required a minimum absence of seven minutes, allowing that Simon Treace was a fit rugby player. 'I'm sure you're right,' he went on, without meaning it, 'but we'll need to check the information, of course.' Earlier, he'd had misgivings about taking Janet Treace's sole word that her father's car had been parked at the vicarage all Wednesday evening. Now he was certainly not ready to accept her as the lone witness to her brother's movements. It might have been unfair on the girl, but there was too much coincidence involved. He looked across at Davies. 'And now your daughter's had time to think about it, perhaps she'll have other suggestions to make to us, sir.'

'I have to say I doubt it,' Treace interposed – with too much certainty for Lloyd's taste. 'And if I'm impersonated again on the telephone, now we're alerted to the possibility, I hope the police will track down the caller by electronic means, swiftly and surely. One is always reading about the technical advances you've made in these matters. And now, if you'll excuse me, parish duties call,' the clergyman completed, without allowing time for a reply to his pompous observations, not that either of the policemen was immediately disposed to make one.

'Another thing we need your help on, Mr Davies,' said Lloyd, after Davies had returned from seeing Treace to the door, 'your daughter mentioned earlier that you were at the Waggoner on Wednesday, playing in a darts match. That was from about 7.30 to 10.30, she said. Except we now understand the match didn't start till 9.15. You were noticed at the bar at 7.30, but did you leave for a bit after that and come back later, in time for the match?'

Davies blinked and searched in a pocket for his pipe. 'That's right enough, yes.' He looked up with a twinkle in his eye. 'When we were told two of the visiting team were going to be late, I nipped off for an hour or so. To see a man about a dog.' He blew down the stem of the pipe. 'Oh, except it was a lady I saw.'

'My question was a serious one, sir,' the sergeant replied, solemnly.

'And so was my answer, Mr Lloyd. You see, at about quarter to eight, I drove over to Caerphilly, to choose a nice little bitch from a litter of lovely thoroughbred Welsh spaniels. A surprise birthday present for my daughter next Monday.' He searched in his pocket for his tobacco pouch. 'That's why I never mentioned it to her, of course. I'd planned to go Thursday morning, but it was more convenient to go when I did, when the chance arose, like. The breeder's name is Alice Matthews. Very nice lady. No doubt she'll confirm what I've told you. I've got the address and telephone number here somewhere.' He moved towards a bureau. 'Expensive present these days, I can tell you, but worth it. Maud loves animals. Having a puppy will . . . well, it'll take her mind off things. Give her something else to think about besides religion and . . . church people. But please don't let on to her, will you? Mrs Matthews is delivering the animal Sunday night.'

In physical appearance, Mrs Ann Elliott was a sixty-year-old version of what Parry imagined her daughter Delia must have been. She was probably a touch shorter than Delia, he thought, but with the same fair colouring and controlled, well-developed figure – a homely figure in her case – evident in photographs of the doctor. Only the eyes, behind rimless spectacles, lacked the alertness in those of the dead woman. The mother's eyes betokened a placidity bordering on vagueness. She had taken some time to answer the door bell, eventually opening the door only a cautious fraction, but after incautiously removing the security chain. She was wearing an oatmeal cardigan over a plain white blouse and flared brown skirt.

'It's good of you to call, Mr Parry,' she said, as she was leading the two policemen towards the kitchen. 'The lady officer, Mary . . . Morris, is it?' A raised hand had made a quivering interrogative movement.

'Actually it's Norris, ma'am. Detective Sergeant Norris,' replied the chief inspector, tolerantly.

'Yes, of course, silly of me to forget, after all her kindness. I remembered the Mary all right. Well, she was here earlier on to take me to . . . to the hospital, as I'm sure you know. For the identification. So understanding, she was. Mif is the same. Everybody's so kind.' She looked from side to side of the hall as if seeking others to include in the endorsement.

'Mif has been here, has she, Mrs Elliott?'

'Oh, yes. She's here today, only she's gone to do a bit of shopping for me. Back soon, I expect. Did you want to see her?'

'Probably not, ma'am, no. Not for any official reason, at least.'

'I know you're all doing your best to catch whoever did this dreadful thing to my daughter. I'm sorry I can't be more help than I have been.'

'Bringing your daughter's will was a great help, Mrs Elliott,' said Lloyd, who was behind the other two as they entered the kitchen.

She stopped and turned, fingering the large cameo pinned to her blouse. She used her hands a lot. 'I'm so glad. My son said it might be. He knows about these things. I spoke to him last night, on the telephone. And the day before. He'll be on his way now from Australia.'

'He lives there, does he, ma'am?'

She looked vaguely surprised at the question. 'Oh, yes,' she answered, but as though she wasn't quite sure. 'He's a doctor, too. A surgeon. It'll be such a comfort to have him with me over the . . . the funeral, and . . . and the rest. I'm a widow, but I expect you know that too.' She paused. 'I may even move to Australia myself now that . . . now that my daughter's . . . now that she's gone.' She straightened her shoulders in what was evidently a revivifying gesture. 'Except you think twice about uprooting at my age.' Then both hands lifted suddenly in support of an apology. 'I'm so sorry, going on about myself when you have work to do. Sit down, won't you? Forgive me asking you in here, but I can't bring myself to use the sitting room. Not yet. Silly of me, I expect. And, you see, I remember her so much better in here. She was a wonderful cook, you know?' She pulled a handkerchief from her sleeve. 'Oh, dear, whoever could have done those terrible things to her?' There were tears welling now in her eyes, showing that the lady wasn't nearly so inured against grief as her unexpectedly composed, if slightly vaporous, demeanour had suggested so far.

'Who indeed, ma'am. But we'll find out, never fear,' Parry replied, a confidence in his voice that Lloyd at least found reassuring in spirit, if presently lacking in body. 'And we shan't keep you long now. Could you tell us, has any name come to mind since you were with Mary Norris? Anyone who might have borne a grudge against your daughter?'

She shook her head. 'Delia never harmed a living soul.'

Curiously, the platitude invented more of a question than it provided any kind of answer in Parry's mind – but not the kind of question it was necessary or desirable to put to Mrs Elliott at this point.

'And she'd told you about her engagement to Mr Treace, ma'am?' said Lloyd.

'Oh, yes. We had no secrets from each other. Not since she was quite a small child. He came to meet me at the station, you know? Such a lovely man. I can see why Delia was attracted to him. Not that I approved of what they were doing. But it wasn't my business, was it?'

'You'd told your daughter that, ma'am?' asked Parry.

'She knew, all right. She understood. Nowadays, I know it's no use saying anything to young people about marriage being forever in God's sight. And, I mean, you couldn't blame Delia for asking where God was when a loving husband was taken from her in that accident, could you? To his credit, I know Mr Treace tried to explain that to her. He may have succeeded, too, but it didn't stop them falling for each other in the process.' She shook her head. 'It's a funny old world, when a clergyman . . . well.' She left the rest of that sentence unsaid before beginning another. 'Mrs Treace, Sybil, she's been kindness itself to me, as well. She came to the station with her husband. The tragedy's brought them together again, you know?

203

Well, it's an ill wind, I suppose, but I'm glad. I must be, mustn't I?' She looked a little doubtful.

'You're being very brave and understanding, Mrs Elliott,' Parry put in reassuringly. He rose from his chair, while wondering, with a touch of cynicism, if the vicar of Bryntaf had gone back to his wife out of Christian charity, or as part of an attempt to help salvage his job from the damaging dramas of the last few days. 'Anyway, we don't need to trouble you any longer, but you won't mind, will you, if we have another quick look round your daughter's bedroom? There's a few things there we'd like to see again.'

'Of course not. And I'm not using it. Mif got the guest suite ready for me. I'm used to being in there. So Delia's things are just the way she left them. On the dressing table and everything.'

But it wasn't the things on the dressing table that concerned the chief inspector. It was the list of brand names in his pocket, provided by Mary Norris from another source, that he was anxious to check.

Mrs Thora Anstey, deep-voiced, jolly daughter of octogenarian Ianto Price, was a big woman, and looked to be over sixty herself. 'More tea, Mr Parry, Mr Lloyd?' she encouraged. 'And another square of my *teisen lap*, made this morning? The name means "moist cake", doesn't it? I hope this isn't too moist for you. It's what the miners' wives used to make for their men to take down the pit.'

'Nothing more for me, thanks, Mrs Anstey,' Parry replied.

Lloyd passed his cup gratefully after watching their hostess lift another square of the flat, browned cake on to his plate. 'It's delicious. Best I've had for ages,' he said. 'Other cake dried out too fast underground, of course,' he added, knowledgeably.

'Can't beat home-made,' mumbled Ianto Price, his mouth full.

The policemen had come to Valley Lane directly from

Kingfishers, just as Mrs Anstey had been making tea for her father. She had invited the callers into her small, warm kitchen where they were all now seated at the scrubbed table.

'So you did mention your father had reported seeing Miss Maud Davies and a car in Picton Grove, ma'am?' questioned the chief inspector now. The earlier part of the interview had been taken up with an unnecessarily long, but unstoppable recitation by Ianto Price of his experience on Wednesday night.

'Oh, yes. Don't often get a bit of juicy gossip to share, do you?' the lady responded with a chuckle, as she gave the sergeant his tea. 'Never about a murder, come to that. Well, not before this. It's very sad, of course, about Dr . . . Bewen, is it? Never met her myself, but I must have seen her, mustn't I, her living just up the road from here?'

'I expect so. And the conversation we're referring to was at St Gregory's School, mid morning yesterday, ma'am?'

'That's right.' The lady's cheek muscles had twitched slightly in probably pleased reaction to the chief inspector's mode of addressing her. 'About quarter to eleven, it was,' she went on. 'There's a break then, when the free teachers always come to my kitchen for coffee and a biscuit.'

Parry wondered why the Welsh seemed always to gravitate towards a kitchen, as he had been obliged to do now: for instance, didn't teachers have common rooms any more? 'And yesterday those teachers included Dilys Hughes?' he asked. It was his earlier checking through yesterday's reports that had provoked the not immediately significant realization that Dilys and Mrs Anstey worked at the same school in Greychapel.

'Dilys, and about four others, yes. She's Mrs Bronwyn Hughes's daughter, from the village here. Well, you know that, I expect. Dilys is young to be teaching, really. But she only looks after the very little ones. Don't believe she's trained for anything else, come to that. She could have gone to university, but dropped out, or so her mother told me. But that was some time back.'

'Was Dilys all right when you saw her?' asked Lloyd, sipping his tea.

'Oh, yes. She wasn't later, though. Never came in to lunch. She'd gone home with a bad migraine, they told me.'

'Nasty thing, migraine,' put in Ianto Price, who was having difficulty keeping up with the exchanges, switching from head to head, like a bee in lavender.

'Can you remember saying your father hadn't seen who was driving the car, Mrs Anstey?' Lloyd questioned next.

'I think so. Yes,' the woman replied, then looked up sharply. 'Shouldn't I have done? I didn't think –'

'No reason at all, Mrs Anstey,' Lloyd put in quickly, patting Ida, the mongrel who, like most domestic pets finding themselves in his vicinity, had settled beside him rather than beside anyone else present, and was resting a slavering muzzle on his knee beneath the table. 'Did you, by any chance, say Miss Davies might have seen who was driving?' the sergeant completed, slipping the dog a morsel of cake.

'No. But someone else did, I think. One of the other teachers. Just in conversation, like.'

Parry leaned forwards. 'Did you notice if Dilys reacted in any special way to that, ma'am?' he asked.

Mrs Anstey shook her head slowly. 'I don't remember. Oh, but . . . yes, come to think, she left straight away after. Didn't finish her coffee, either.' Her normally agreeable expression hardened suddenly as she demanded: 'Here, you're not suspecting Dilys of doing something wrong, are you?'

'Certainly not, ma'am,' Parry replied, not quite as truthfully as he might have been, but satisfied that the case was solved.

It was shortly after 5.30 when Parry drew up the Porsche in one of the empty, free street parking spaces in front of

Top Notch, the boutique owned by Bronwyn Hughes. This was the most sophisticated-looking emporium in the short Station Road that ran eastward, off the wide and usually busy Valley Road, down to the railway station. Lloyd was in the car with his chief. At this lower end of the thoroughfare, there were shops on one side only. Buildings on the other side stopped higher up, giving way to the big station car park. The estate agency next door to the Bryntaf boutique was the last of the shops altogether. After that, the road angled to the left, between the car park and the station forecourt, and then swung sharply right before it disappeared from sight, under the railway bridge.

'Not as busy as you'd expect, late on a Friday afternoon, boss,' remarked the sergeant, undoing his seat belt and regarding the almost deserted, windswept scene outside. The setting sun was offering an impression of warmth, but against the much more evident bite of a strong easterly breeze. 'People do their weekend shopping earlier these days, I suppose,' Lloyd completed.

'Or find other ways of doing it,' said Parry, reflectively.

The only other occupied street parking spaces were those fronting the Craig-Owen self-service grocery, and the post office-cum-newsagents. They were further up, and next door to each other. The station car park was still fairly full.

Since leaving Ianto Price and his daughter, the two policemen had been at the incident room in Fairwater, testing and corroborating new evidence. Parry had decided against bringing in Alex Vespucci and Dilys Hughes for questioning – although he might have been more confident about getting a fast result from what was immediately ahead if he had seen those two first. It had been a question of balancing greater surety against the advantage of surprise – against the risk of too many people being alerted. He was glancing at his watch as his cellphone rang.

It was Lloyd who answered the call with a brief: 'OK,

Mary.' He looked across at Parry. 'DS Norris and DC Vaughan are at Isabella Street, boss.'

The chief inspector nodded. 'Right. Let's get it over with, Gomer,' he said.

20

Top Notch had a mock Dickensian frontage – a deep bow window with heavy, dark wood glazing bars and one or two opaque, bulls-eye panes to heighten the illusion of antiquity, without seriously diminishing the chances of outsiders studying the display beyond. The hanging notice, behind the single glass panel in the otherwise solid wood and coffered door, stated that the shop was already closed – but the door opened easily enough to Parry's push.

'I'll just drop the latch. Then we shan't be disturbed,' said Mrs Hughes, who had come from the rear of the long and quite wide, softly carpeted interior as soon as she saw the two men enter. The door secured, she turned, and directed her callers back to the antique desk, where she had been sitting, with its three plush-covered gilt reproduction chairs. 'Do sit down, won't you? And tell me what I can do to help,' she went on. Her manner was businesslike, even a touch brusque – and her appearance was as chic and well groomed as might have been expected in the proprietor of a high-price fashion store.

'First of all, thanks for seeing us at such short notice, Mrs Hughes,' said Parry. 'When I rang just now, I wasn't sure what time you closed. We didn't want to interrupt your Friday afternoon trade.'

She shrugged, then fingered the red and yellow silk scarf gathered at the side of her neck, which added colour and contrast to the simple black dress she had on. 'Late Friday isn't exactly boom time in this village, as you'll have noticed. We close officially at 5.30.' She smiled, her expression remaining alert and expectant.

'When we spoke at your house, with Mrs Treace, we were mostly concerned with her movements on Wednesday night,' Parry began to explain.

'But you also checked on mine,' the lady put in promptly, with a mildly questioning movement of her head.

'Quite. And you gave us very satisfactory answers at the time.'

'Good. So?'

'Since then, as you probably know, I've interviewed your daughter and her boyfriend, Mr Vespucci.'

Mrs Hughes frowned. 'I'm afraid Dilys and I aren't in touch very often.'

'So I understand, Mrs Hughes. But I expect you've heard that I saw them both in Isabella Street?'

She hesitated, before admitting: 'It was mentioned to me, yes.'

'I gathered you don't like Mr Vespucci?' Parry had been ready for her to challenge his right to ask such a thing, but she didn't.

'Who told you that?' she questioned instead, with an indulgent smile.

'He did.'

'I thought so. Well he's wrong. Quite mistaken.'

'You mean you do like him?'

Her already quite straight back became even straighter, and the head lifted even higher as she let out a breathy sigh. 'I liked him well enough to have him stay at my house – often, and not so very long ago.'

'Would that have been when he was still a student in London?'

'Yes. He used to come for weekends. Longer in the vacations.'

'And went to church with you and your daughter, perhaps? To St Samson's?'

'Oh, yes. But I'm afraid we've . . . we've had a parting

210

of the ways since those days. Something that's upset me a good deal,' she completed earnestly, and almost as though she were talking to herself.

'Is that why your daughter's left home and gone to live with Mr Vespucci, ma'am?' Lloyd put in, looking up from his notebook.

The expression hardened. 'Dilys is old enough to make up her own mind about that. About who she lives with.'

'So you'd no basic objection to their relationship? His being . . . from the Caribbean, for instance?' asked Parry carefully.

'His being black, you mean? Certainly not. I find any form of racism repugnant. You'll find my views on that are well known locally.'

'We already have, ma'am,' said Lloyd. 'All the same, some parents can be extra choosy about the social or ethnic backgrounds of their daughters' boyfriends.'

'Well, not this parent,' she returned roundly. 'Not on those scores, anyway. I've always thought Alex a charming, intelligent young man. Well brought up, and very talented.'

'But you've had a serious disagreement with him?' said Parry stonily.

'Yes, over something that couldn't be of the slightest interest to the police,' she responded, again with firmness, but still no acerbity.

The chief inspector's brow creased before, with a half-smile of resignation, he appeared to accept the point by changing the subject. 'Can you tell us whether it was your daughter who phoned you here at ten past eleven, yesterday morning?'

'I shouldn't think so. She'd have been teaching at school then.' But the answer had been uncertain.

'The call was from near the school. From a phone box in Greychapel High Street. She'd just left for home, suffering from a migraine.'

'Ah, yes. Sorry, I remember now.'

211

'And is that what she phoned about? Her migraine? From a street phone?'

'Sort of, yes. She's . . . er, she's always been a bit of a crybaby where illness is concerned. She'd just missed a bus, that was it. As you know, they're not very frequent at that time of day. Alex was at the university, apparently, and she'd wanted me to pick her up in the car.'

'And did you?'

'I couldn't, no. I had no help here. I could have gone over at noon, but she'd have got a bus by then.'

'So you're not so estranged she doesn't turn to you for help in an emergency?' Parry asked quietly.

'She's my daughter, after all.' Mrs Hughes made it plain she was not going to enlarge further on the point.

'Quite so,' said the chief inspector. 'And did she mention, on the phone, what the school cook had been saying? About Maud Davies being very close to the scene of the crime on Wednesday night?'

Mrs Hughes appeared to think deeply. 'It's not likely, no. But honestly I don't remember. You see, I had customers here when she rang.'

'But you knew yesterday about Miss Davies being there in Picton Grove?'

She blinked. 'Yes, I think I must have done.'

'So if it wasn't your daughter who told you, who did?'

'Oh . . . er, I heard about it at the grocers in the afternoon. Something old Ianto Price had been retailing, about what he'd told the police.' The fingertips of one hand went to touch the carefully arranged hair at the nape of her neck.

Lloyd cleared his throat. 'Going back a minute to your own movements Wednesday night, ma'am. I've got a note that you left your house to come here to the shop at 8.15, or thereabouts. Anyway, it was before Simon Treace left the house as well.'

'That's right.'

'Only Simon now thinks you must have left earlier than that. More like five past eight.'

'Does he? His mother may be able to help on that. Does it matter?'

'It's just that we like to have everything as accurate as we can, see? And Mrs Treace doesn't remember,' Lloyd went on, in a concerned voice. 'And we don't have an exact time for when you came back either. Just your estimate that it was before 8.45. Only Mrs Treace was asleep by then, so she can't confirm the time either.'

'I see. And . . . and what you call my estimate alone isn't exact enough?' After the lips had closed, the lower one made several small contracting movements.

'We need independent confirmation of such things, Mrs Hughes,' Parry offered. 'So we can eliminate people from our inquiries. Is there anyone else who might have seen you coming back to the house?'

She frowned. 'No one I can remember. Not offhand. I'm sorry I can't be more specific than I've been already.'

Parry nodded. 'I understand, Mrs Hughes. But I'm afraid it means we have to ask you a few more questions.' She shrugged apparent indifference before he continued. 'I wonder, could you tell us what your attitude was to Dr Bewen?'

The woman's perfectly arched eyebrows rose a fraction. 'She seemed a pleasant enough person, what little I knew of her.'

'She was a customer?'

She hesitated. 'Yes . . . yes, she bought a few things from me.'

'In fact quite a lot of things, Mrs Hughes. Most of the clothes in her wardrobe are from makers you stock here. Our Sergeant Mary Norris noticed that. She said you only buy from the best fashion houses, and it was obvious you and Dr Bewen had the same taste.'

'Well that was nice of your sergeant. But I'm not the only buyer of quality fashion in the Cardiff area.'

'Except Dr Bewen kept sales receipts in her files. They show that in the last two years, more than half the clothes she bought actually came from here.'

Mrs Hughes smiled, leaned back a little, and crossed her legs. 'You surprise me. Of course, I'm not always here myself. I have two part-time assistants.'

'Perhaps you didn't need to be here yourself. We've been told Dr Bewen didn't patronize shops in the village because she wasn't here much in the daytime. But she'd found there are ways round that, of course.' As Perdita's equally busy mentor Dr Reynald-Kane had also discovered, Parry was thinking as he put the point. 'For instance, her cleaner used to get most of her groceries at Craig-Owen's. I wondered, perhaps, did she send anyone here to pick up things for her to try? Or did you, or one of your assistants, ever take clothes to her?'

Mrs Hughes smoothed the hem of her dress with her right hand, her eyes watching the movements. Then she looked up. 'I don't believe she ever sent anyone here, but now I come to think of it, I did once take a dress for her to see at the hospital, in Cardiff. One lunchtime, it was. It meant closing the shop, as I had no help at the time. I don't make a habit of that sort of thing, of course. But it was an exclusive model, rather expensive, and, I'd thought, perfect for her.'

'To the hospital, ma'am? That's service beyond the line of duty all right, isn't it?' Lloyd put in.

'I suppose it is. It paid off, though. She bought the dress.'

Parry smiled. 'Of course, there was a simpler way of getting things to her. Her home isn't far away.'

'But by all accounts she was rarely in it, Mr Parry.'

'Of course.' The chief inspector folded his arms. 'Going back to your personal relations with her, you said just now you found her a pleasant enough person.'

For an unguarded moment the woman's eyes showed something between surprise and relief at the switch in subject. 'Yes. But I never knew her intimately.'

'I see. Even so, did you, for instance, approve of her . . . of her liaison with Mr Treace?'

'It wasn't for me to approve or disapprove, was it?'

'But as a very active member of the congregation, and

214

in view of your close friendship with Mrs Treace – '

'We're not particularly close friends,' Mrs Hughes broke in. 'I feel sorry for her, that's all. Always have.'

'And that's why you took her in on Wednesday morning, after Mr Treace's announcement at the parish meeting?'

'Yes. She seemed helpless and alone. I was once deserted by . . . by my own husband. Peter Treace was . . . well, let's just say I knew what Sybil was going through.' Her lower lip began its spasmodic tightening movements again after she had finished speaking – after she had clearly stopped herself saying something disparaging about Treace.

'And did the situation Mrs Treace was in produce any special antagonism in your mind toward Dr Bewen?'

She breathed slowly in and out. 'It was only Sybil Treace who concerned me.'

Sergeant Lloyd leaned forwards. 'Mr Treace said you had an appointment to see him at lunchtime on Tuesday, ma'am. Except he had to cancel it. Did what you were seeing him about have anything to do with him and Dr Bewen?'

'No. I had no more idea than anyone else about their plans. Not at the time.'

There was a longish silence until it became plain that Mrs Hughes was not going to volunteer specifically why she had wanted to see the vicar.

'And did you have any special feelings about Dr Bewen's work, Mrs Hughes?' Parry asked next.

'She was a gynaecologist. A very necessary job, of course,' she answered, sucking in her cheeks a little.

'But as deanery secretary for . . . PLUC?' They were the initials that Maud Davies's writing had made it hard to decipher. 'That stands for Protecting the Life of the Unborn Child, doesn't it?' Mrs Hughes gave a slight affirming nod before Parry continued. 'You must have had . . . misgivings about the part of her work that dealt with ending pregnancies? I assume you knew she did abortions?'

'Yes, I knew. And I believe abortion is horribly wrong and . . . and against God's ordinances.'

'All abortions? Even of malformed embryos, for instance?'

'I don't see the relevance or . . . or the necessity for such questions as that, Mr Parry,' Mrs Hughes answered stiffly.

'Then, with respect, I've got to say you'll have to put up with them, ma'am. In investigating a brutal and callous murder, the police have to be the best judges of what's relevant and necessary.'

She swallowed. 'Very well. In answer to your question, I can't help my convictions, and I don't excuse them.'

'But you knew, of course, that Dr Bewen performed an abortion on your daughter?'

'How did you find that out?' she snapped back, showing real resentment for the first time.

'Not from your daughter, Mrs Hughes, and not because anyone at the Bryntaf Cottage Hospital has parted with confidential information. We know Dilys had a surgical appointment with Dr Bewen there at 3.20 p.m. on Tuesday, March 21st last year. We know also that there were seven other surgical appointments the doctor had at the hospital that afternoon, at fifteen-minute intervals, which is consistent with the time normally taken to do simple terminations –'

'Well, that's a . . . a very careless assumption for a start,' she broke in. 'Dilys was –'

'We also know your daughter left home the day before the appointment, Mrs Hughes,' Parry interrupted in turn, without raising his voice, 'and that she's been living with Mr Vespucci ever since. So putting two and two together, we believe Dilys had an abortion, that you tried to stop her, and that you had an almighty row over it. We believe the rift between the two of you has gone on, even though your daughter and her boyfriend would like to see it healed. You haven't forgiven them –'

'That's not true, they put me in an impossible –'

216

Although Mrs Hughes had broken in again, loudly, the tirade had stopped in mid sentence.

'An impossible situation, yes,' Parry completed for her. 'And it's something we believe had built up in your mind, Mrs Hughes. Got worse. Festered. Of course you had no objection to Alex Vespucci as a person. You've made that plain enough. So was the fact he'd deprived you of a grandchild the reason you turned against him?'

There had been a dead silence for several seconds before the cellphone on the table in front of Lloyd began to burp. He picked it up, and, rising, moved away to the front of the shop with it. Meantime Mrs Hughes had looked up slowly. 'It wasn't anything as selfish as you suggest,' she almost whispered to Parry. 'It was because he condoned the murder of a defenceless unborn child. His child. He could easily have persuaded Dilys not to go through with it. She'd have listened to him. Instead he actually encouraged her.' She let out a deep sigh. 'They both know how I feel about what they did.'

'And about what Dr Bewen did,' said Parry.

The last words could have been a comment, or a question. Either way they produced no audible response from Mrs Hughes, who was now staring down hard at the hands folded in her lap.

'Did you go to see the doctor? Before Dilys's termination?' Parry went on. 'At Bryntaf Cottage Hospital, or at her home, more likely? To try to get her to join you in dissuading Dilys? And was the result negative? Did she turn you away, saying your daughter was of age, legally entitled to make her own decisions? Or did she say it was a professional matter she couldn't discuss with anyone else, not even Dilys's mother?'

Mrs Hughes had looked up for a moment at the mention of Dilys being of age. Her lips had moved, but still she had said nothing.

'Coming to lunchtime last Tuesday, Mrs Hughes,' Parry resumed doggedly. 'Was the rift with Dilys what you wanted to see Mr Treace about? Were you going to him for counsel as your parish priest? Only he let you down by cancelling the appointment, for a trivial reason – and only hours before he announced he was leaving his wife for the woman who had . . . who'd desecrated your daughter's body in a way you found so very . . . sacrilegious. That must have been hard to accept. Worse than hard, probably. Maddening . . . maddening in the true sense,' he added pointedly, and because this still hadn't elicited a response, he continued: 'And was it tempting then to transfer all the guilt from Dilys and Alex on to the doctor who did the abortion? And did you give in to the compulsion?'

'No, I . . .'

When the words stopped as abruptly as they had begun, Parry urged: 'Yes, Mrs Hughes? What was it you didn't do?' But when she was obviously not prepared or able to go on, he tried a different tack. 'When Dr Bewen was killed,' he said, 'she was wearing bra, panties, and white high-heeled shoes. It took us till today to figure why. She'd simply got herself ready to try on dresses, summer dresses, from the collection you'd had delivered here in the afternoon. We believe you phoned her at just after eight, from one of the phone boxes in the car park opposite here, on the chance she'd be in, and she was. You suggested you come up with some new things for her to try, before anyone else had seen them. She agreed, but she never did try them, did she? When you arrived, she showed you to the sitting room, not up to her bedroom, because it was in such a mess after the hurried shower she'd taken following your call, and, anyway, there were plenty of mirrors downstairs. When you were both in the sitting room, when she turned her back on you, probably to drape her dressing gown over a chair, you smashed her skull in with the miner's lamp. And after that, you took a bloodier, more fitting vengeance for your dead grandchild on the doctor's own body, using one of her scalpels.'

Mrs Hughes's lips moved. 'It's not . . .'

'Not true?' Parry put in, when she again failed to complete her sentence. 'I don't believe you're going to deny it, because that would mean lying to us, which you haven't done yet.' He stopped to look at Lloyd, who had returned to his seat. The sergeant nodded in silent response to an understood question.

'I can tell you,' Parry continued, 'we're certain Dilys and Alex concluded you'd worked yourself up into taking Delia Bewen's life in a furious fit of blind, righteous indignation. It's why Dilys rang you yesterday morning, and not over her invented migraine. She'd heard at school that Maud Davies had seen the murderer's car leaving Picton Grove – a small, light-coloured car, like your Ford, with a P in its number, again like yours. Dilys was sure it'd only be a matter of time before Maud, under pressure, was made to identify you as the person in the car, no matter how much she detested Dr Bewen. No doubt you dismissed what Dilys said as nonsense, because you couldn't do anything else. That's why she went home and told Alex what had happened. Alex is an accomplished mimic. Unfortunately for him, it's a talent he just couldn't resist proving to me. It was he who hit on the idea of ringing Maud Davies, of course, pretending to be Mr Treace, and telling her she should never confess to anyone who she saw in the car. Alex knew Treace's voice well enough. He'd listened to it often, with you, at St Samson's. And both he and Dilys believed Treace was the only person in the world Miss Davies would obey implicitly. Except her father overheard the conversation and came to us, which is what let the cat out of the bag.'

Mrs Hughes appeared not to hear the rattle of the street-door handle made by some disappointed shopper. She was still sitting stiffly upright, but with all the colour drained from her face, while the tears that had welled in her eyes now began trickling down her tautened cheeks – like rain-drops over granite.

Parry leaned forward towards her. 'We knew, pretty certainly, which of two people took the doctor's life,' he said. 'That was after we figured who'd done the telephone impersonation – something, incidentally, that's been confirmed since we've been here.'

'That's right enough, Mrs Hughes,' Lloyd interjected. 'Mr Vespucci has admitted it was him, after he was positively identified by someone who saw him using the phone box at the exact time the call was made. By a newspaper vendor with a pitch five yards away.'

Both men waited for Mrs Hughes to react verbally to this detailed account. When she didn't, Parry went on. 'At first we decided Alex made the call to protect you, or possibly because it was Dilys, not you, who killed the doctor, alibied by him and Mif Evans. That could only have been because Dilys badly needed to make things up with you, to make amends for –'

'Dilys had nothing to do with it.' Mrs Hughes had spoken at last, interrupting Parry in a quite subdued voice. She swallowed painfully, then took a long breath. 'I killed Dr Bewen, and I'm . . . I'm sorry.' She paused, looking squarely at the chief inspector before she added. 'And I'm glad you know.'

'A moral obsession that ended in a compulsive homicide, Gomer,' said Parry, much later that evening, as he and Lloyd were getting into the Porsche outside Fairwater police station.

The sergeant slipped a peppermint into his mouth. 'Divine retribution she thought it was at the time, no doubt, boss,' he replied. 'And perhaps even later, in less sane moments. But when it came to it, she made no real attempt to pretend she hadn't done it. Not when she had to deny or admit things outright. If we'd arrested somebody else, would she have come forward and confessed, do you think?'

'Yes, I'm pretty sure she would. And certainly if we'd arrested her daughter. Dilys and Vespucci returned the compliment in a way, by trying to shut up Maud Davies.'

'Who's been insisting again this afternoon she really never saw the car driver, boss.'

'I know, and I'm beginning to think she's telling the truth.' Parry shook his head. 'That Vespucci is quite an actor, as well as a mimic. When I went into their living room last evening, I'd have sworn he'd been hemmed into his armchair, studying for hours before I got there. In fact, he couldn't have been back from making the phone call very long before I arrived.'

Lloyd was fastening his seat belt as he commented, 'Mrs Hughes wouldn't withdraw the confession, would she, like her lawyer wanted?' A lawyer had been found to represent Mrs Hughes shortly after she had been formally arrested. 'Well, he had to try and make her do that, of course. But she wasn't having it. No way. By then, it was like she'd lifted a great weight off her mind.' He sucked on the peppermint. 'They'll plead temporary insanity, won't they?'

'Which for once may be the truth,' the other policeman observed, starting the car. He frowned. 'It was Treace pushed her over the edge, of course. Cancelling his appointment to see her, when she'd worked herself up into asking his advice on how to cope with the abortion.'

'The abortion done by Dr Bewen,' said Lloyd, dourly.

'Who never hurt a living soul,' Parry responded, wistfully quoting Mrs Elliott. 'And then for Treace to announce he was divorcing his wife for the doctor –'

'Put the tin lid on it, no mistake,' the sergeant completed for Parry. 'For a deeply religious woman like her, it must have been like an ungrateful God was making fun of her and everything she stood for.' He sniffed. 'So temporary insanity, boss? A brainstorm? But what about evidence of premeditation?'

Parry frowned. 'Depends if they can prove she originally went up to Kingfishers intending just to show dresses. She took no weapon. The lamp was merely the handiest heavy object to hand, and the scalpel came from the consulting room.' He was moving the car out into Norbury Road as he added: 'It's the call from the station phone box that may sink her.'

'Unless they can show the phone in the shop wasn't working, boss. Or . . . or she forgot to ring before leaving and . . . and used the box, which was easier than going back to the shop, having to unset and reset the burglar alarm, and all that.'

Parry chuckled. 'Well, we'll have to see if her defence lawyers are as creative as you, Gomer,' he said.

Lloyd shrugged. 'Can't help having some sympathy for her, can you? Did she leave Mif's rubber gloves at the shop on purpose, do you think?' They had found the gloves under the stock-room washbasin after making the arrest.

'Not so much on purpose, possibly, as because they were just too good to throw away. Frugal habits die hard.'

'But the gloves she wore to cut up the doctor!' Lloyd expostulated, in a thoroughly shocked voice, then added, 'So the dress she had on then has most likely been washed and put back in her wardrobe. Well, we'll find that for sure, if it's there.'

'I really don't believe the enormity of what she'd done came home to her till this evening, Gomer,' said Parry. 'Before then the whole episode was a . . . an aberration . . . and one she'd managed to block out of her mind like –'

'Like Dr Bewen terminating an unwanted pregnancy, boss?'

'Hm. I think that's possibly a fair analogy, Gomer.' But Parry was half thinking of Perdita Jones and her career aspirations as he added, 'To Mrs Hughes, it's probably what her demented mind made of killing the doctor. A case for termination. Urgent and justified.'